Be sure to read **all** the **BABYMOUSE** books:

#1 BABYMOUSE: Queen of the World
#2 BABYMOUSE: Our Hero
#3 BABYMOUSE: Beach Babe

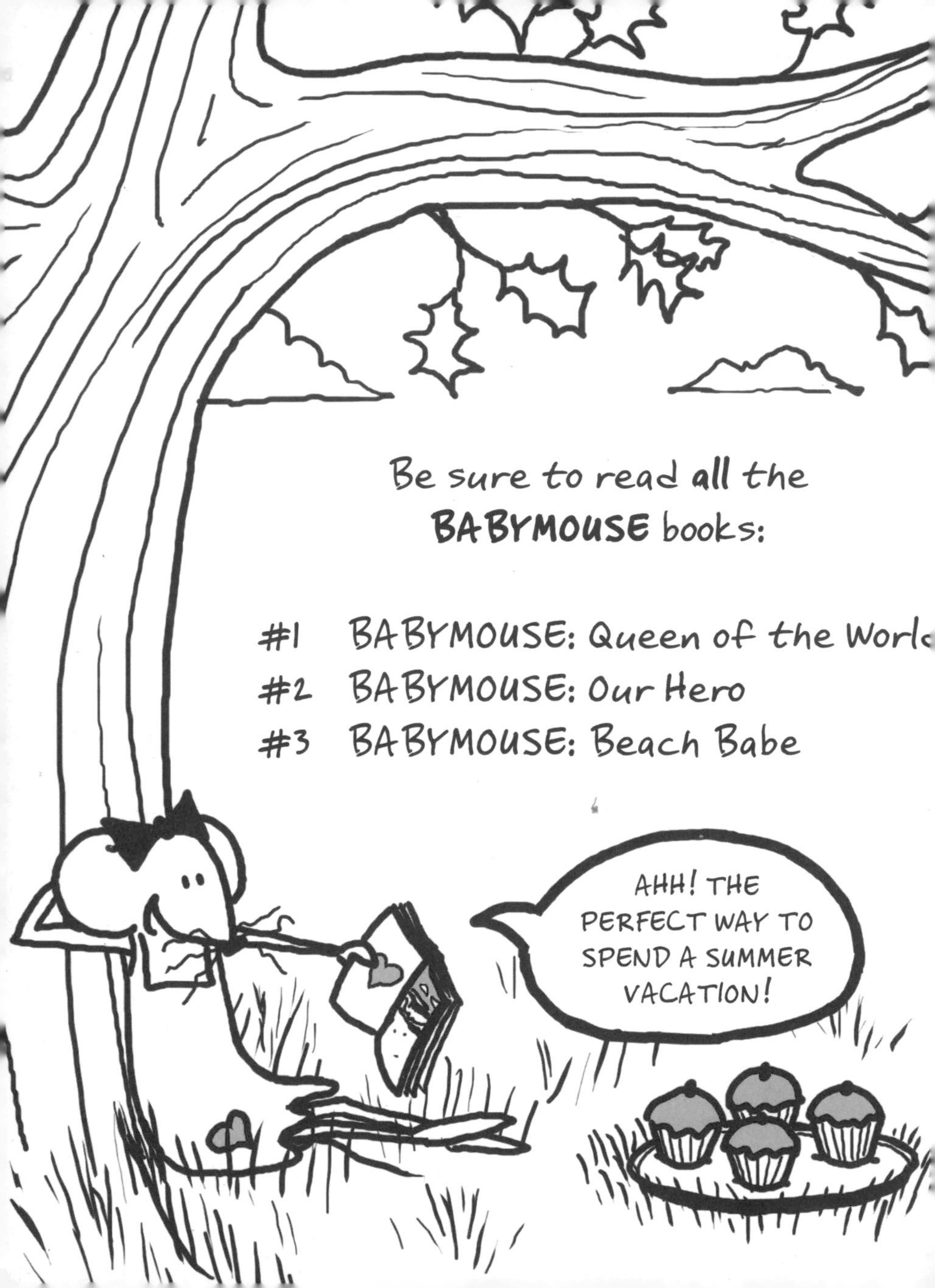
AHH! THE PERFECT WAY TO SPEND A SUMMER VACATION!

BABYMOUSE
BEACH BABE

BY JENNIFER L. HOLM & MATTHEW HOLM

RANDOM HOUSE 🏠 NEW YORK

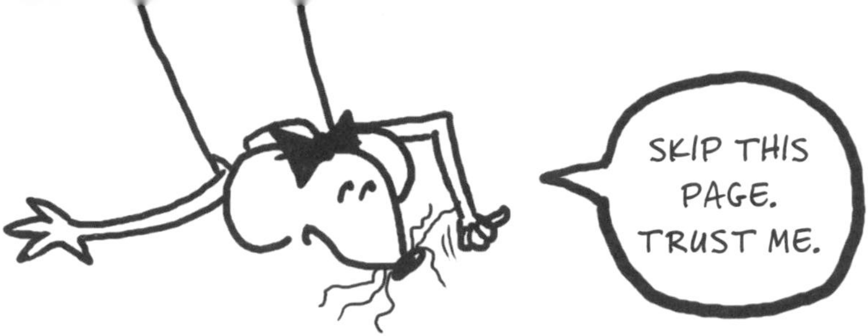
SKIP THIS PAGE. TRUST ME.

This is a work of fiction. Names, characters, places, and incidents either are the product of the author's imagination or are used fictitiously. Any resemblance to actual persons, living or dead, events, or locales is entirely coincidental.

 Published in the United States by Random House Children's Books, a division of Random House, Inc., New York, and simultaneously in Canada by Random House of Canada Limited, Toronto.

www.randomhouse.com/kids
www.babymouse.com

Educators and librarians, for a variety of teaching tools, visit us at www.randomhouse.com/teachers

Library of Congress Cataloging-in-Publication Data
Holm, Jennifer L.
Babymouse : beach babe / Jennifer L. Holm and Matthew Holm.
p. cm.
ISBN 0-375-83231-9 (trade) — ISBN 0-375-93231-3 (lib. bdg.)
1. Graphic novels. I. Holm, Matthew. II. Title.
PN6727.H592B25 2006 741.5'973—dc22 2005046465

PRINTED IN MALAYSIA 10 9 8 7 6 5 4 3 First Edition

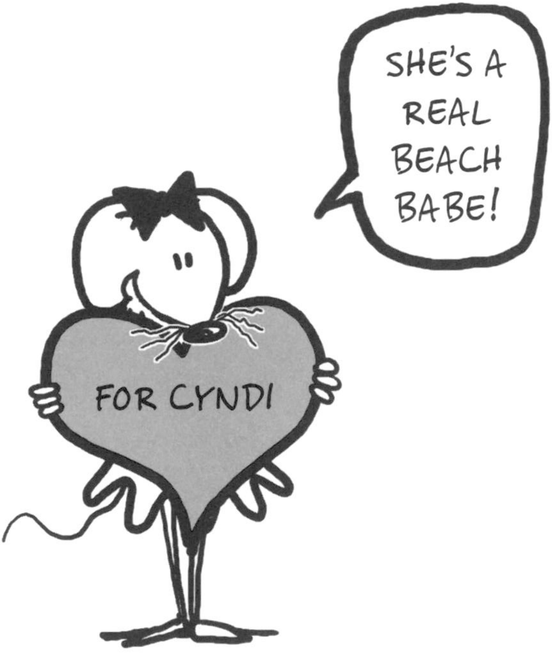
SHE'S A REAL BEACH BABE!
FOR CYNDI

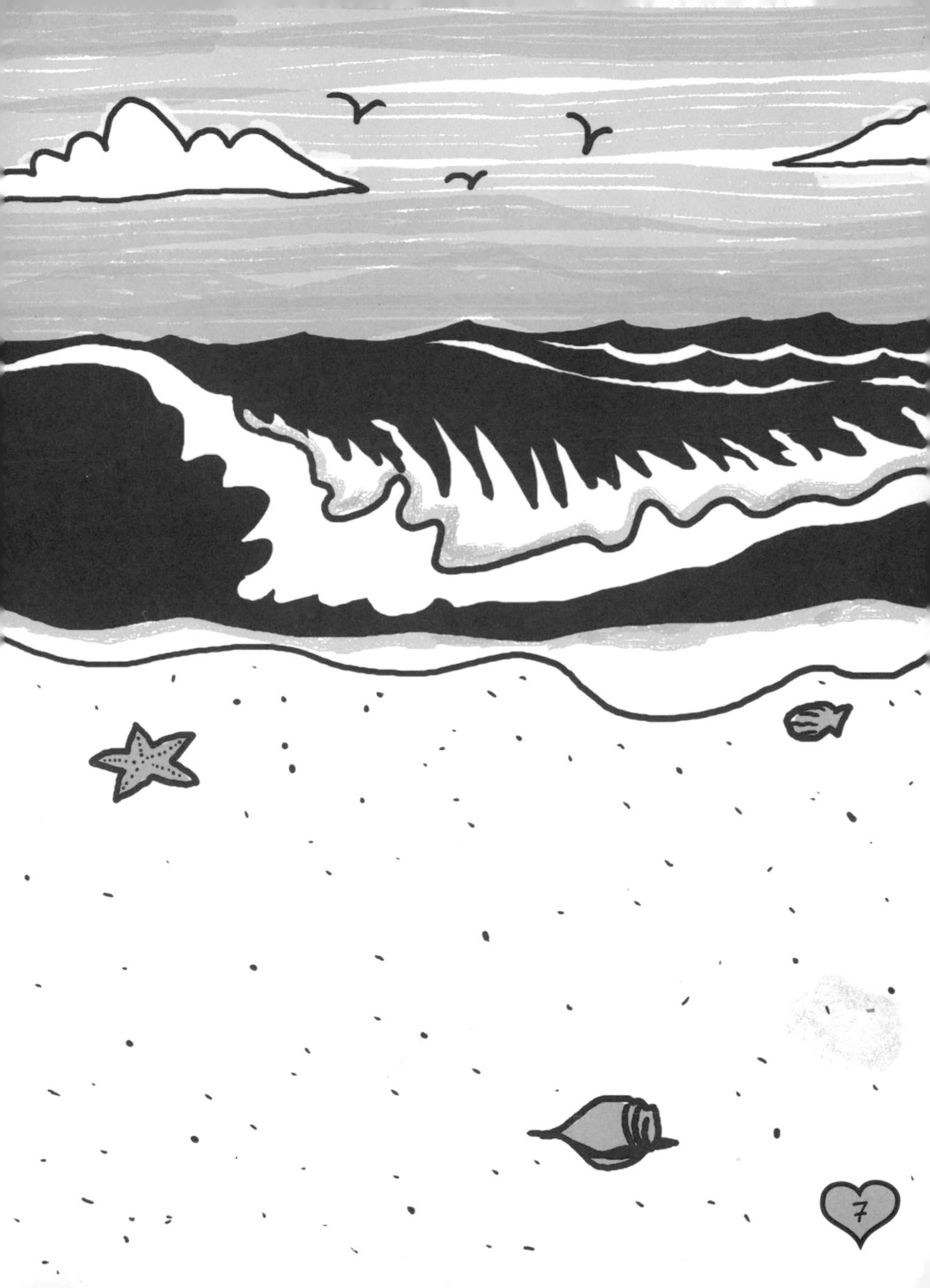

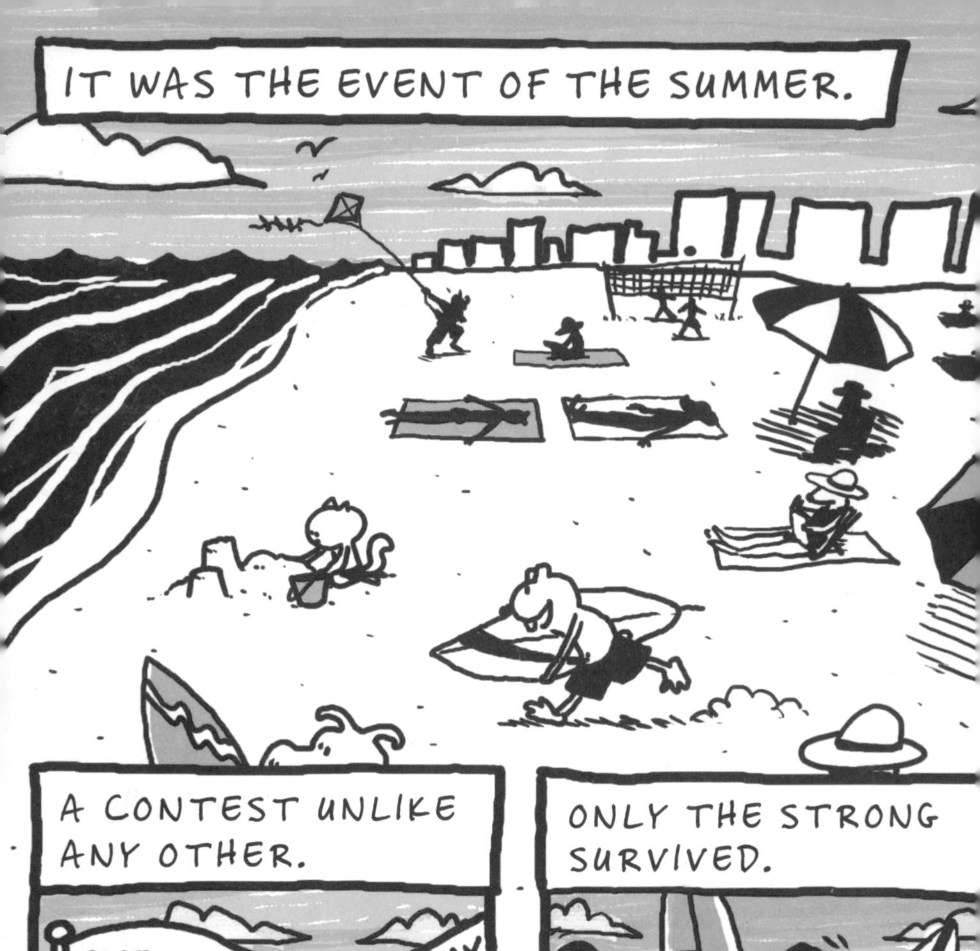
IT WAS THE EVENT OF THE SUMMER.

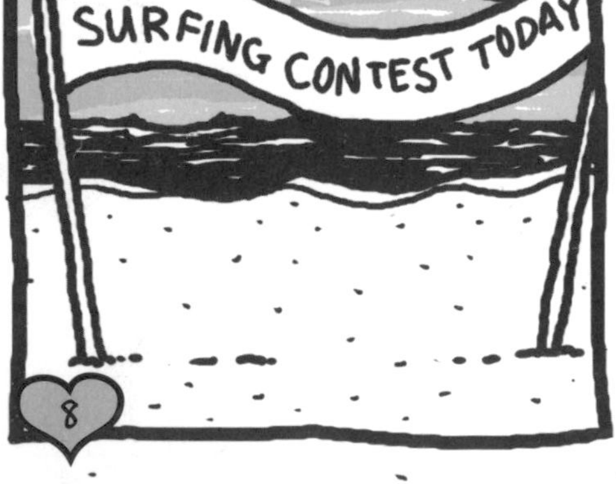
A CONTEST UNLIKE ANY OTHER.
SURFING CONTEST TODAY

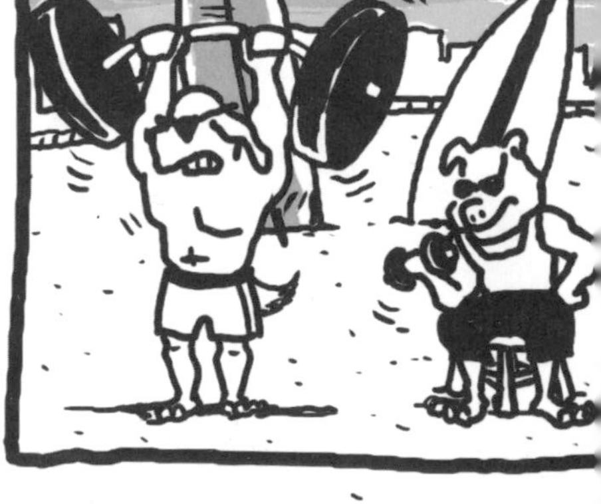
ONLY THE STRONG SURVIVED.

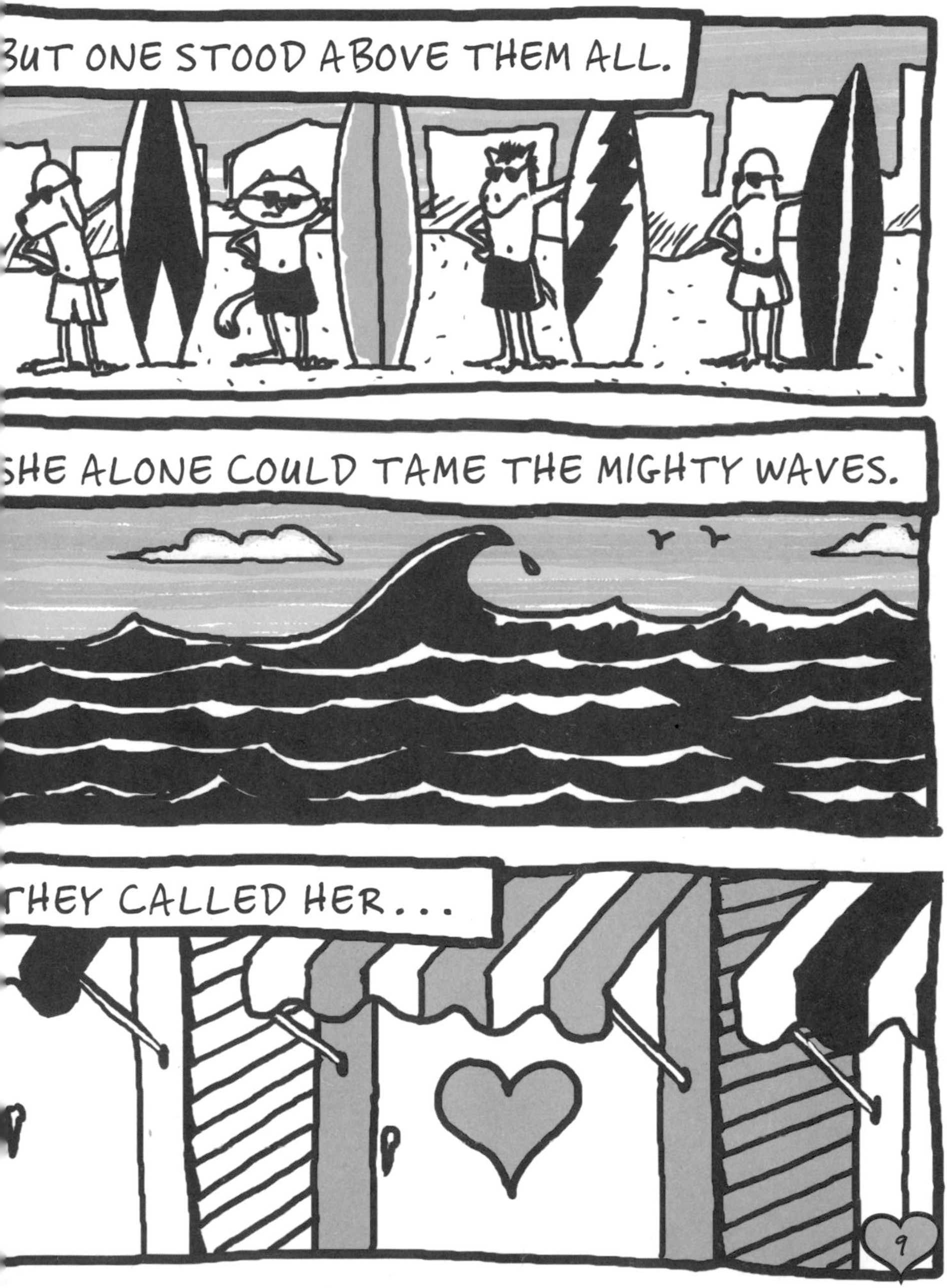
BUT ONE STOOD ABOVE THEM ALL.
SHE ALONE COULD TAME THE MIGHTY WAVES.
THEY CALLED HER . . .

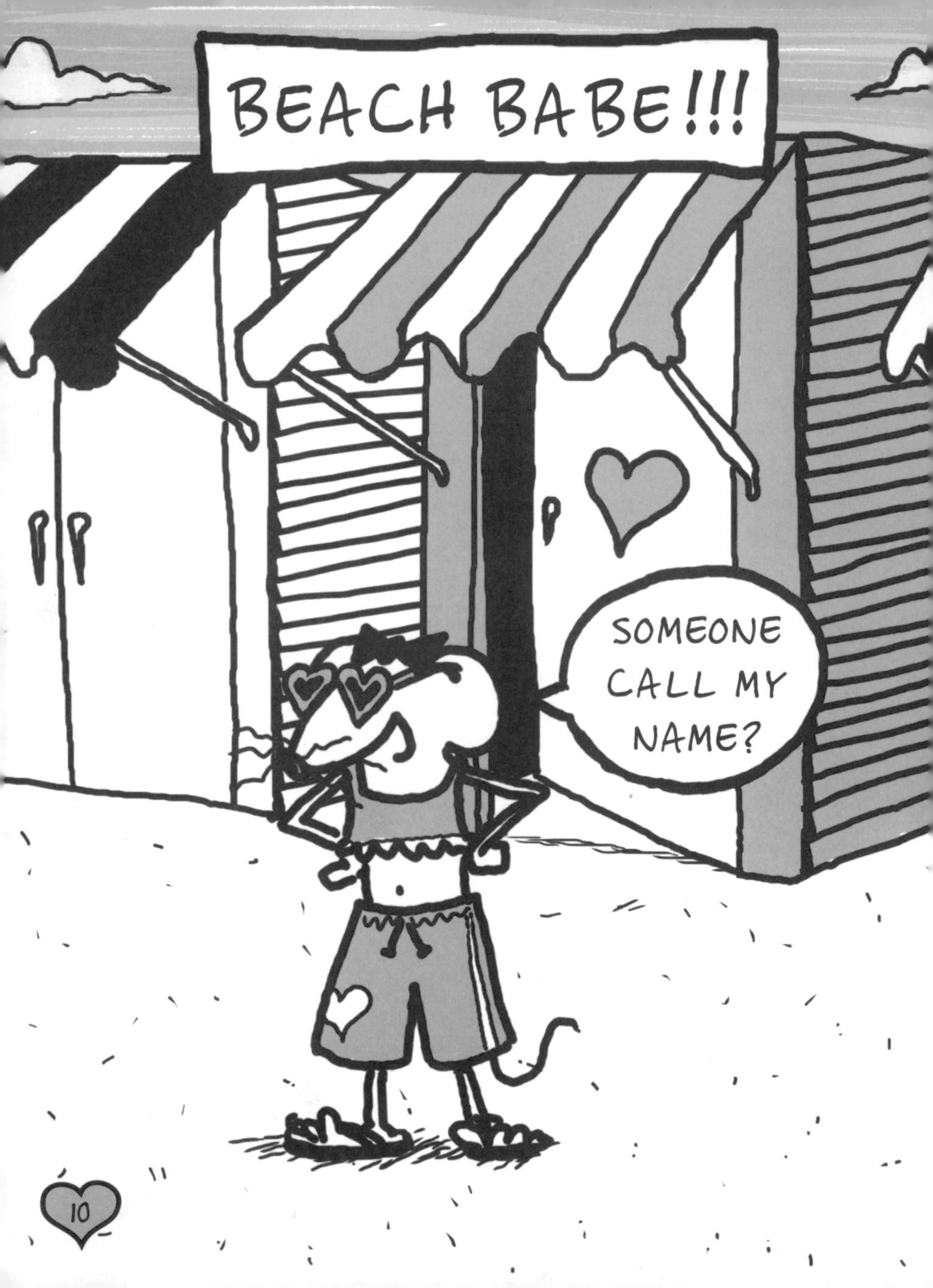
BEACH BABE!!!
SOMEONE CALL MY NAME?

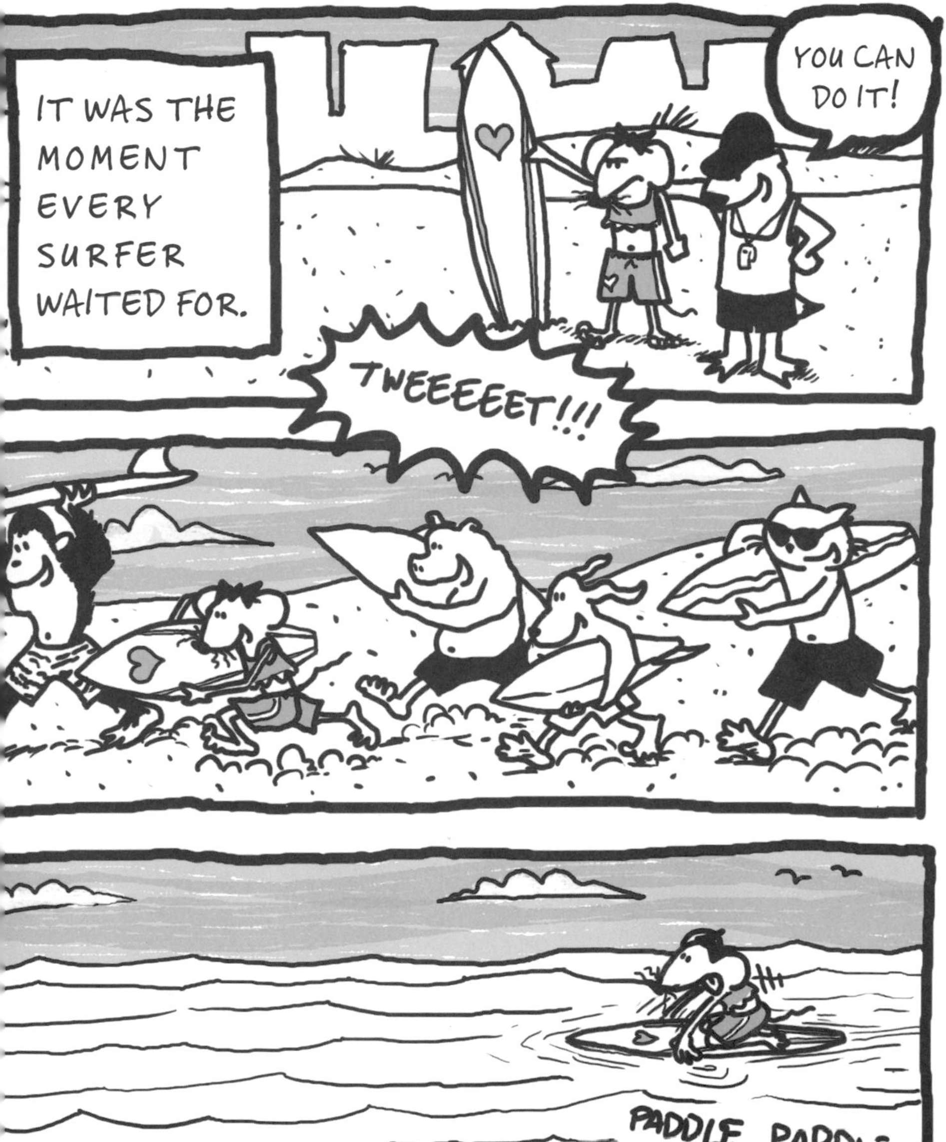
IT WAS THE MOMENT EVERY SURFER WAITED FOR.
YOU CAN DO IT!
TWEEEEEET!!!
PADDLE PADDLE
A ONCE-IN-A-LIFETIME CHANCE.

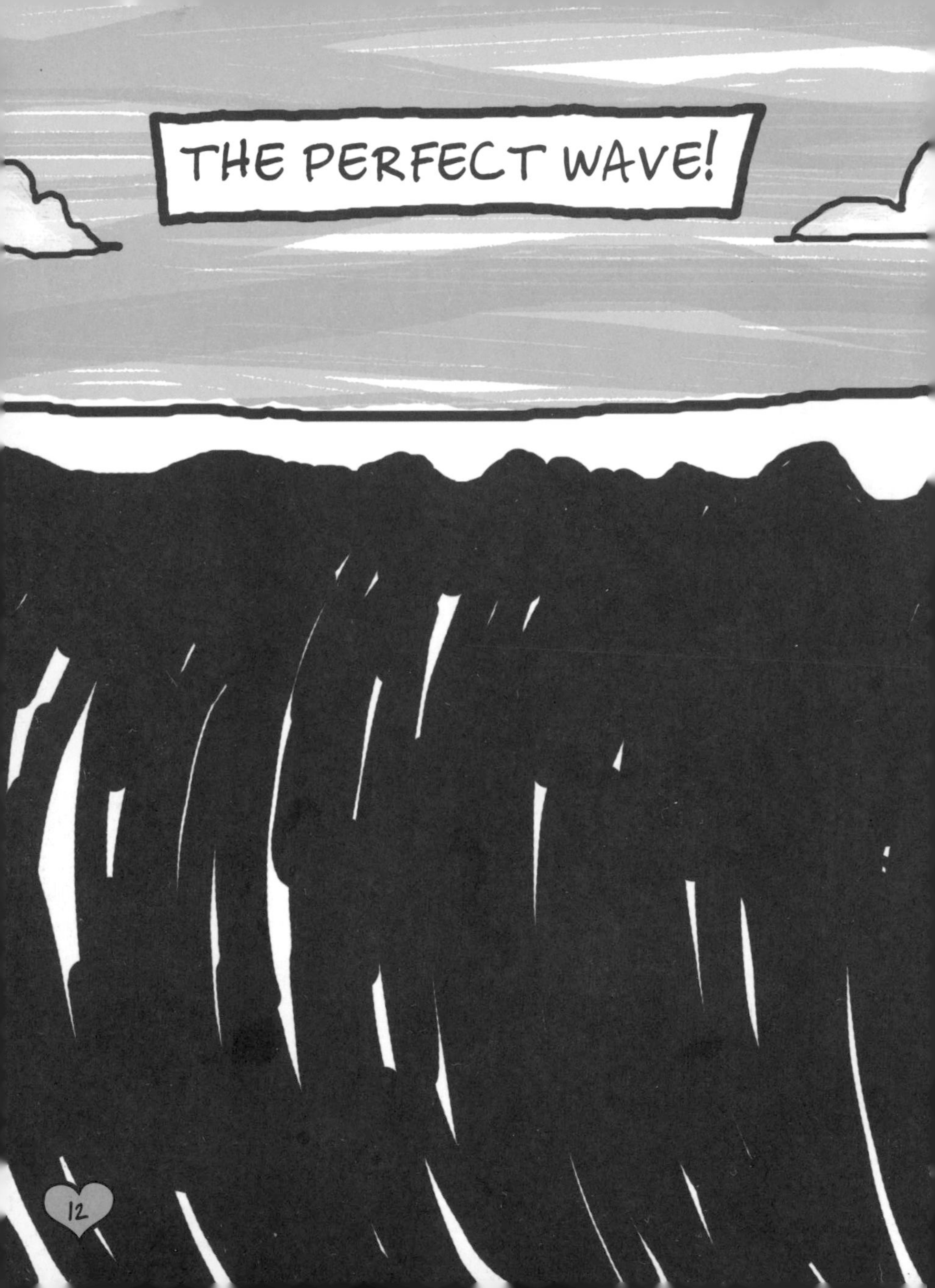
THE PERFECT WAVE!

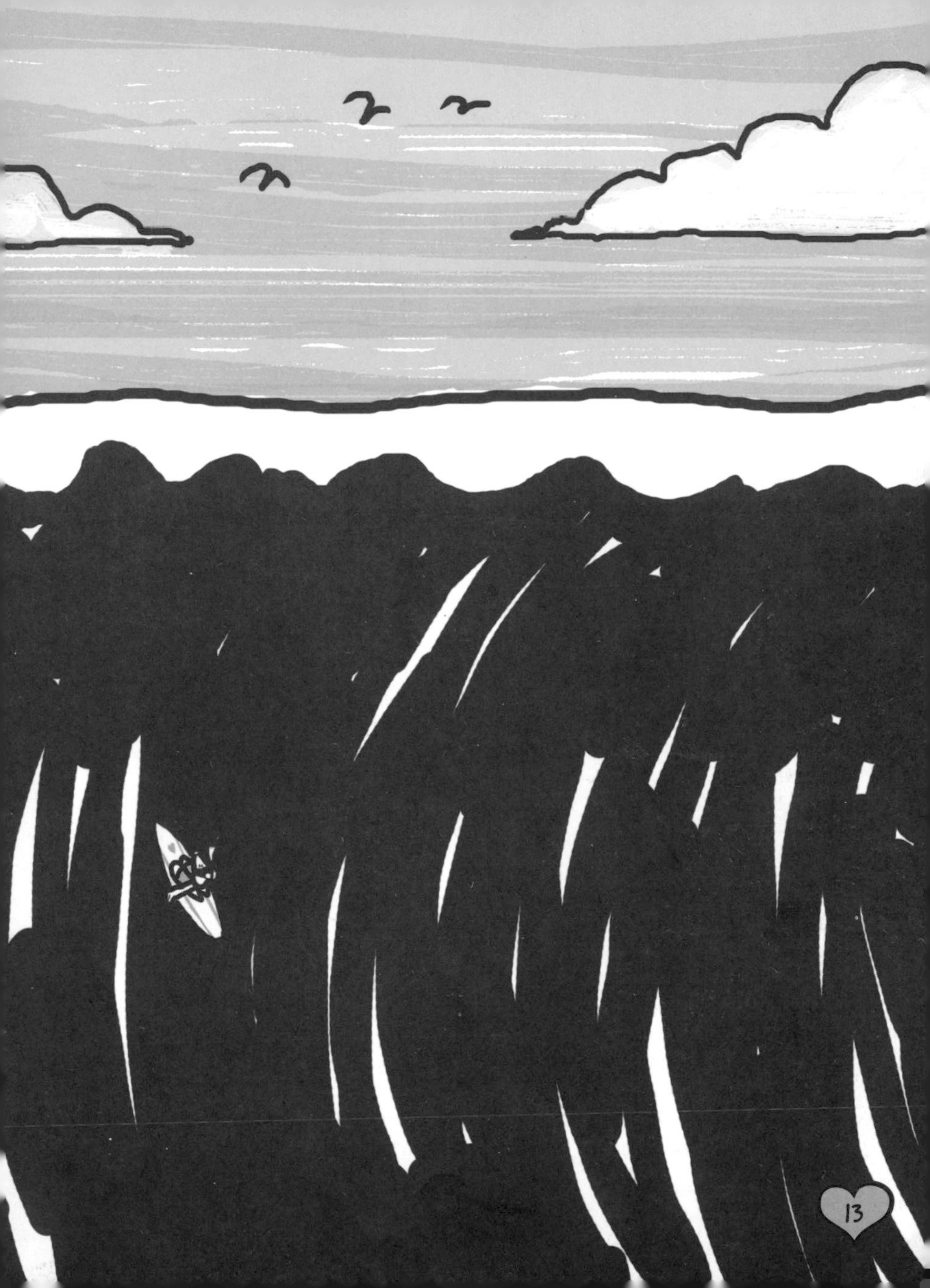

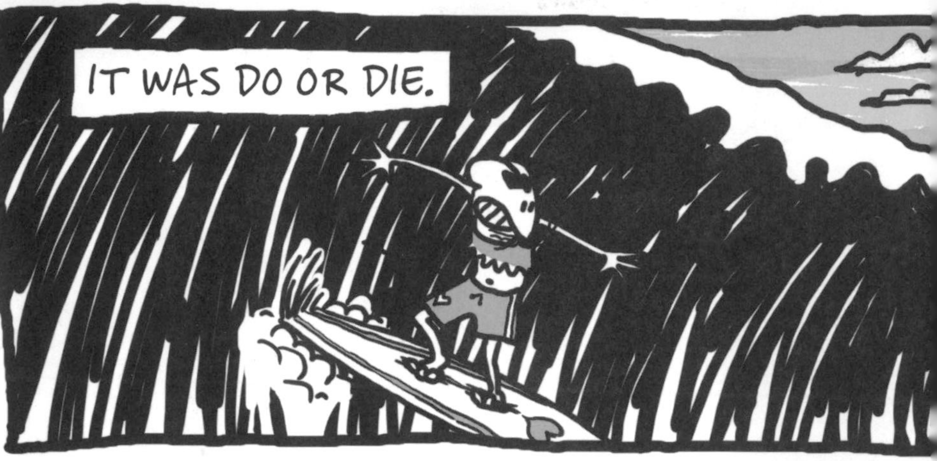
IT WAS DO OR DIE.

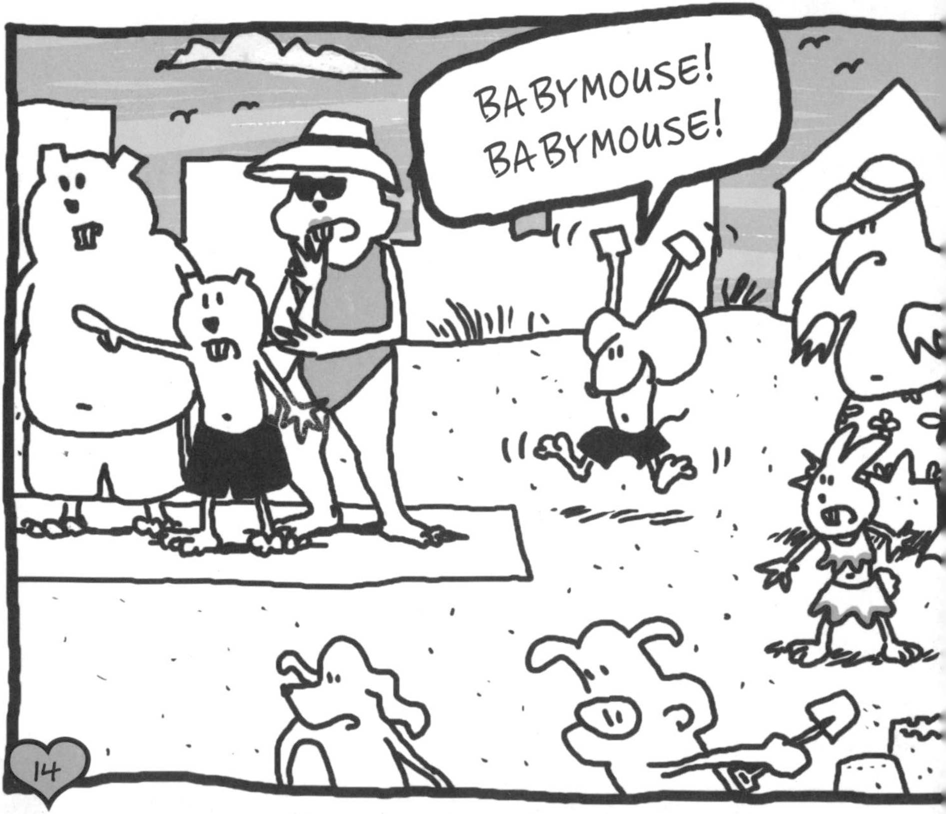
BABYMOUSE!
BABYMOUSE!

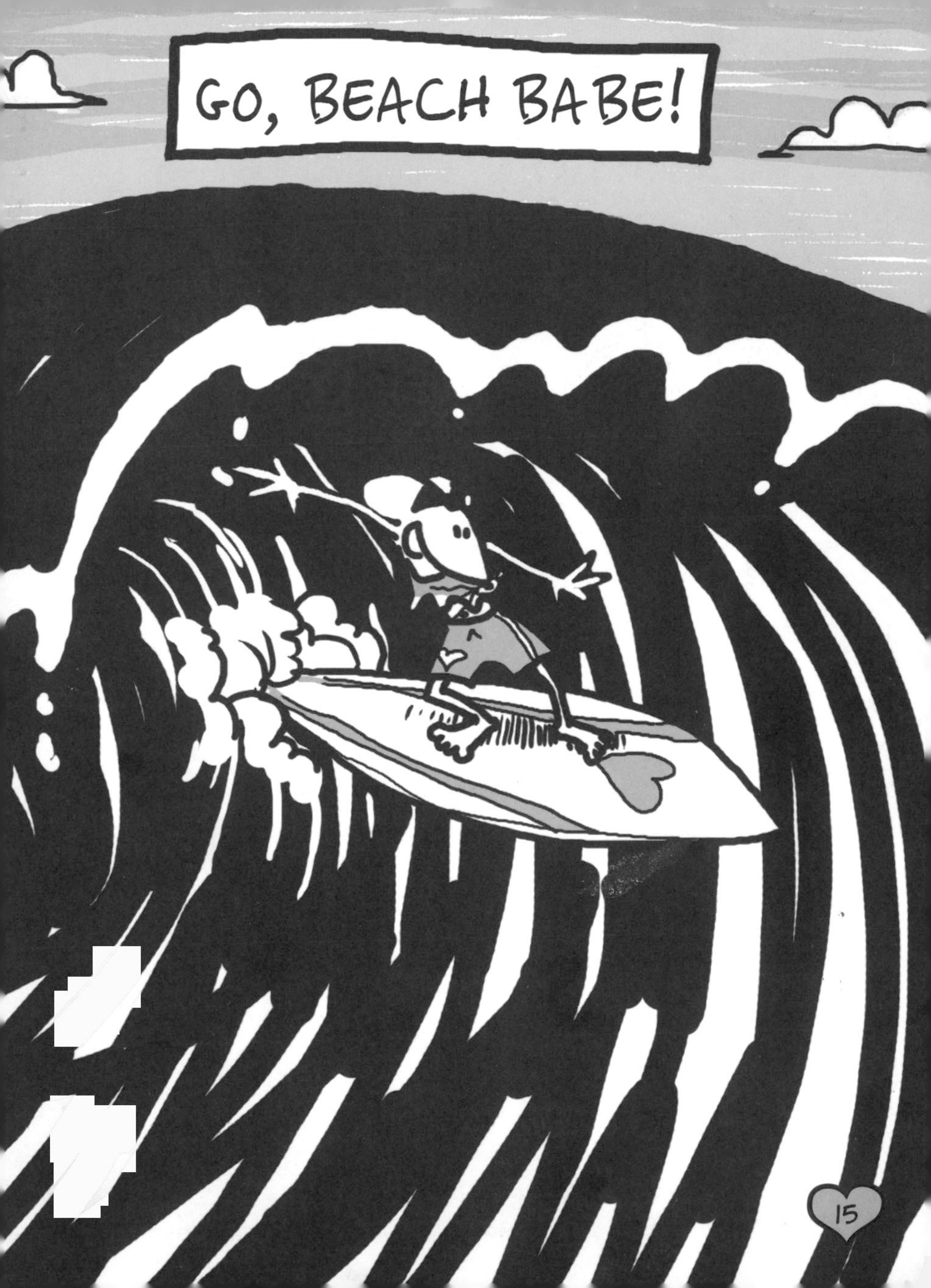
GO, BEACH BABE!

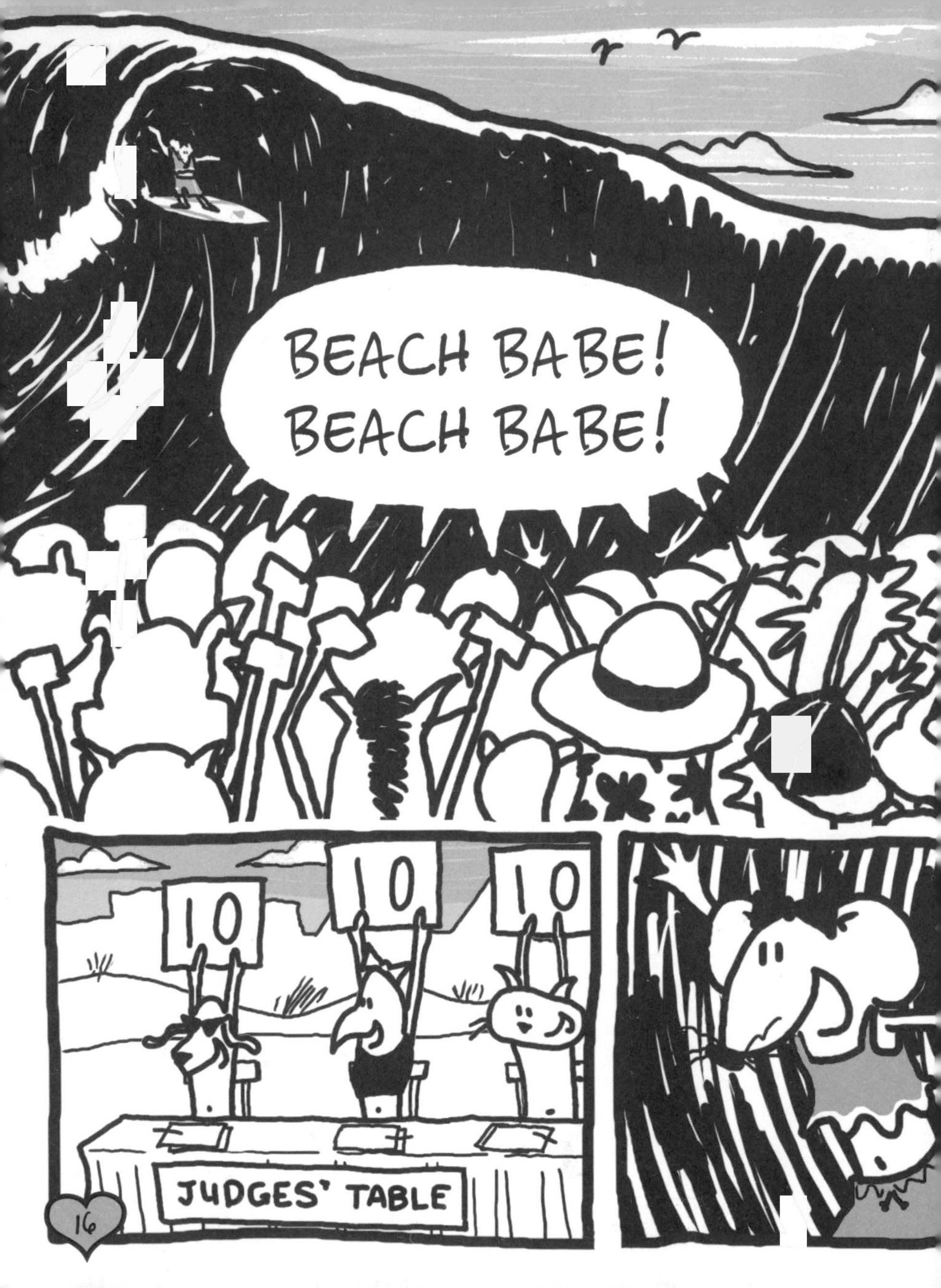
BEACH BABE!
BEACH BABE!
10
10
10
JUDGES' TABLE

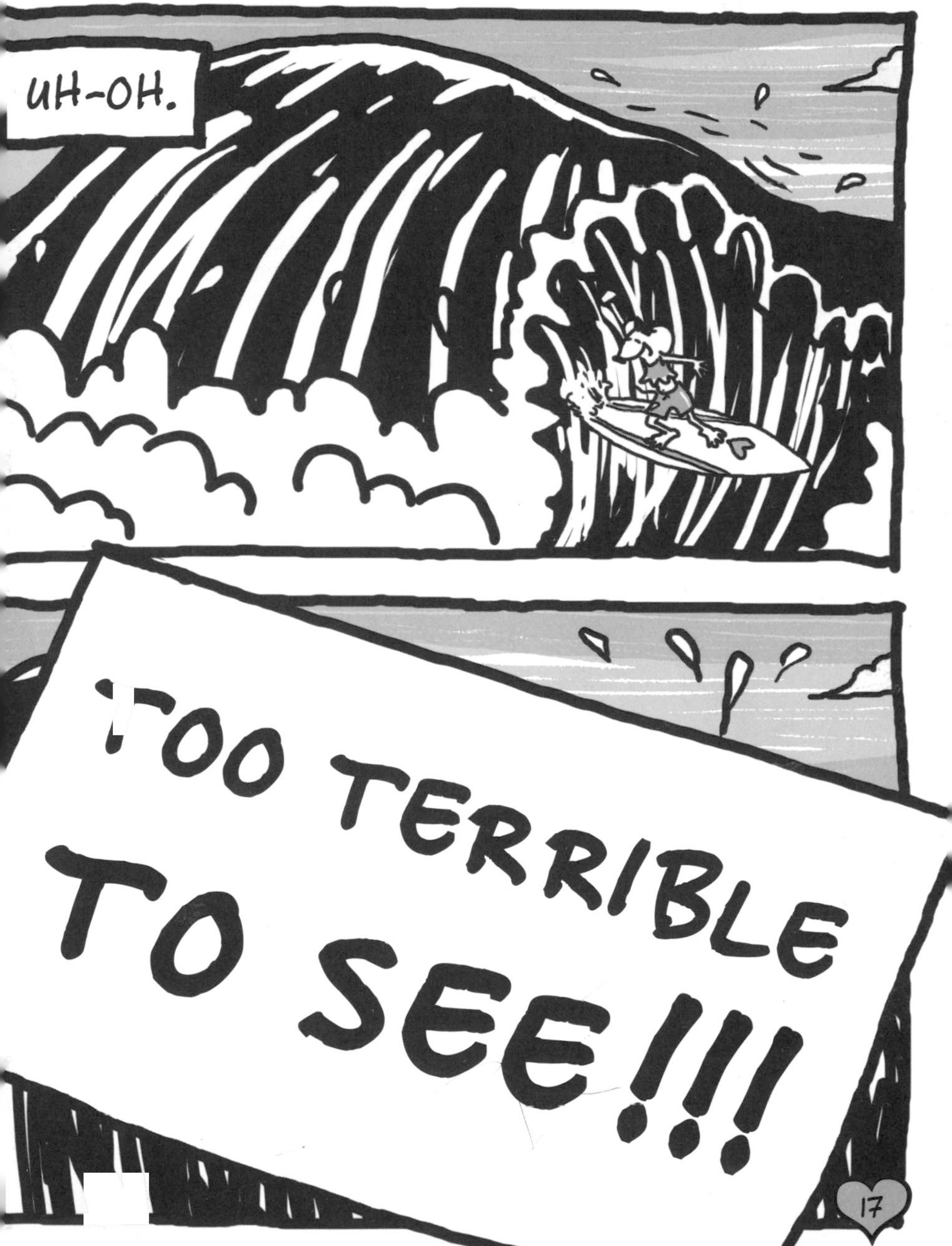
UH-OH.
TOO TERRIBLE TO SEE!!!

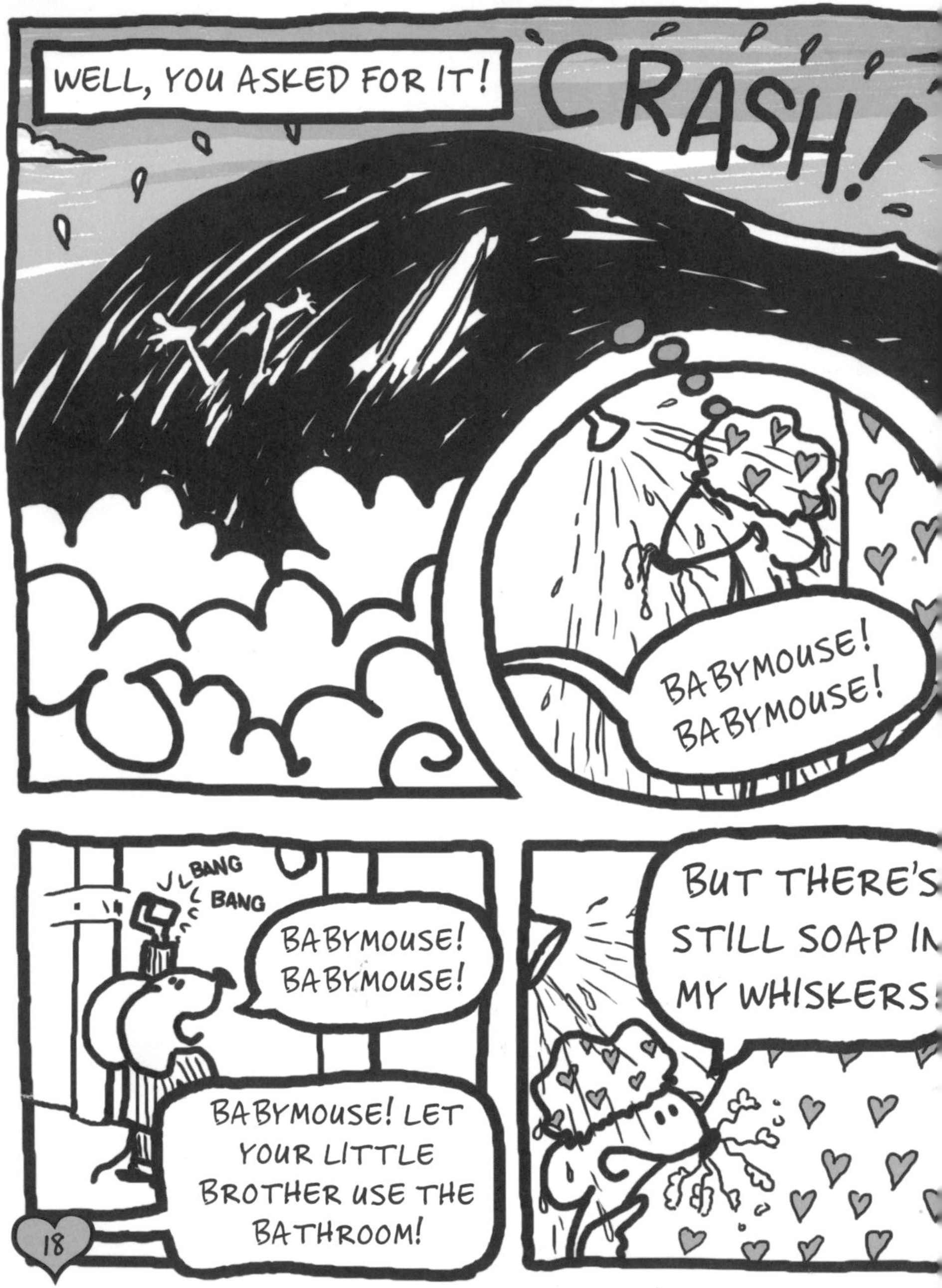
WELL, YOU ASKED FOR IT!
CRASH!
BABYMOUSE! BABYMOUSE!
BANG
BANG
BABYMOUSE! BABYMOUSE!
BABYMOUSE! LET YOUR LITTLE BROTHER USE THE BATHROOM!
BUT THERE'S STILL SOAP IN MY WHISKERS!

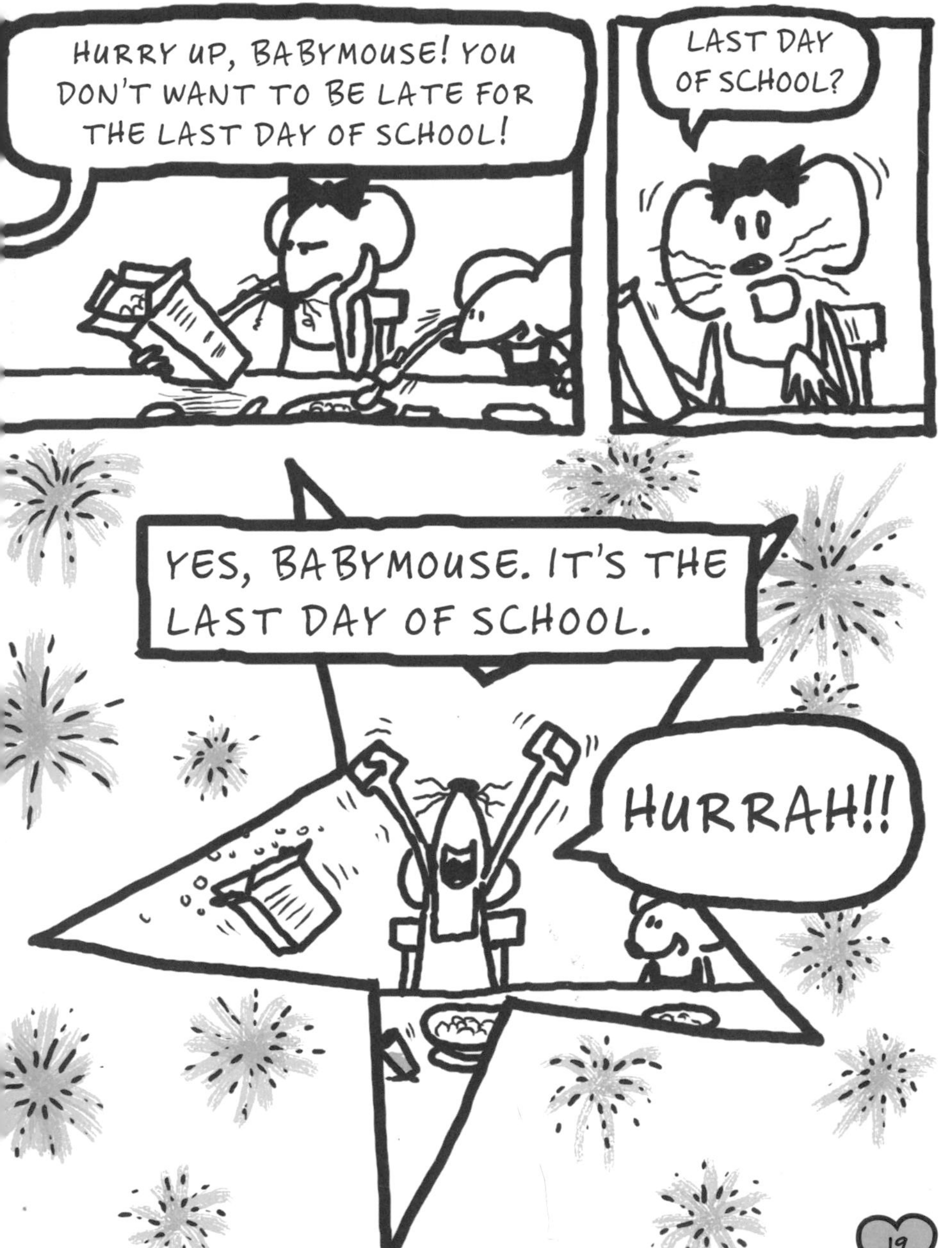
HURRY UP, BABYMOUSE! YOU DON'T WANT TO BE LATE FOR THE LAST DAY OF SCHOOL!
LAST DAY OF SCHOOL?
YES, BABYMOUSE. IT'S THE LAST DAY OF SCHOOL.
HURRAH!!

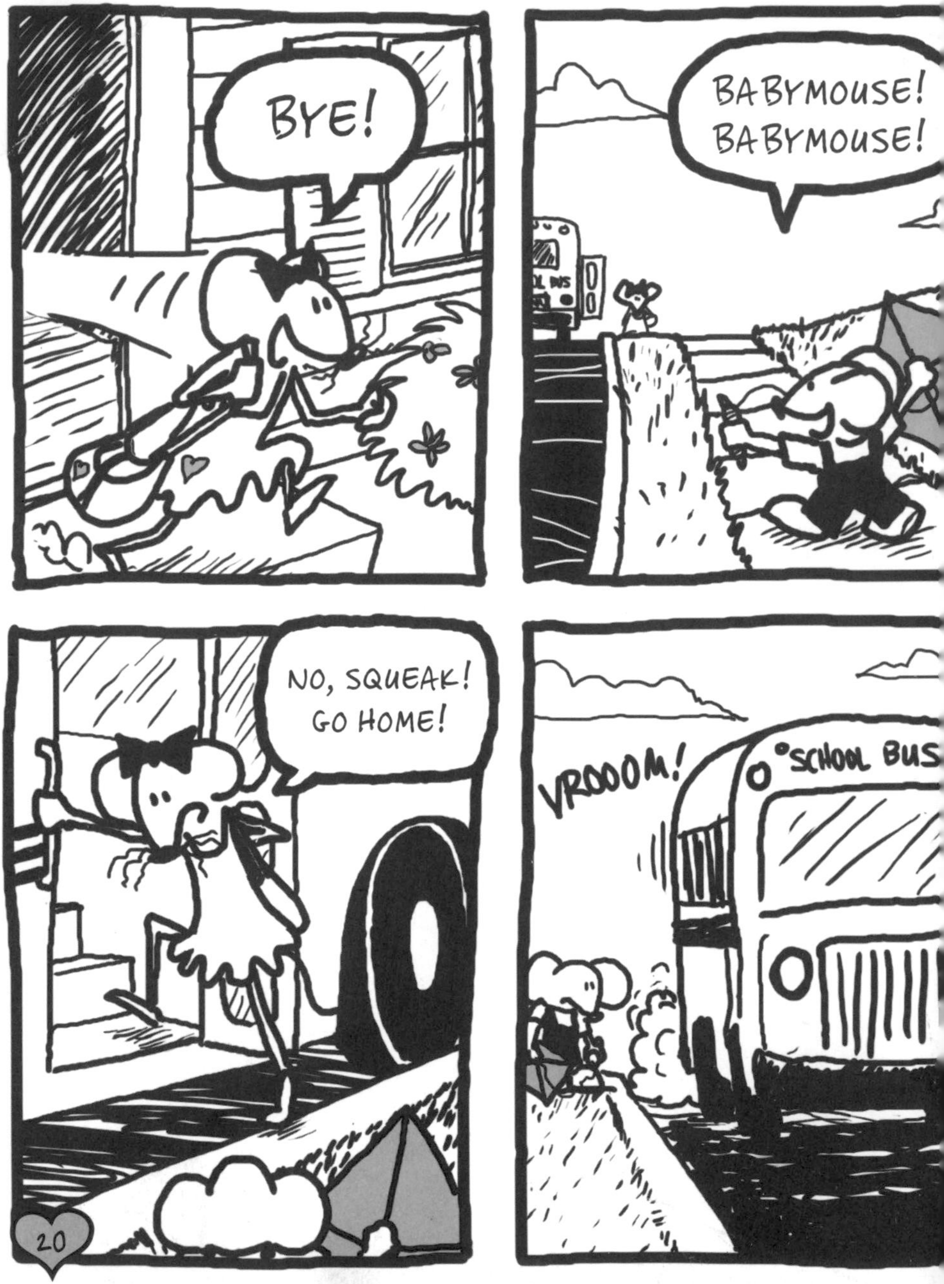
BYE!
BABYMOUSE! BABYMOUSE!
NO, SQUEAK! GO HOME!
VROOOM!
SCHOOL BUS

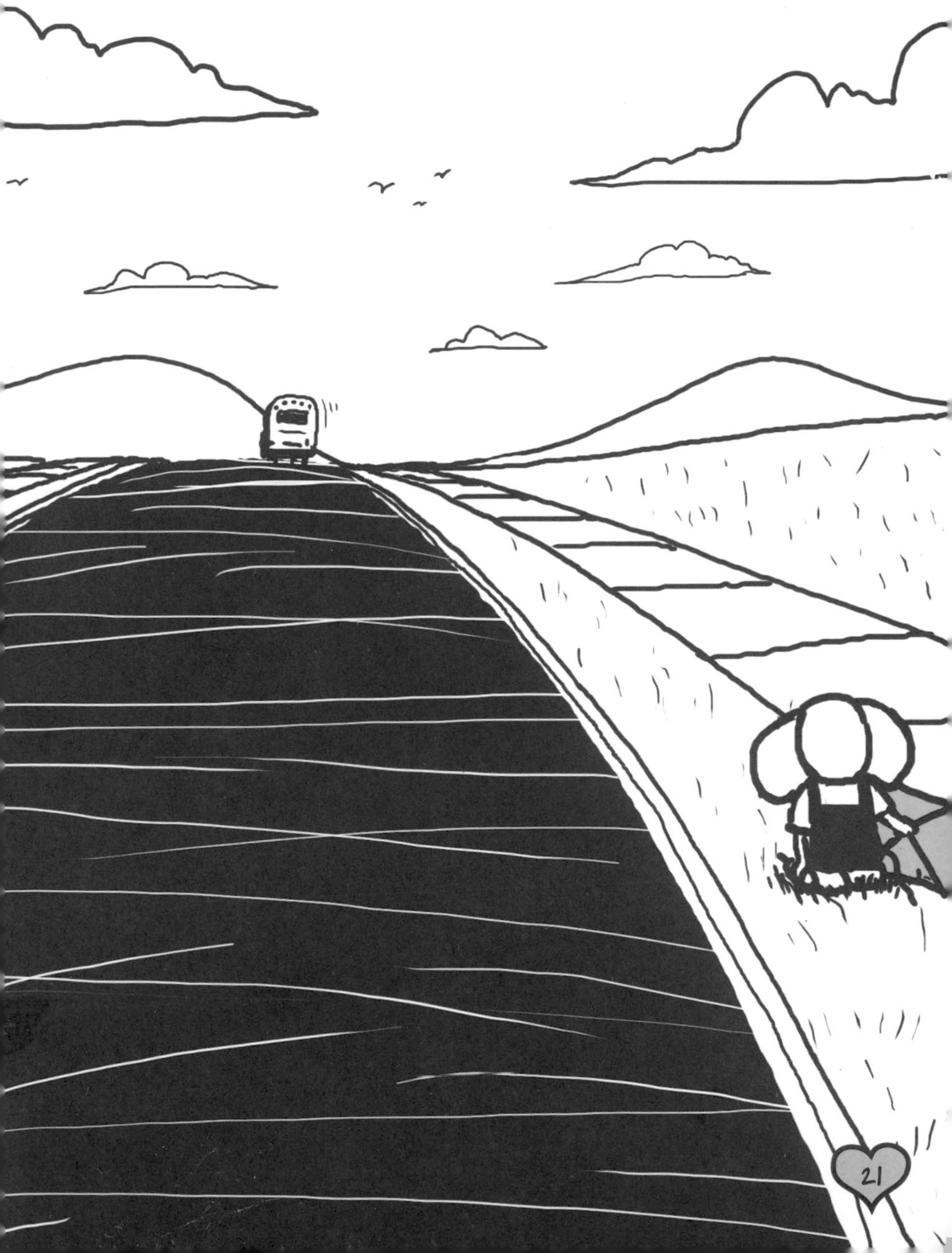

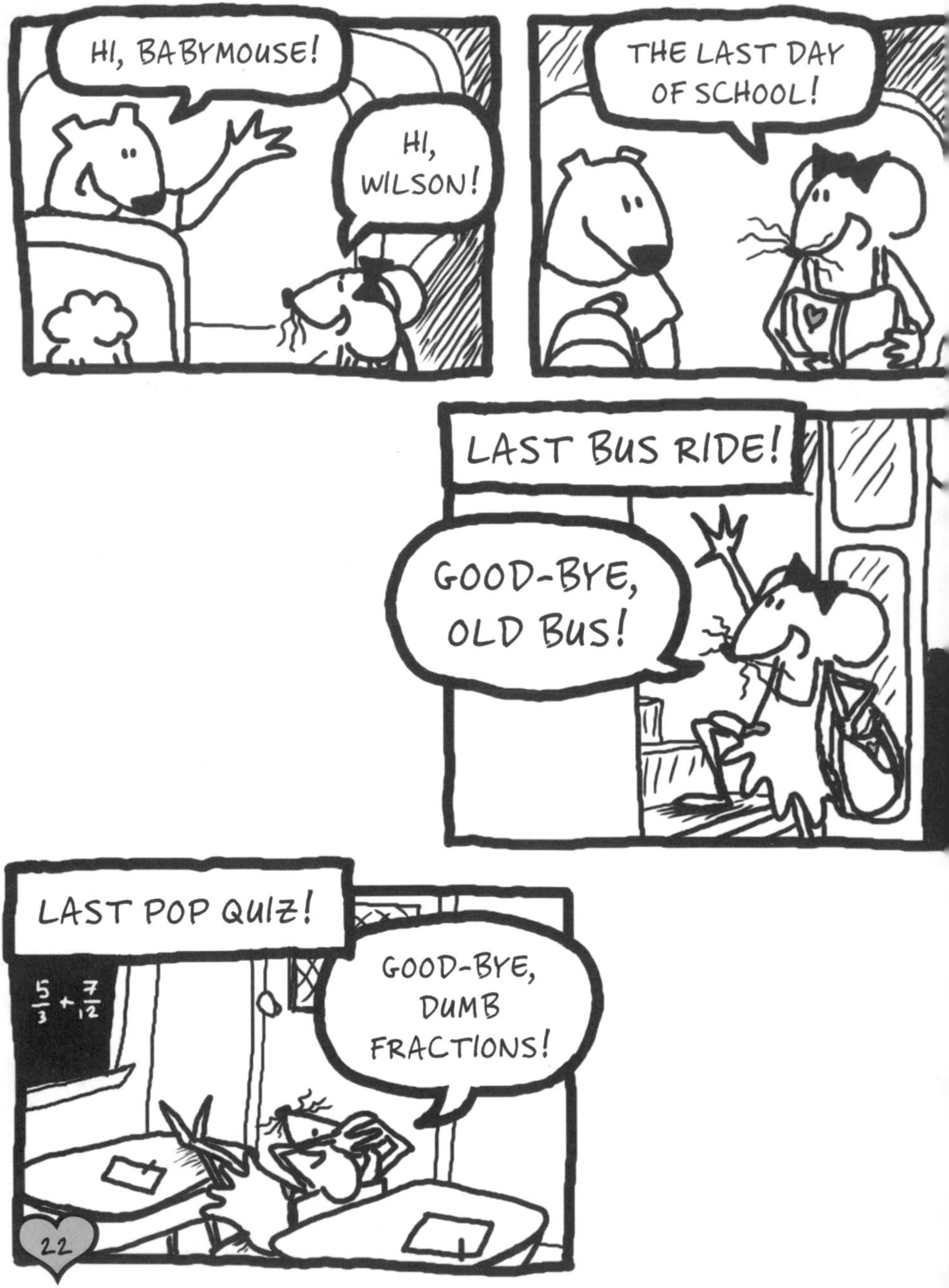
HI, BABYMOUSE!
HI, WILSON!
THE LAST DAY OF SCHOOL!
LAST BUS RIDE!
GOOD-BYE, OLD BUS!
LAST POP QUIZ!
5/3 + 7/12
GOOD-BYE, DUMB FRACTIONS!

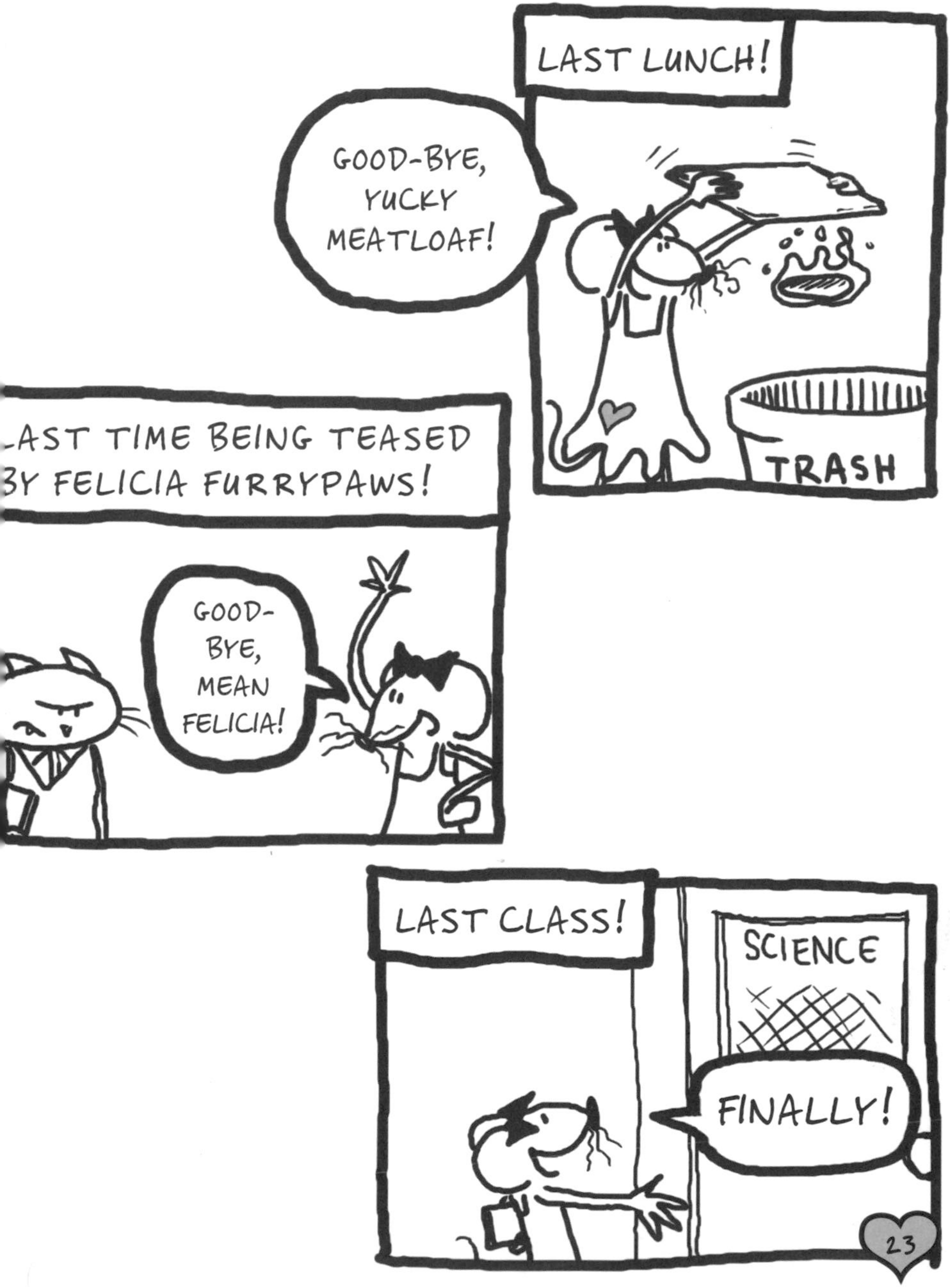
LAST LUNCH!
GOOD-BYE, YUCKY MEATLOAF!
TRASH
LAST TIME BEING TEASED BY FELICIA FURRYPAWS!
GOOD-BYE, MEAN FELICIA!
LAST CLASS!
SCIENCE
FINALLY!

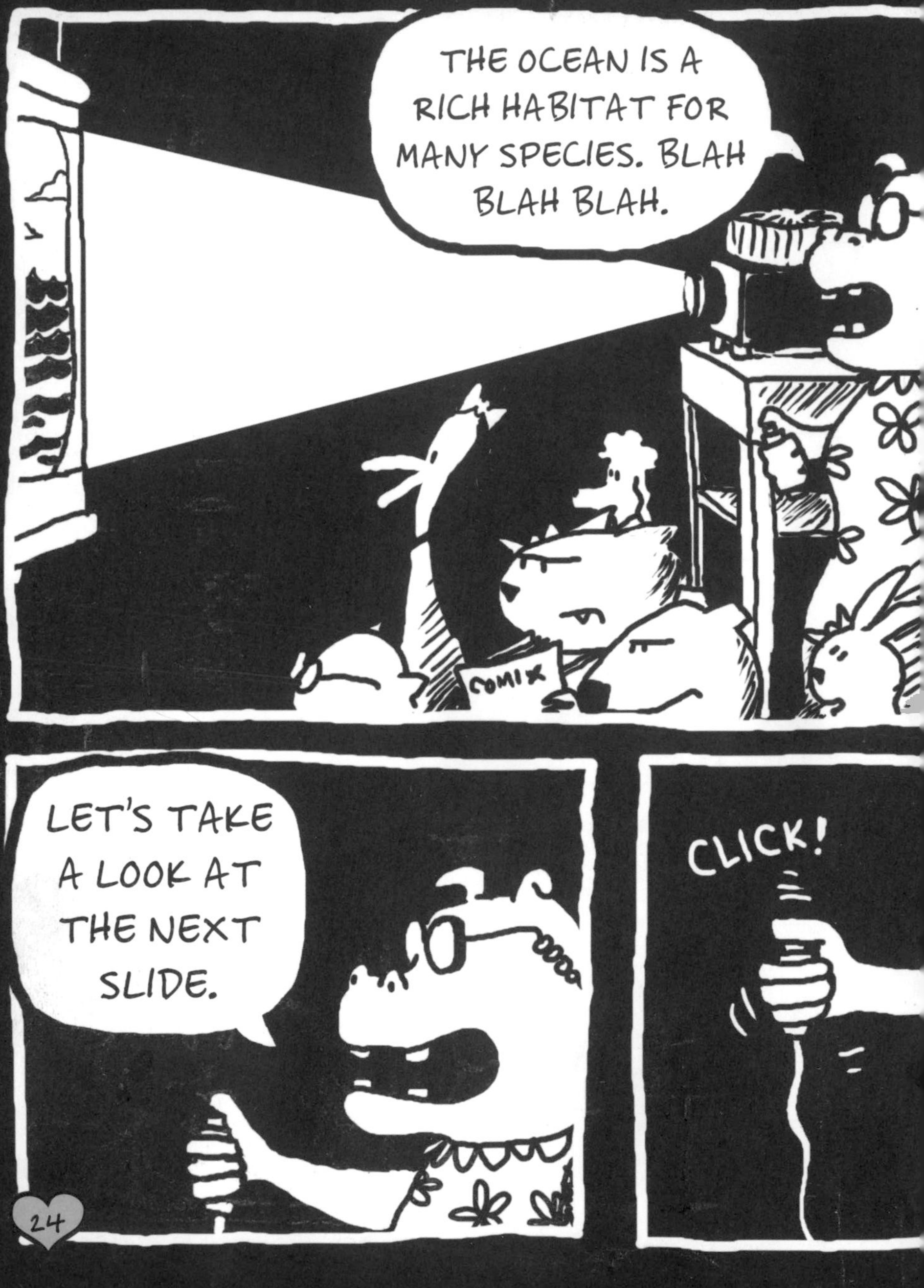
THE OCEAN IS A RICH HABITAT FOR MANY SPECIES. BLAH BLAH BLAH.
COMIX
LET'S TAKE A LOOK AT THE NEXT SLIDE.
CLICK!

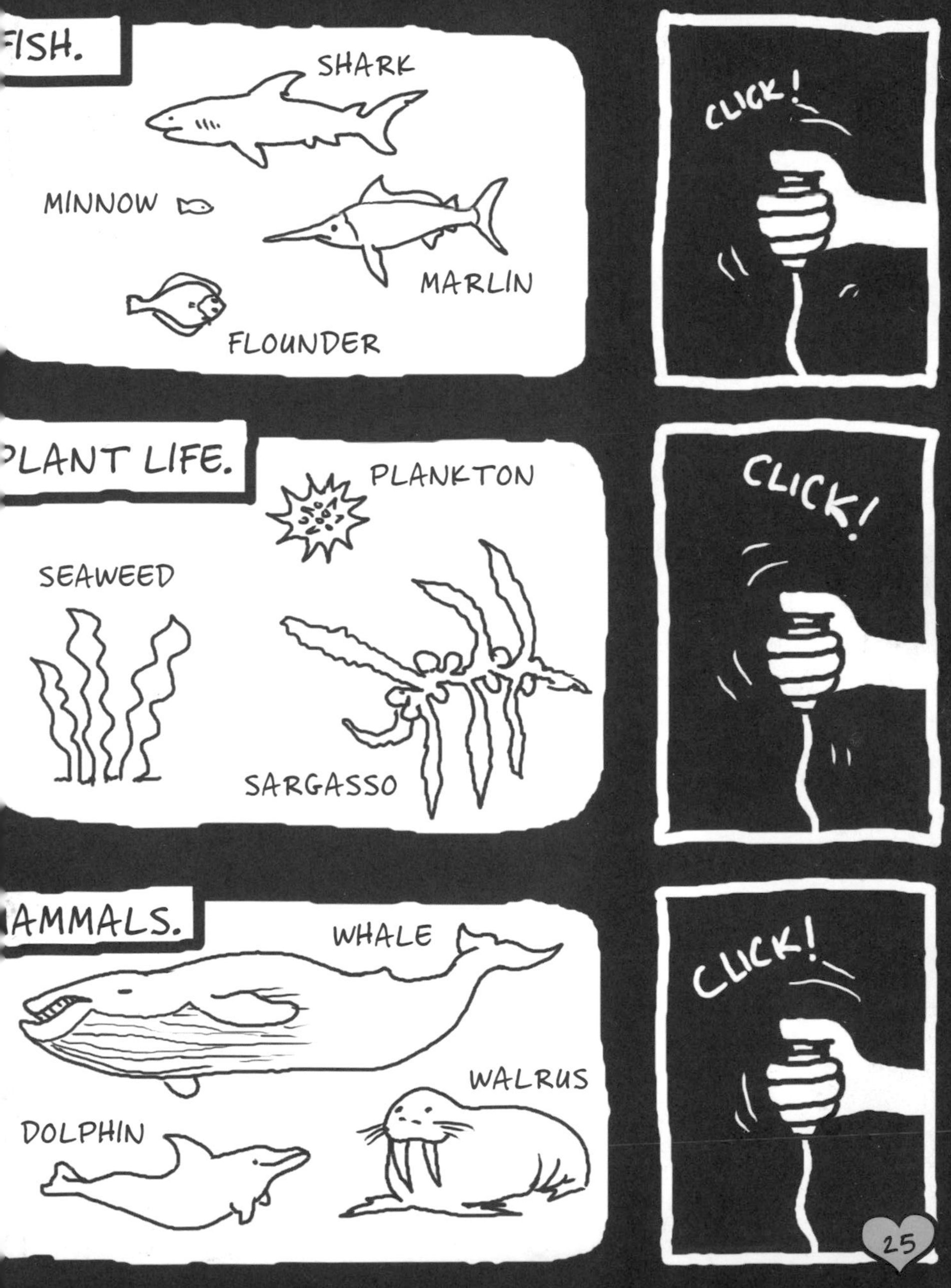

FISH.
SHARK
MINNOW
MARLIN
FLOUNDER
CLICK!
PLANT LIFE.
PLANKTON
SEAWEED
SARGASSO
CLICK!
AMMALS.
WHALE
WALRUS
DOLPHIN
CLICK!

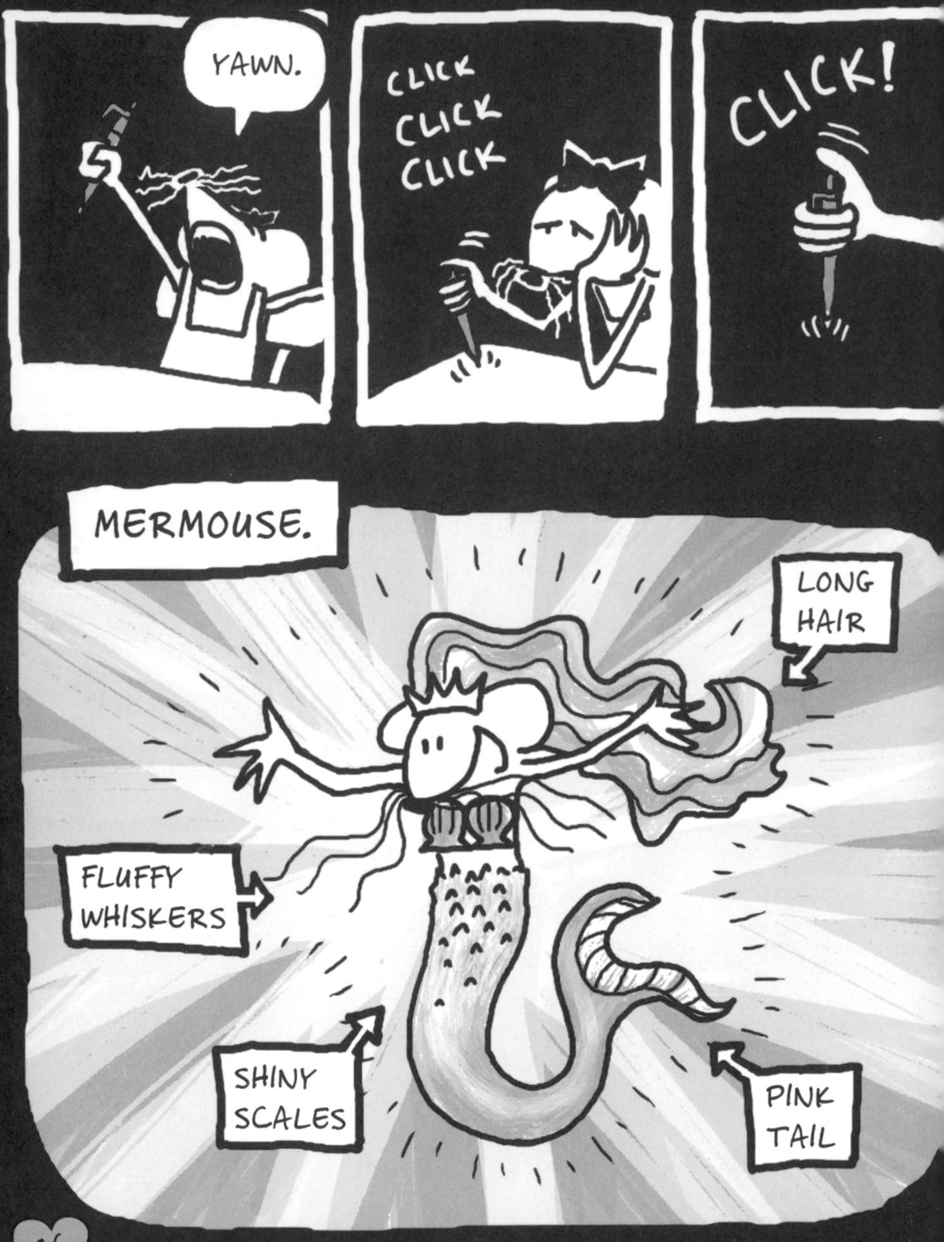
YAWN.
CLICK
CLICK
CLICK
CLICK!
MERMOUSE.
LONG HAIR
FLUFFY WHISKERS
SHINY SCALES
PINK TAIL

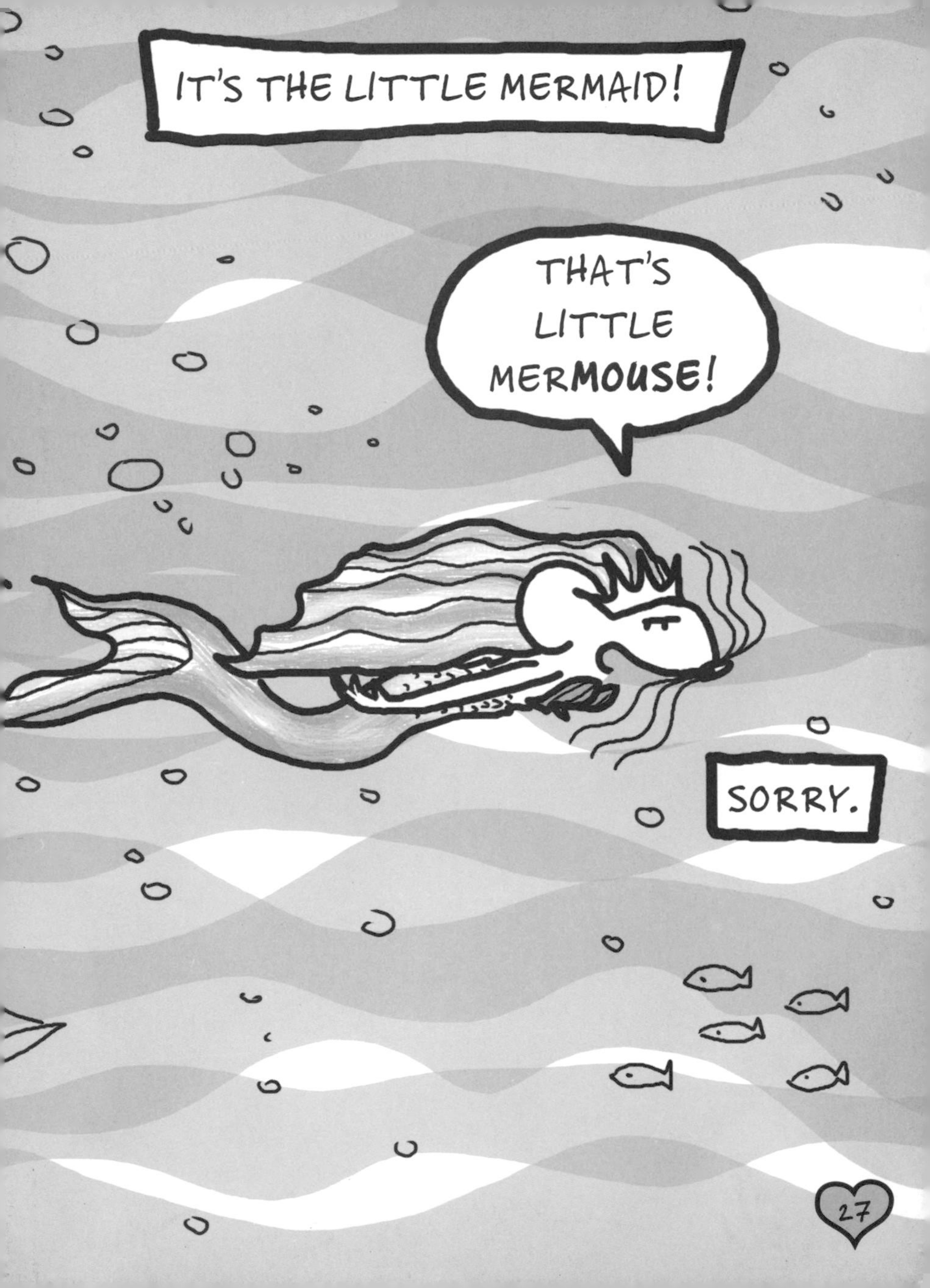
IT'S THE LITTLE MERMAID!
THAT'S LITTLE MERMOUSE!
SORRY.

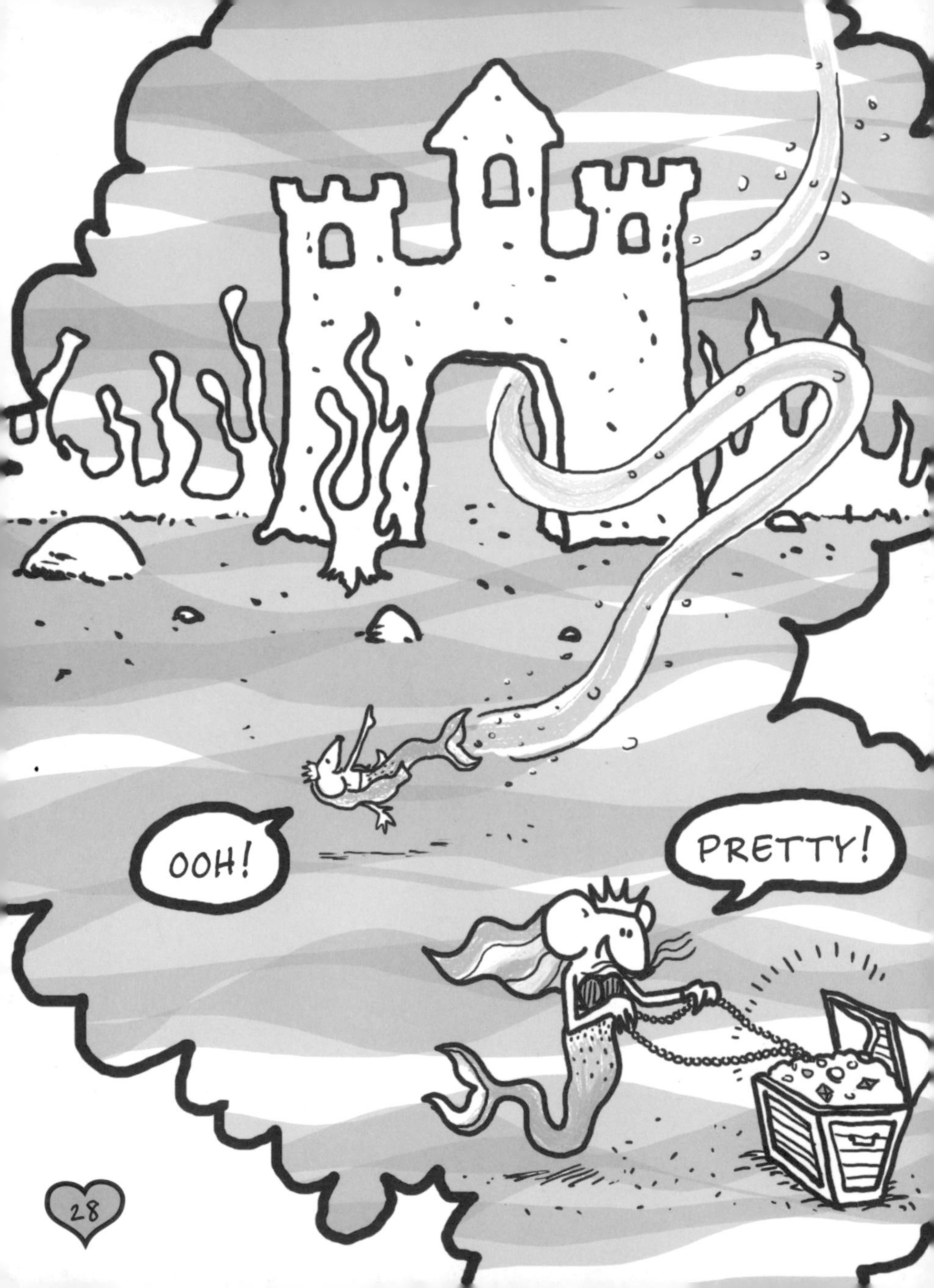
OOH!
PRETTY!

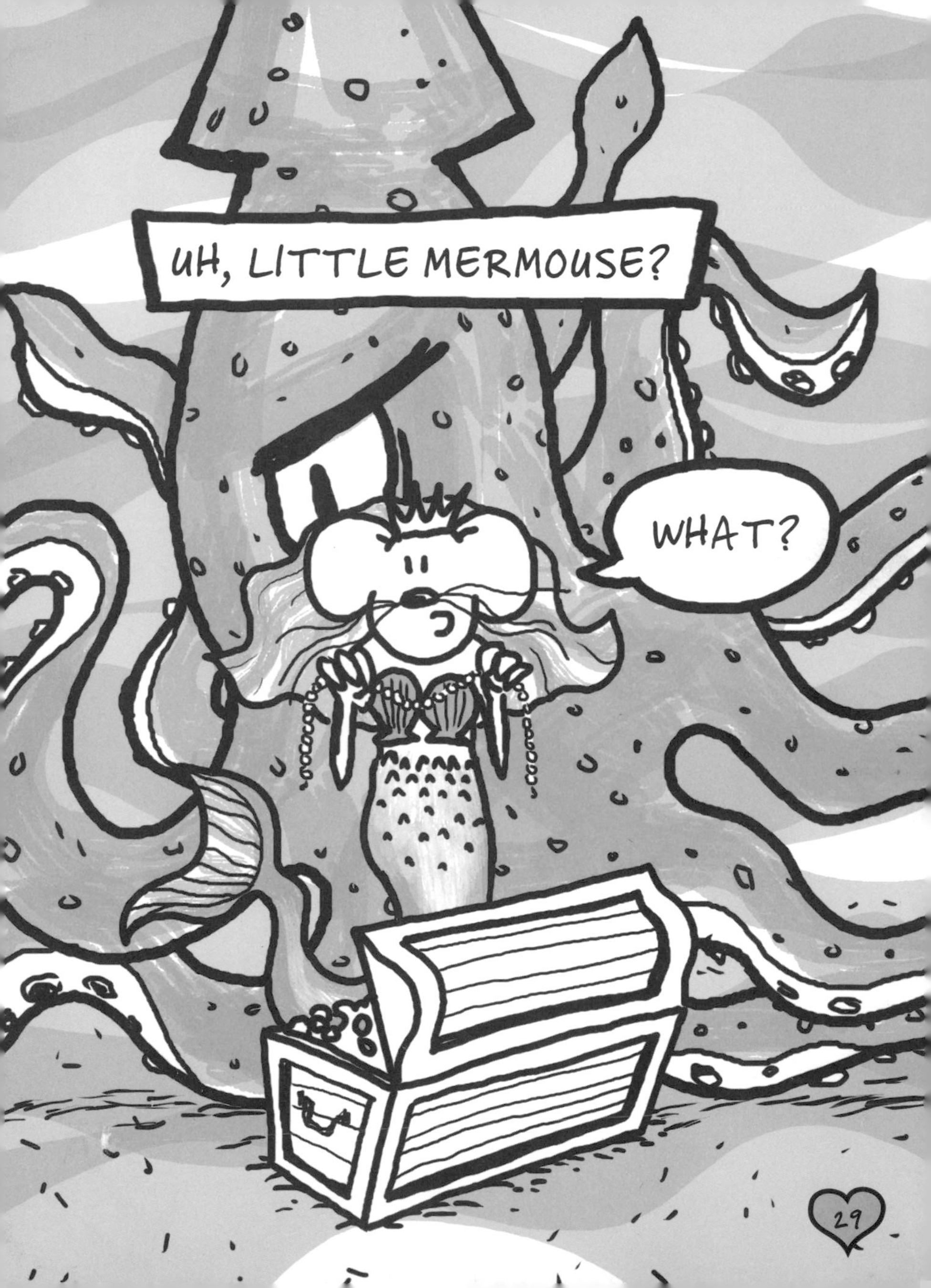
UH, LITTLE MERMOUSE?
WHAT?

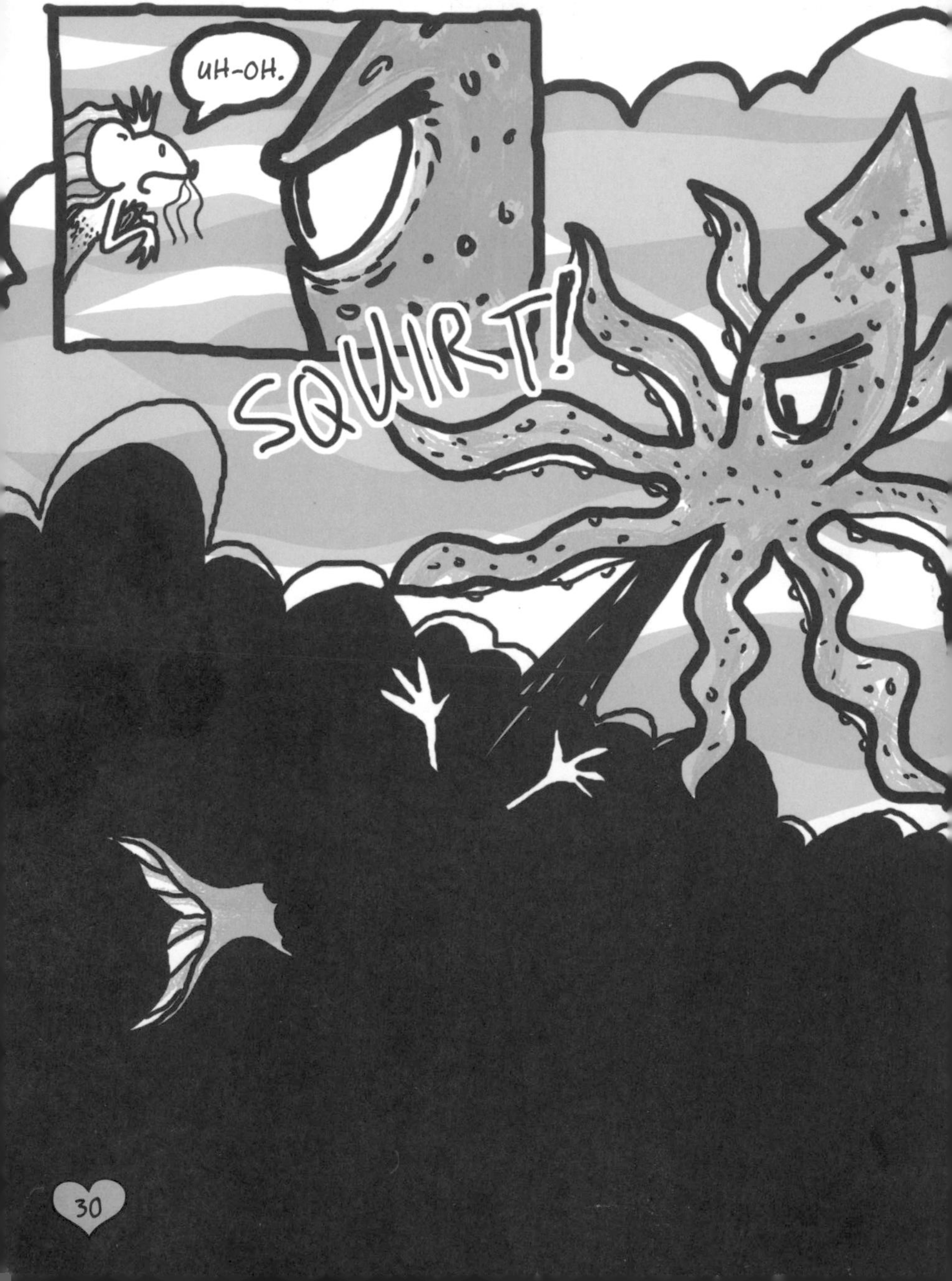
UH-OH.
SQUIRT!

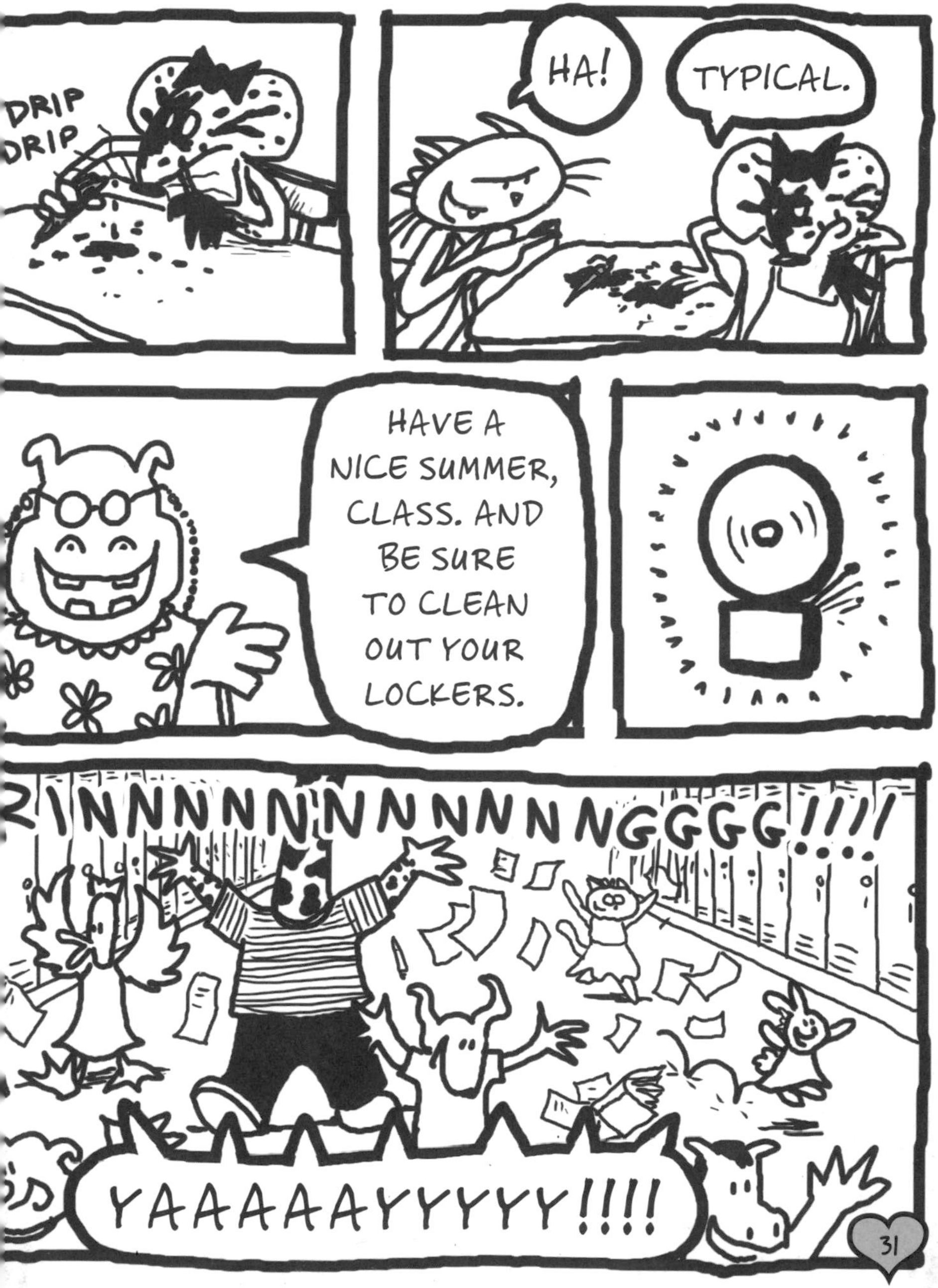
DRIP
DRIP
HA!
TYPICAL.
HAVE A NICE SUMMER, CLASS. AND BE SURE TO CLEAN OUT YOUR LOCKERS.
RINNNNNNNNNNNGGGG!!!!
YAAAAAYYYYYY!!!!

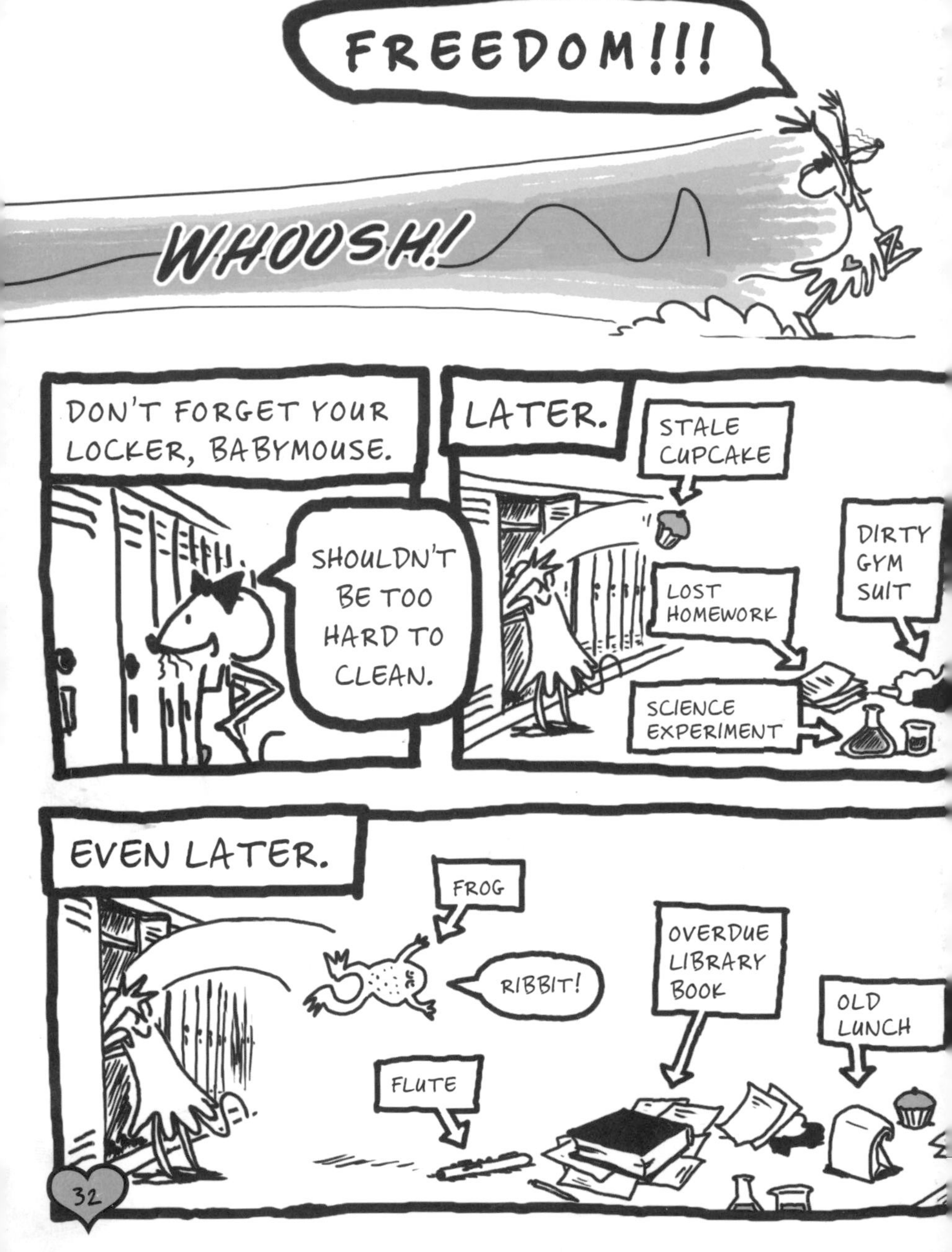
FREEDOM!!!
WHOOSH!
DON'T FORGET YOUR LOCKER, BABYMOUSE.
SHOULDN'T BE TOO HARD TO CLEAN.
LATER.
STALE CUPCAKE
LOST HOMEWORK
DIRTY GYM SUIT
SCIENCE EXPERIMENT
EVEN LATER.
FROG
RIBBIT!
OVERDUE LIBRARY BOOK
OLD LUNCH
FLUTE

MUCH LATER.
METEOR
KING TUT'S SARCOPHAGUS
BIGFOOT
ALIENS
ROUBLESOME
JOMES
DISH THAT RAN AWAY WITH THE SPOON
WE'RE NO TROUBLE AT ALL!

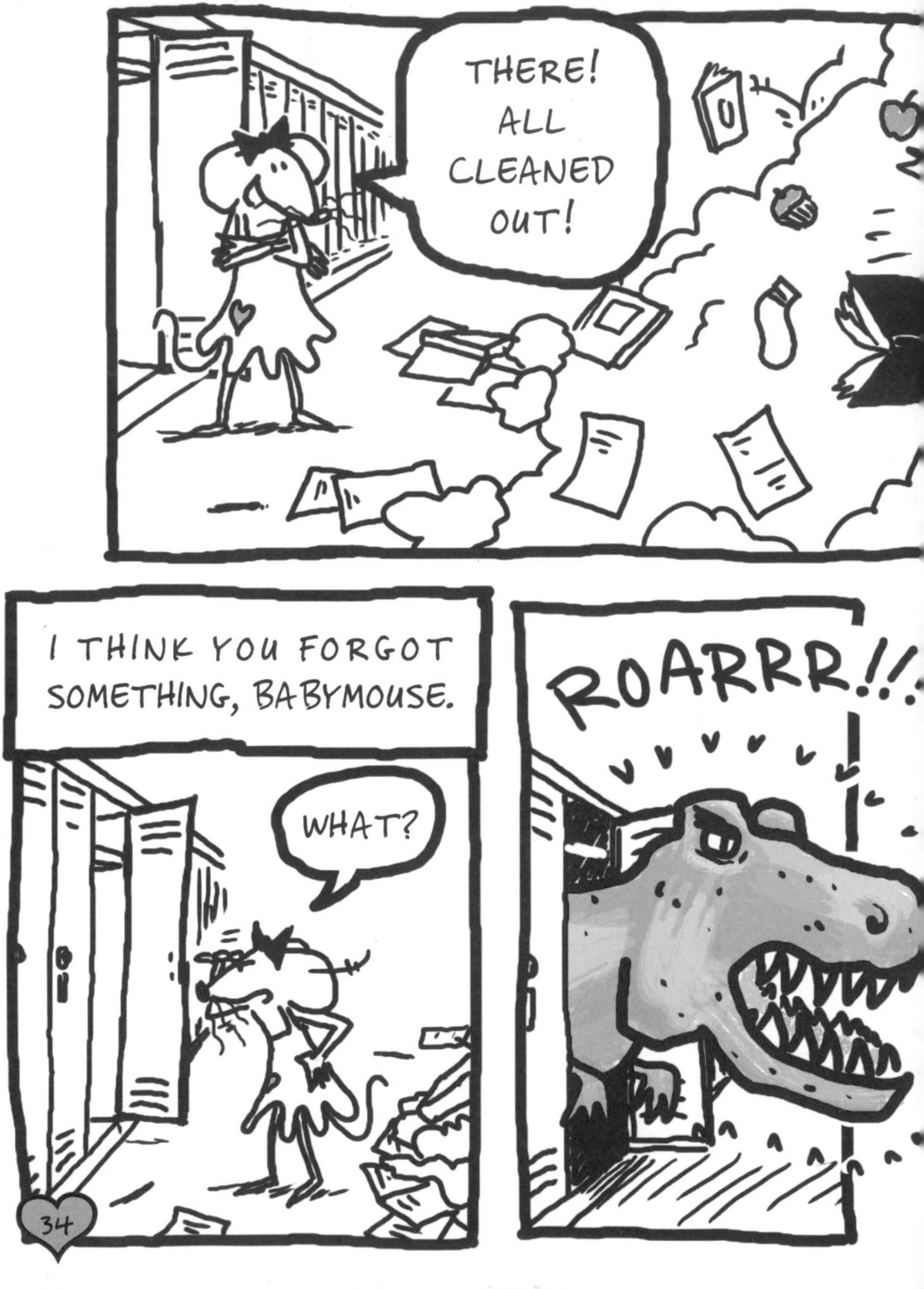
THERE! ALL CLEANED OUT!
I THINK YOU FORGOT SOMETHING, BABYMOUSE.
WHAT?
ROARRR!!!

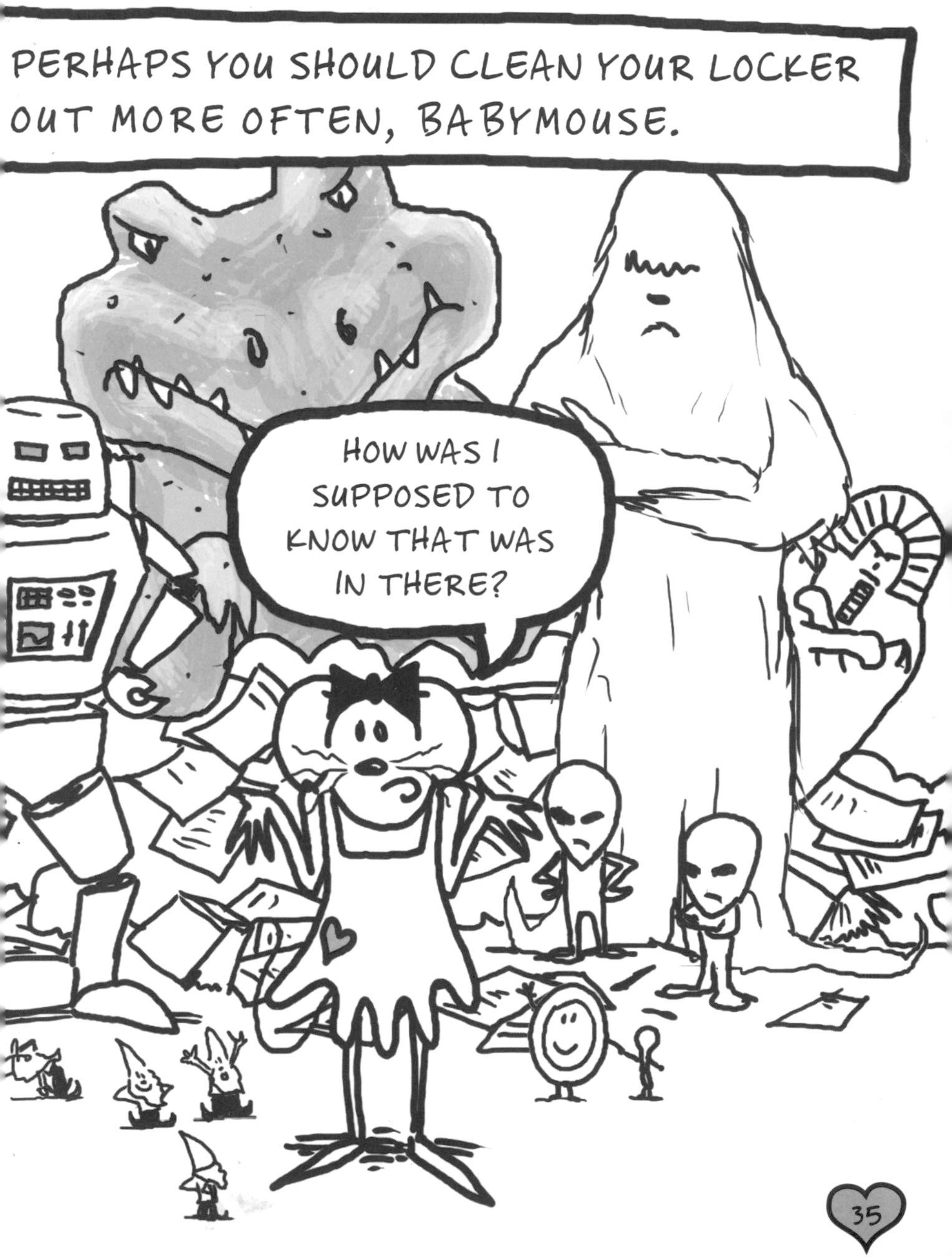
PERHAPS YOU SHOULD CLEAN YOUR LOCKER OUT MORE OFTEN, BABYMOUSE.
HOW WAS I SUPPOSED TO KNOW THAT WAS IN THERE?

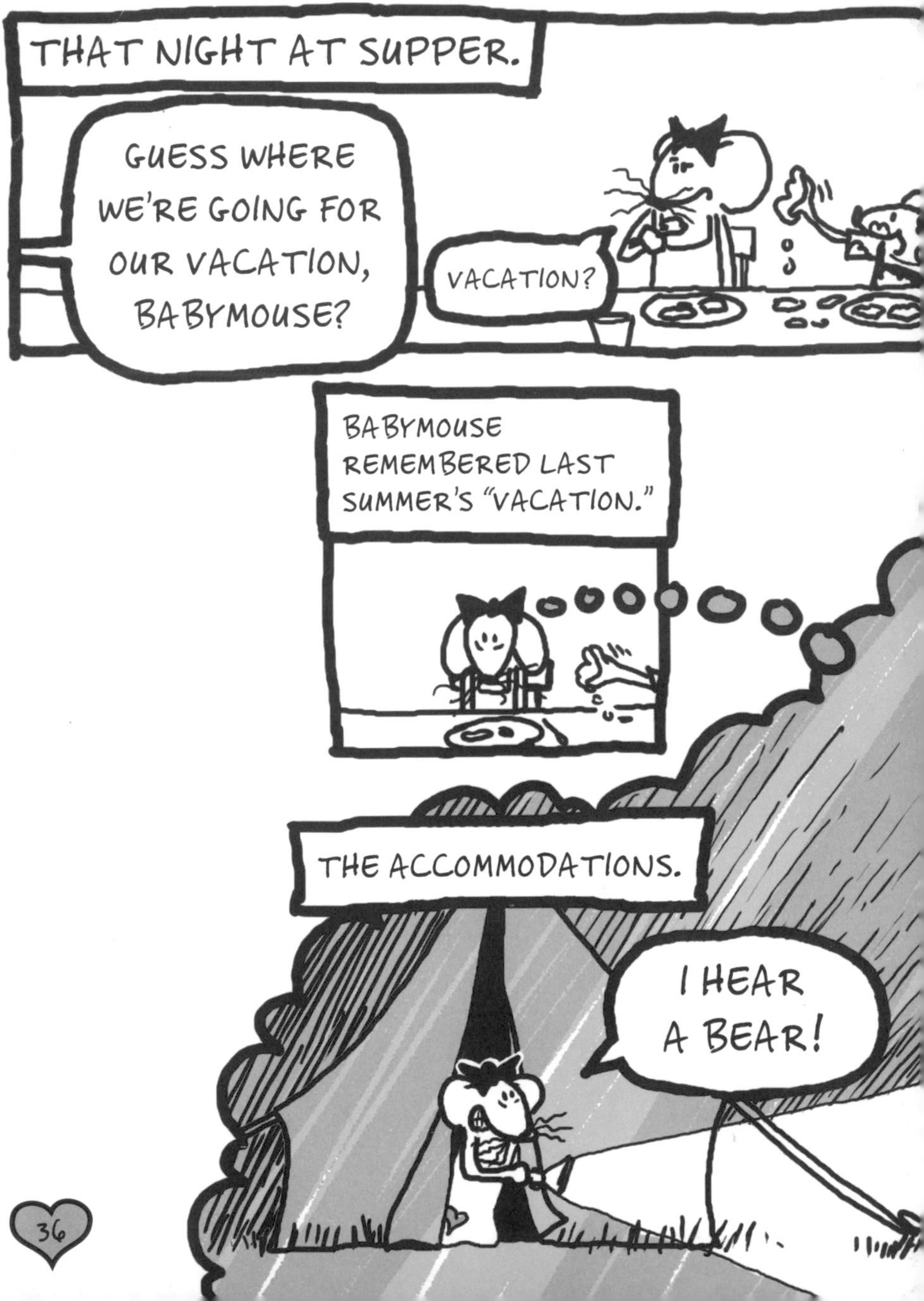
THAT NIGHT AT SUPPER.
GUESS WHERE WE'RE GOING FOR OUR VACATION, BABYMOUSE?
VACATION?
BABYMOUSE REMEMBERED LAST SUMMER'S "VACATION."
THE ACCOMMODATIONS.
I HEAR A BEAR!

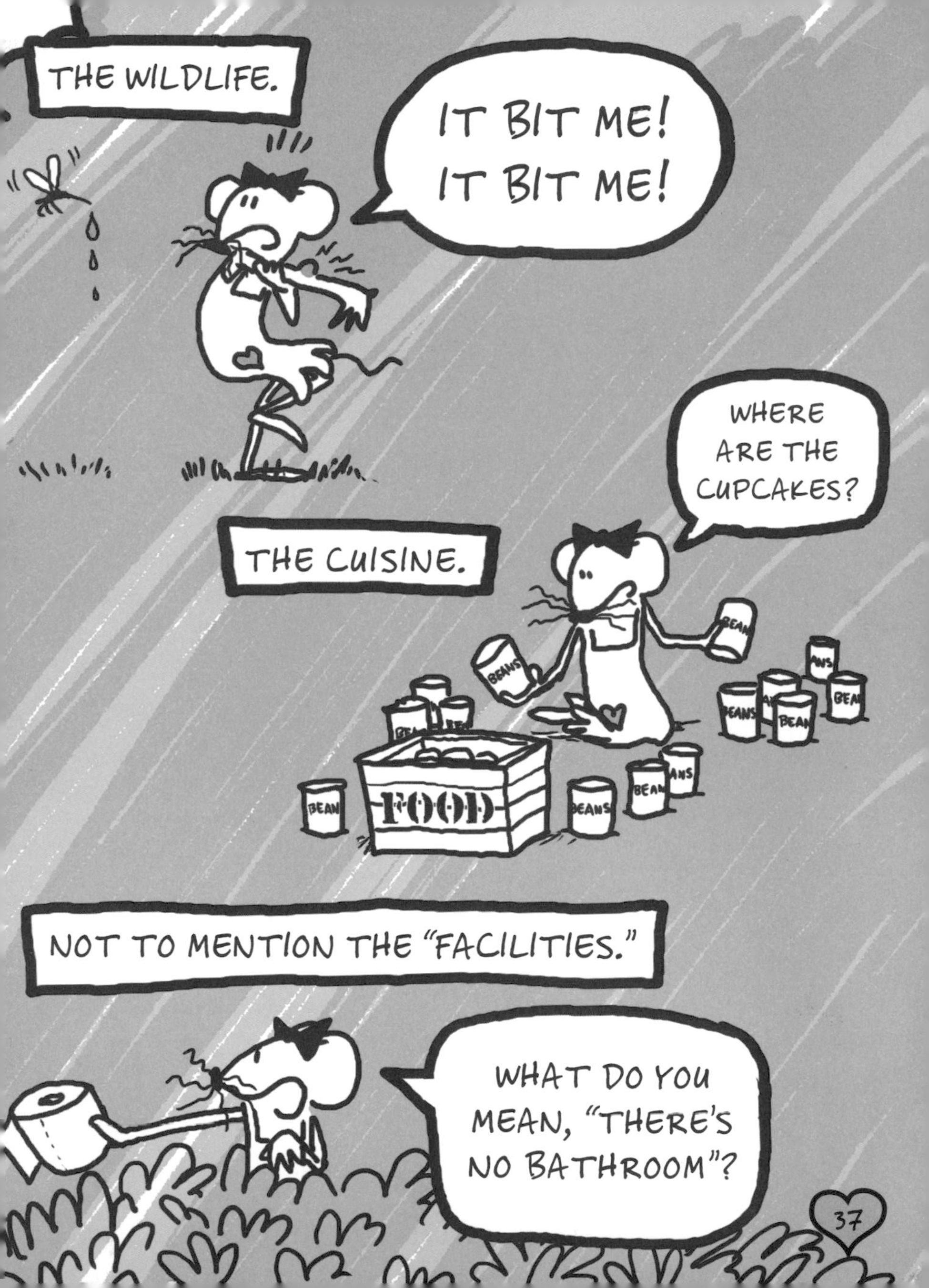
THE WILDLIFE.
IT BIT ME! IT BIT ME!
THE CUISINE.
WHERE ARE THE CUPCAKES?
FOOD
BEANS
NOT TO MENTION THE "FACILITIES."
WHAT DO YOU MEAN, "THERE'S NO BATHROOM"?

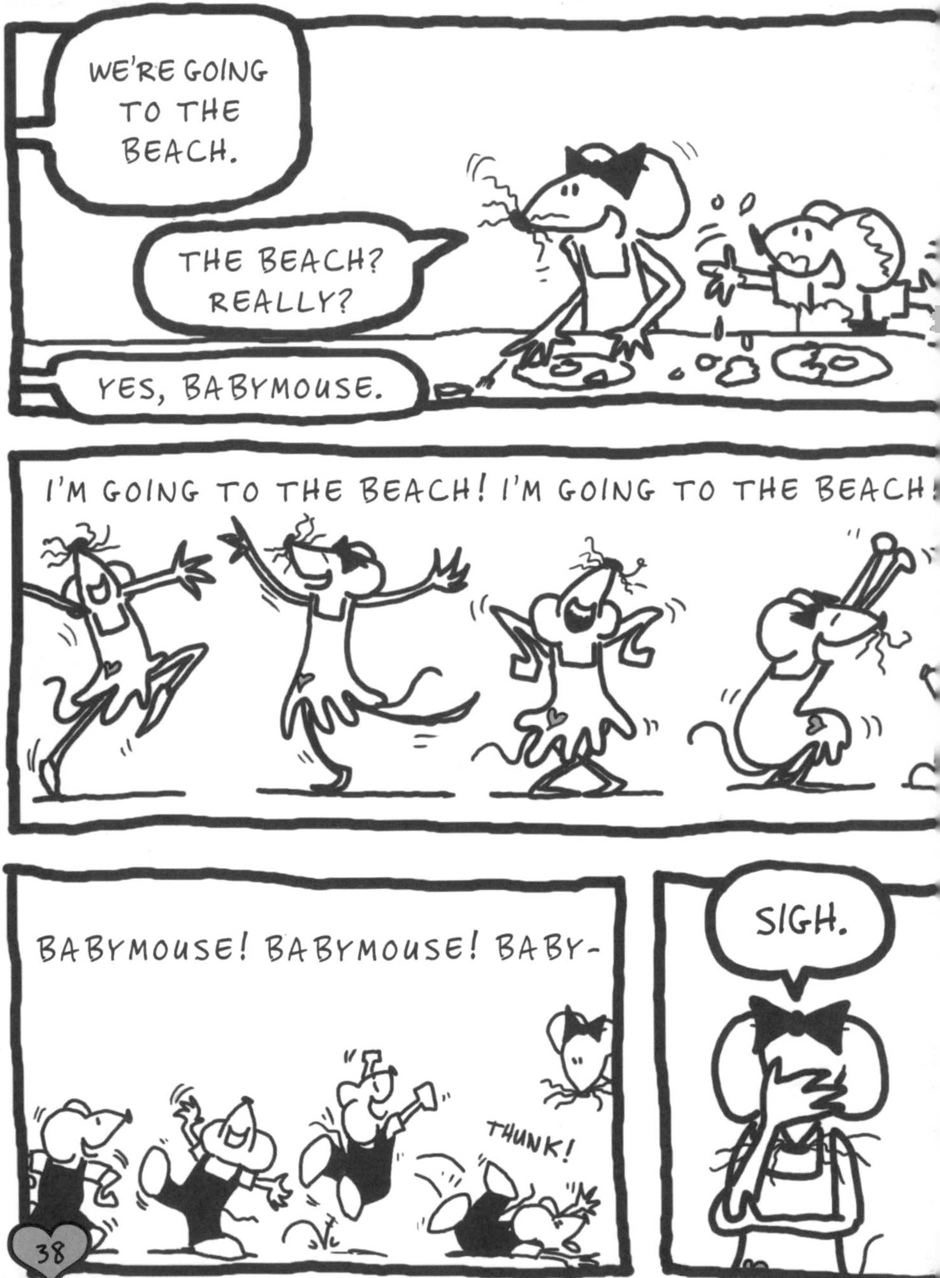
WE'RE GOING TO THE BEACH.
THE BEACH? REALLY?
YES, BABYMOUSE.
I'M GOING TO THE BEACH! I'M GOING TO THE BEACH!
BABYMOUSE! BABYMOUSE! BABY-
THUNK!
SIGH.

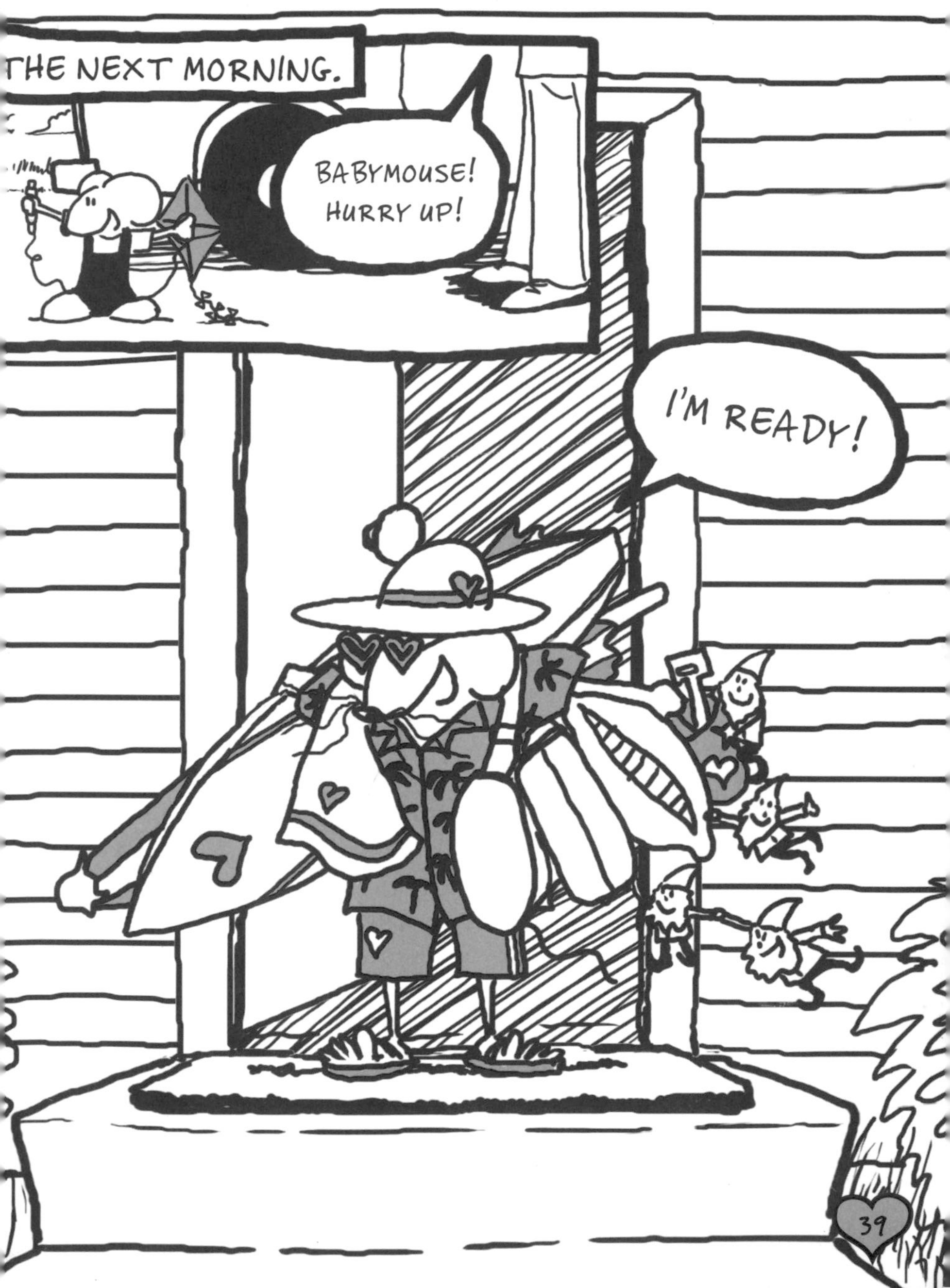
THE NEXT MORNING.
BABYMOUSE! HURRY UP!
I'M READY!

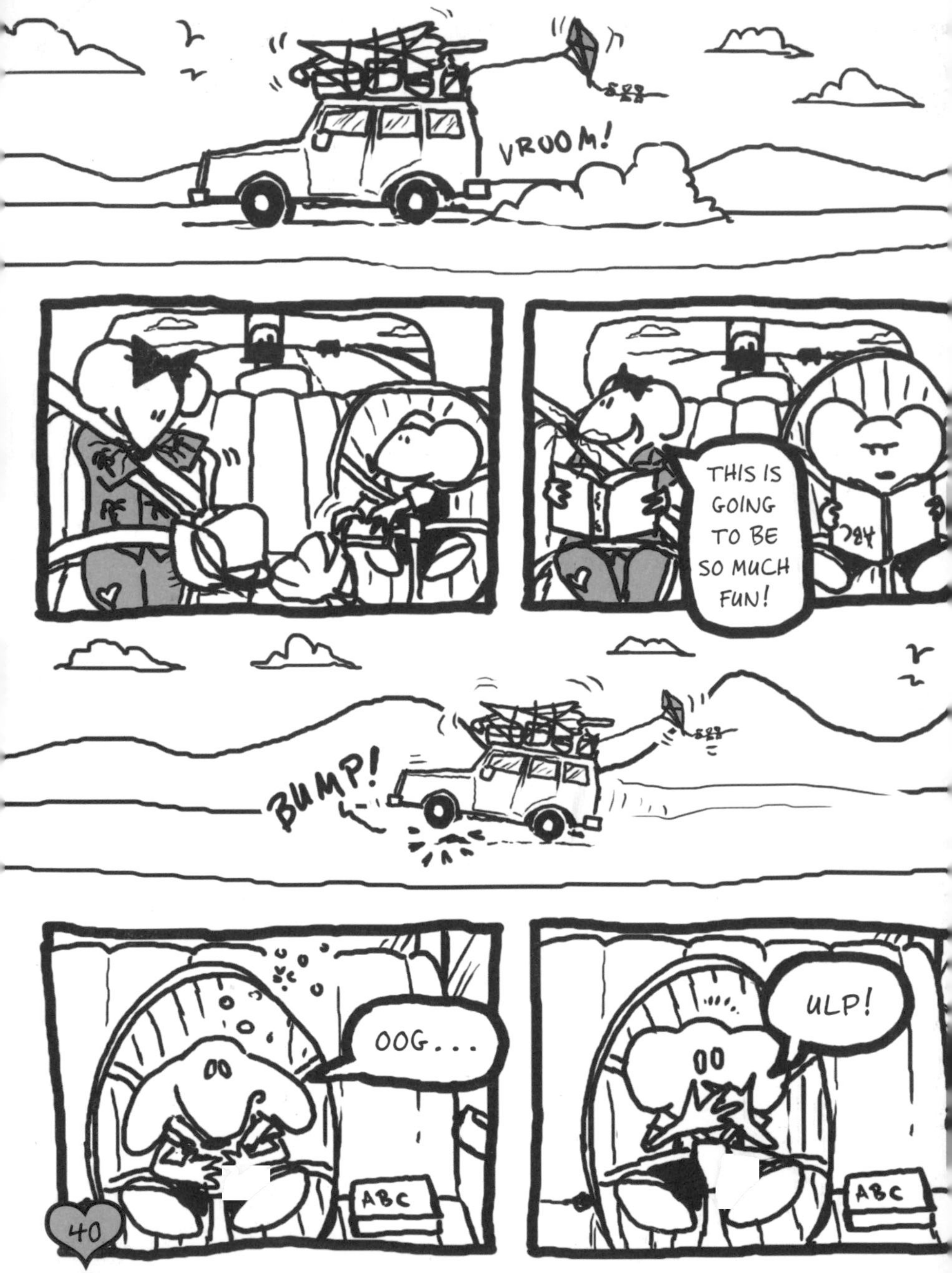
VROOM!
THIS IS GOING TO BE SO MUCH FUN!
BUMP!
OOG...
ABC
ULP!
ABC

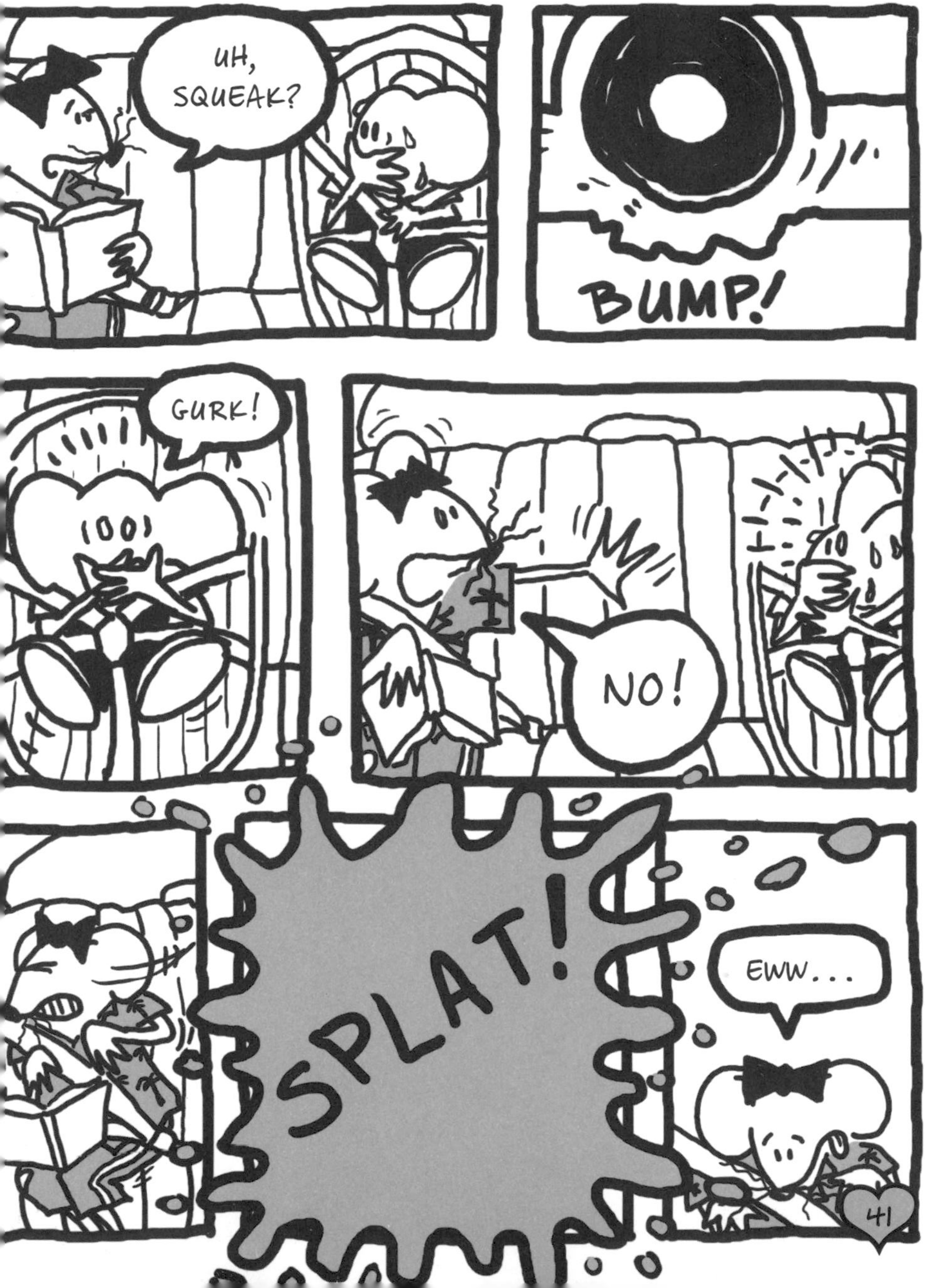
UH, SQUEAK?
BUMP!
GURK!
NO!
SPLAT!
EWW...
41

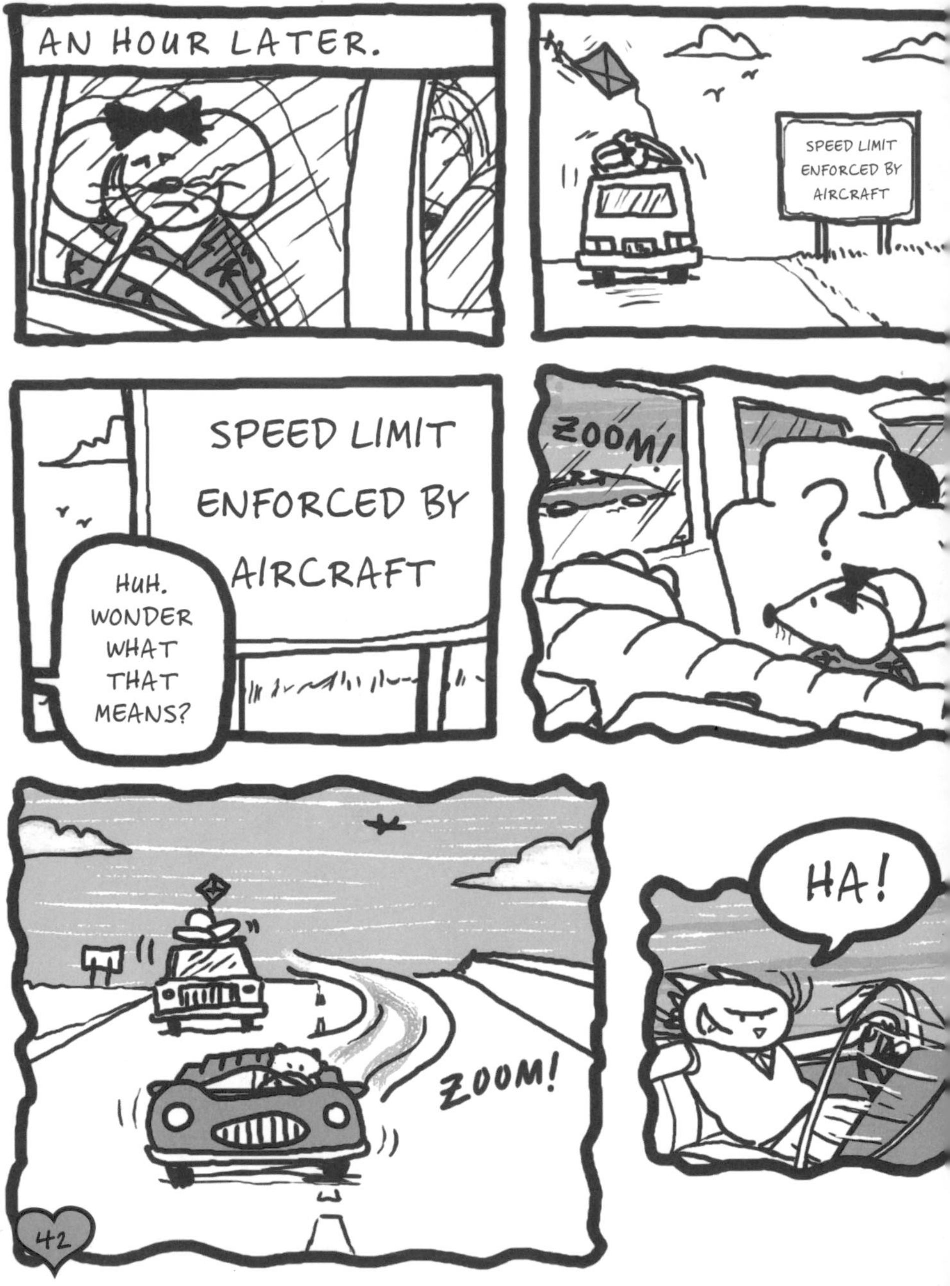
AN HOUR LATER.
SPEED LIMIT ENFORCED BY AIRCRAFT
SPEED LIMIT ENFORCED BY AIRCRAFT
HUH. WONDER WHAT THAT MEANS?
ZOOM!
ZOOM!
HA!

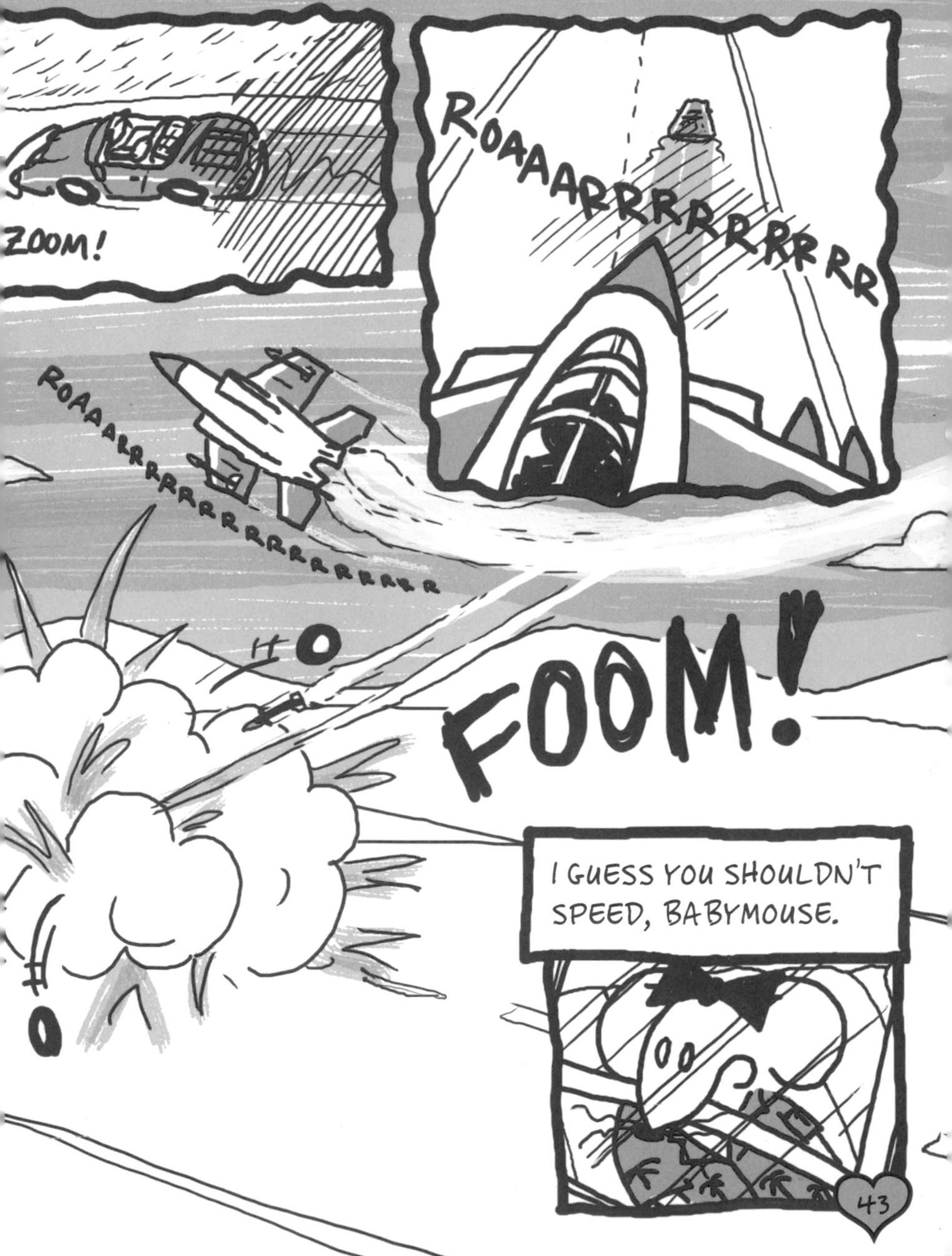
ZOOM!
ROAAAARRRRRRRRRR
ROAAAARRRRRRRRRRRRRRRRRRRRR
FOOM!
I GUESS YOU SHOULDN'T SPEED, BABYMOUSE.

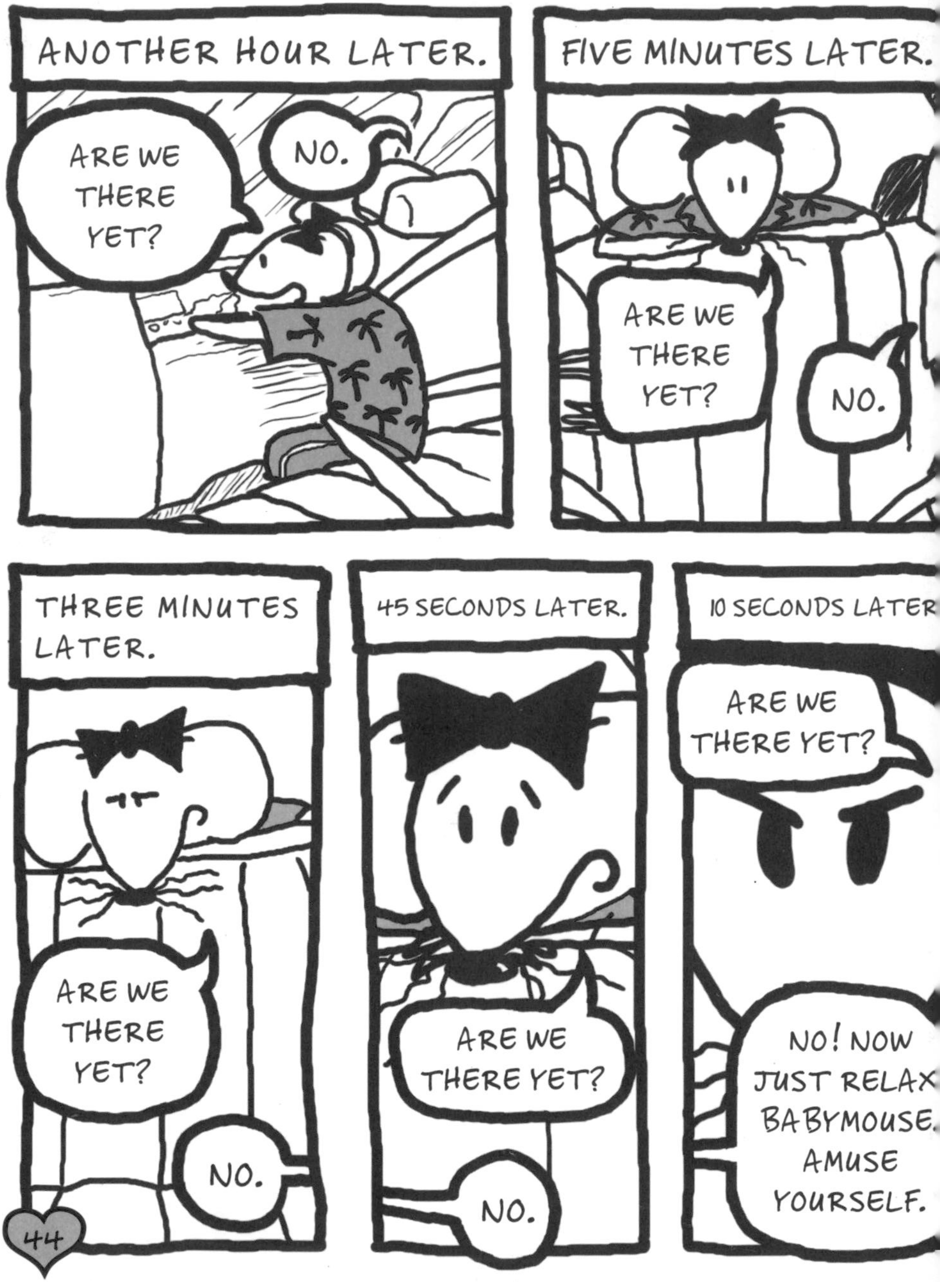
ANOTHER HOUR LATER.
ARE WE THERE YET?
NO.
FIVE MINUTES LATER.
ARE WE THERE YET?
NO.
THREE MINUTES LATER.
ARE WE THERE YET?
NO.
45 SECONDS LATER.
ARE WE THERE YET?
NO.
10 SECONDS LATER
ARE WE THERE YET?
NO! NOW JUST RELAX BABYMOUSE. AMUSE YOURSELF.

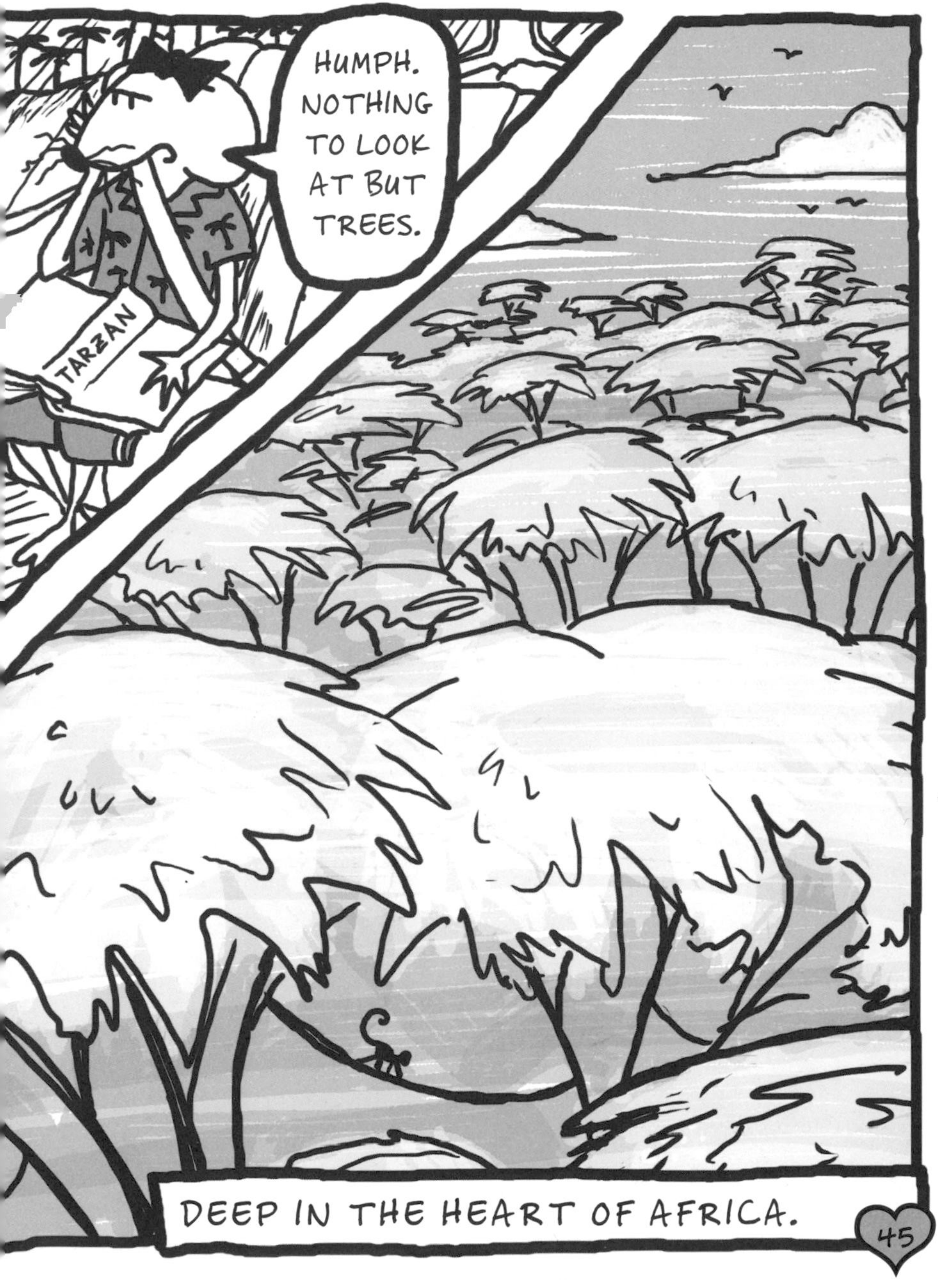
HUMPH. NOTHING TO LOOK AT BUT TREES.
TARZAN
DEEP IN THE HEART OF AFRICA.

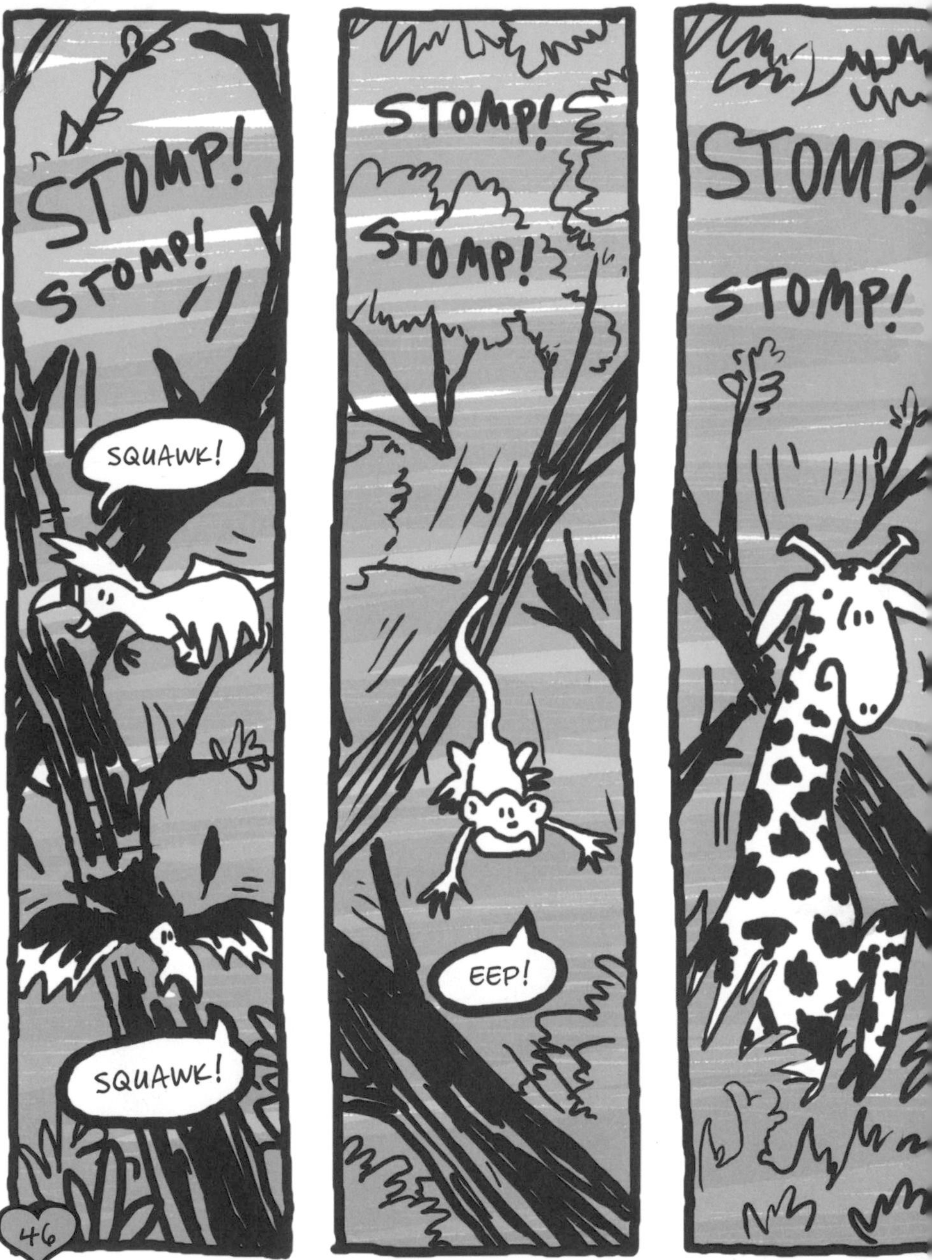
STOMP!
STOMP!
SQUAWK!
SQUAWK!
STOMP!
STOMP!
EEP!
STOMP!
STOMP!

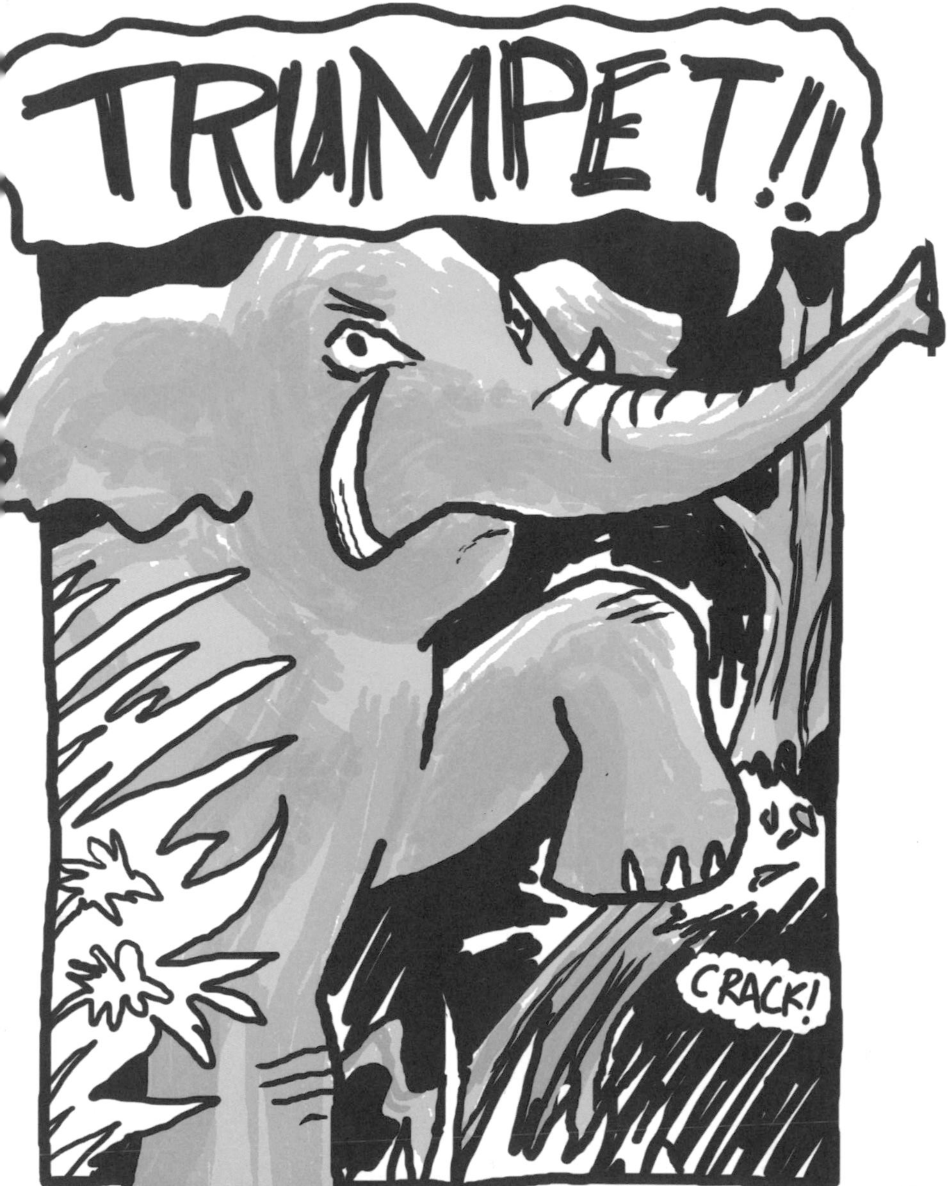
TRUMPET!!
CRACK!

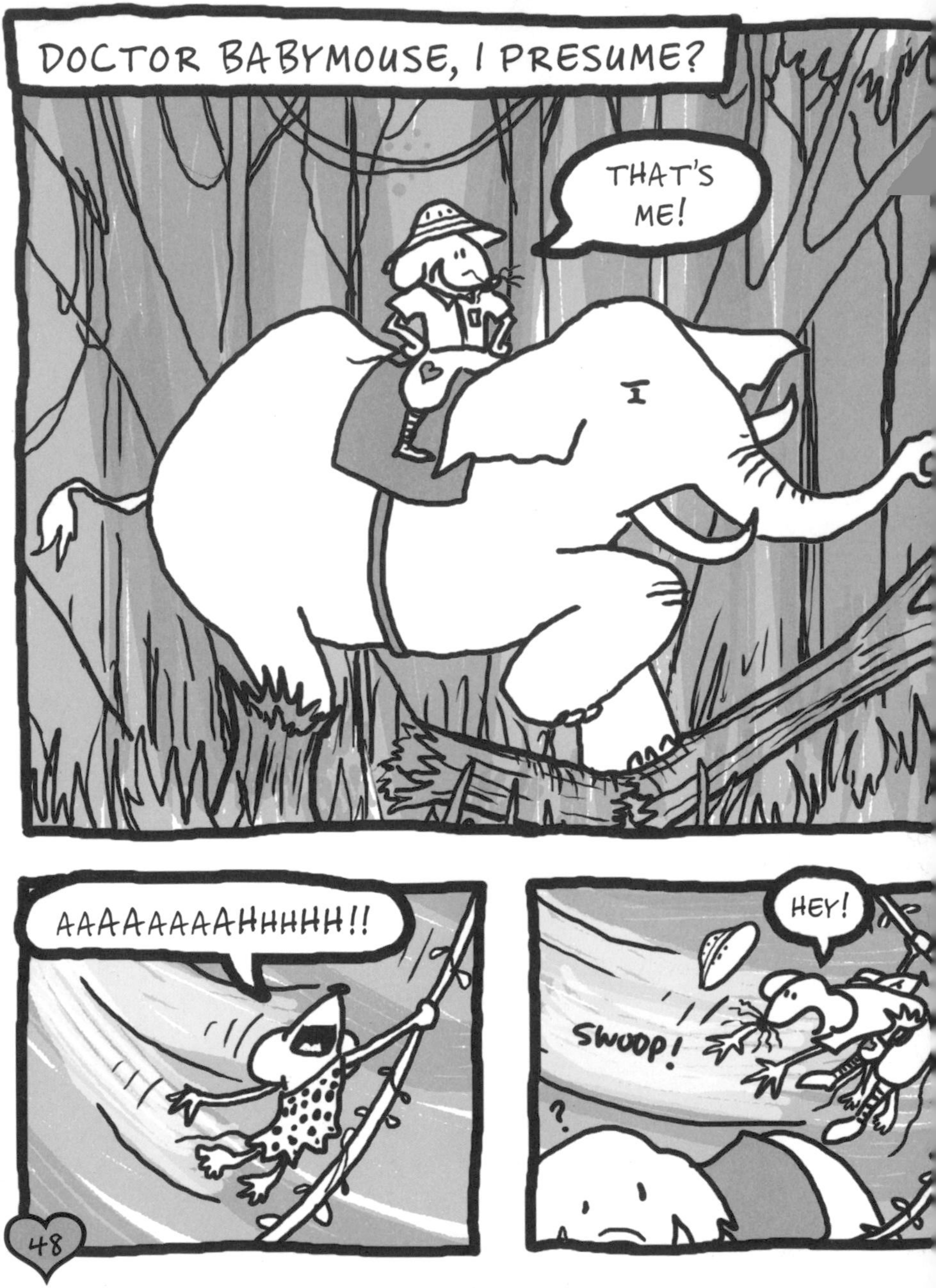
DOCTOR BABYMOUSE, I PRESUME?
THAT'S ME!
AAAAAAAAHHHHH!!
HEY!
SWOOP!
?

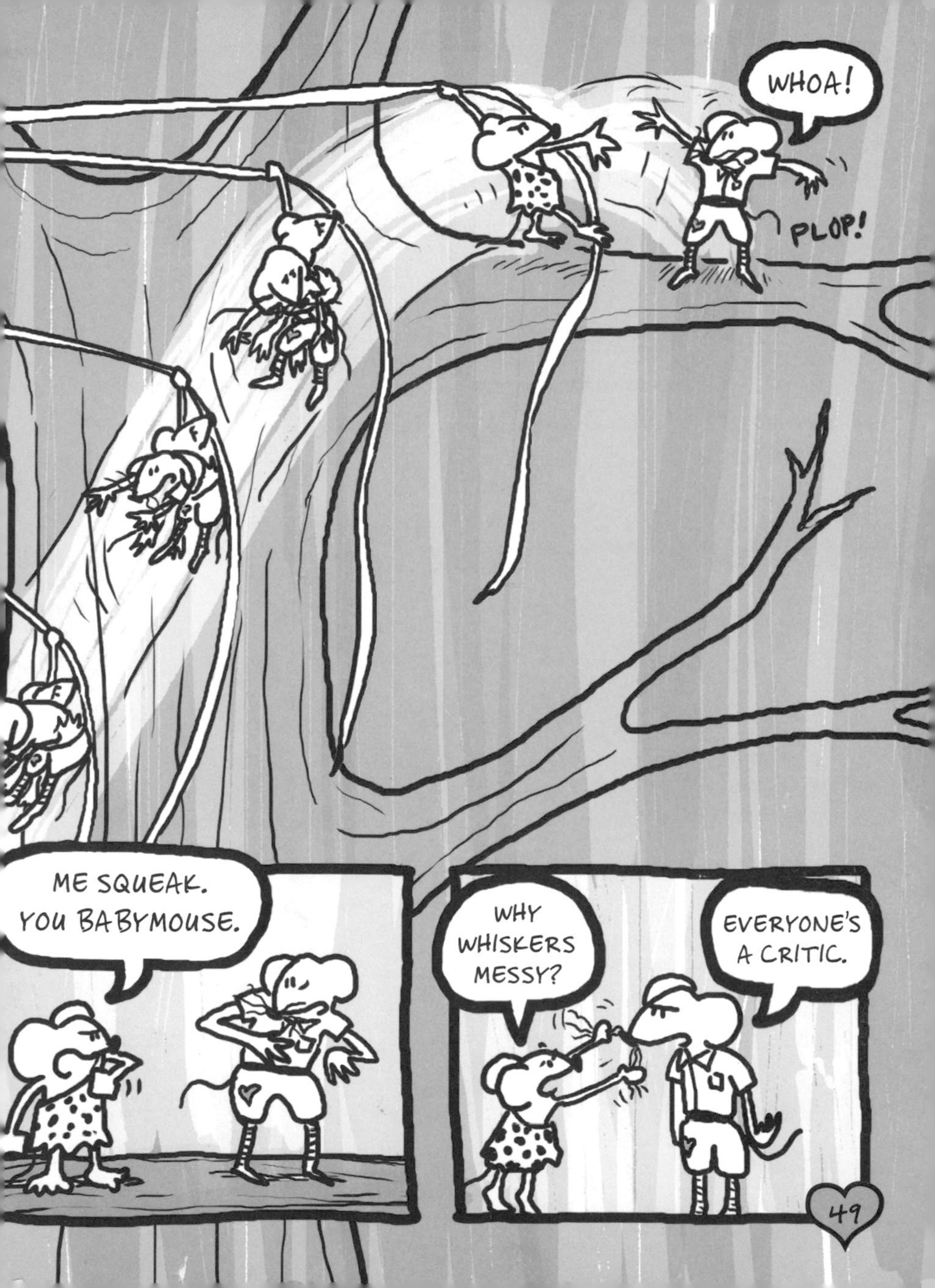
WHOA!
PLOP!
ME SQUEAK.
YOU BABYMOUSE.
WHY
WHISKERS
MESSY?
EVERYONE'S
A CRITIC.

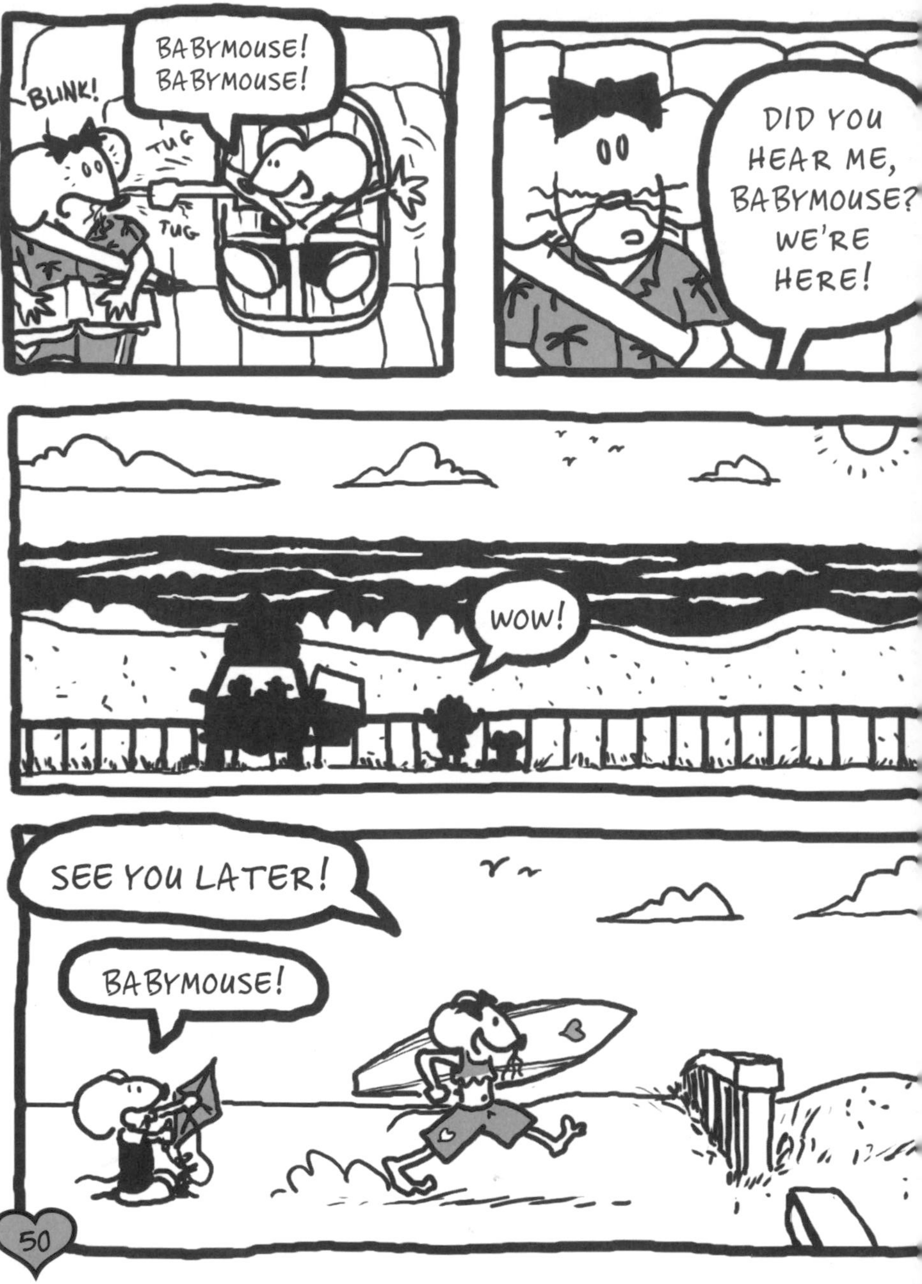
BABYMOUSE! BABYMOUSE!
BLINK!
TUG
TUG
DID YOU HEAR ME, BABYMOUSE? WE'RE HERE!
WOW!
SEE YOU LATER!
BABYMOUSE!

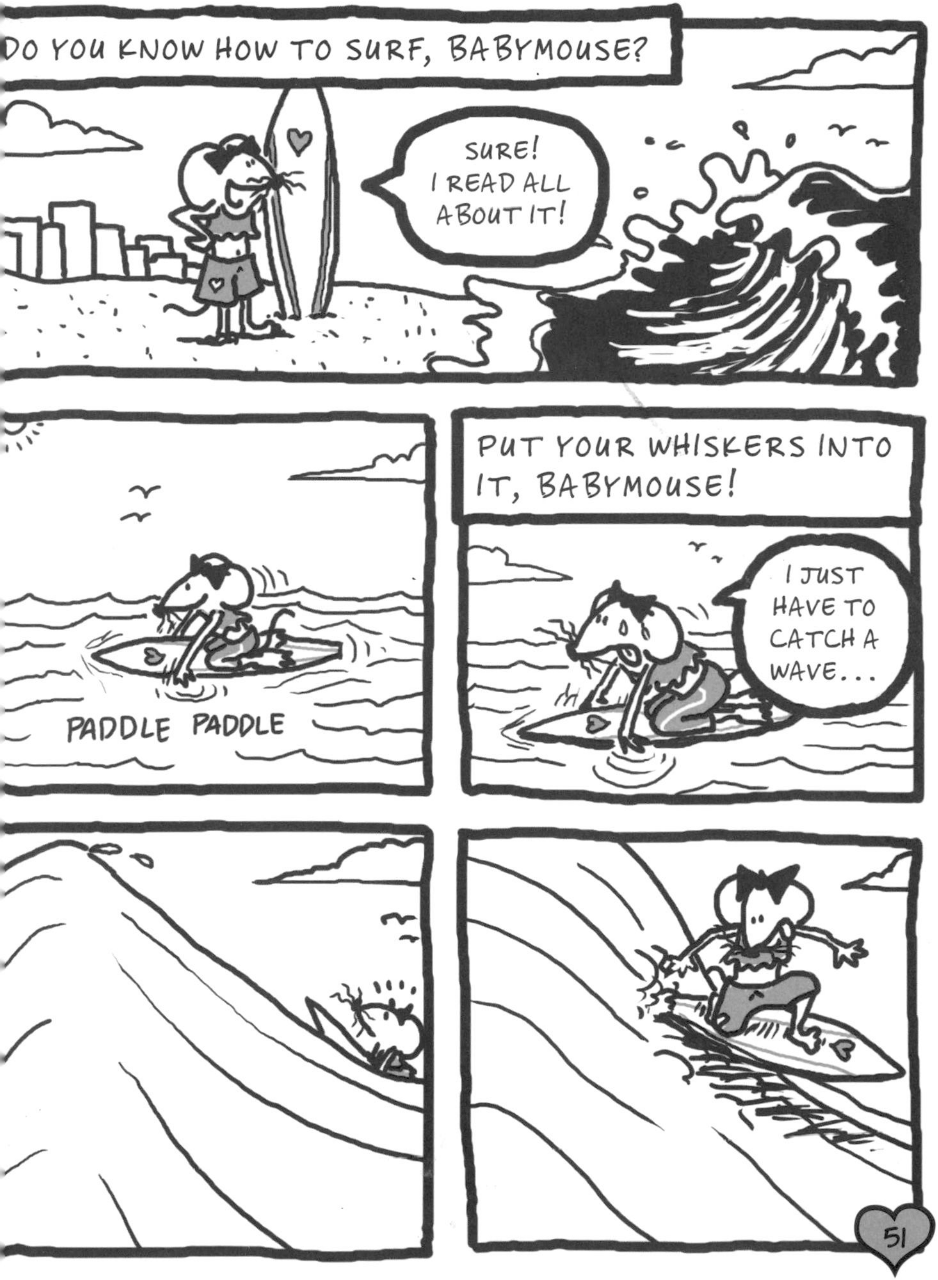

DO YOU KNOW HOW TO SURF, BABYMOUSE?
SURE! I READ ALL ABOUT IT!
PADDLE PADDLE
PUT YOUR WHISKERS INTO IT, BABYMOUSE!
I JUST HAVE TO CATCH A WAVE...

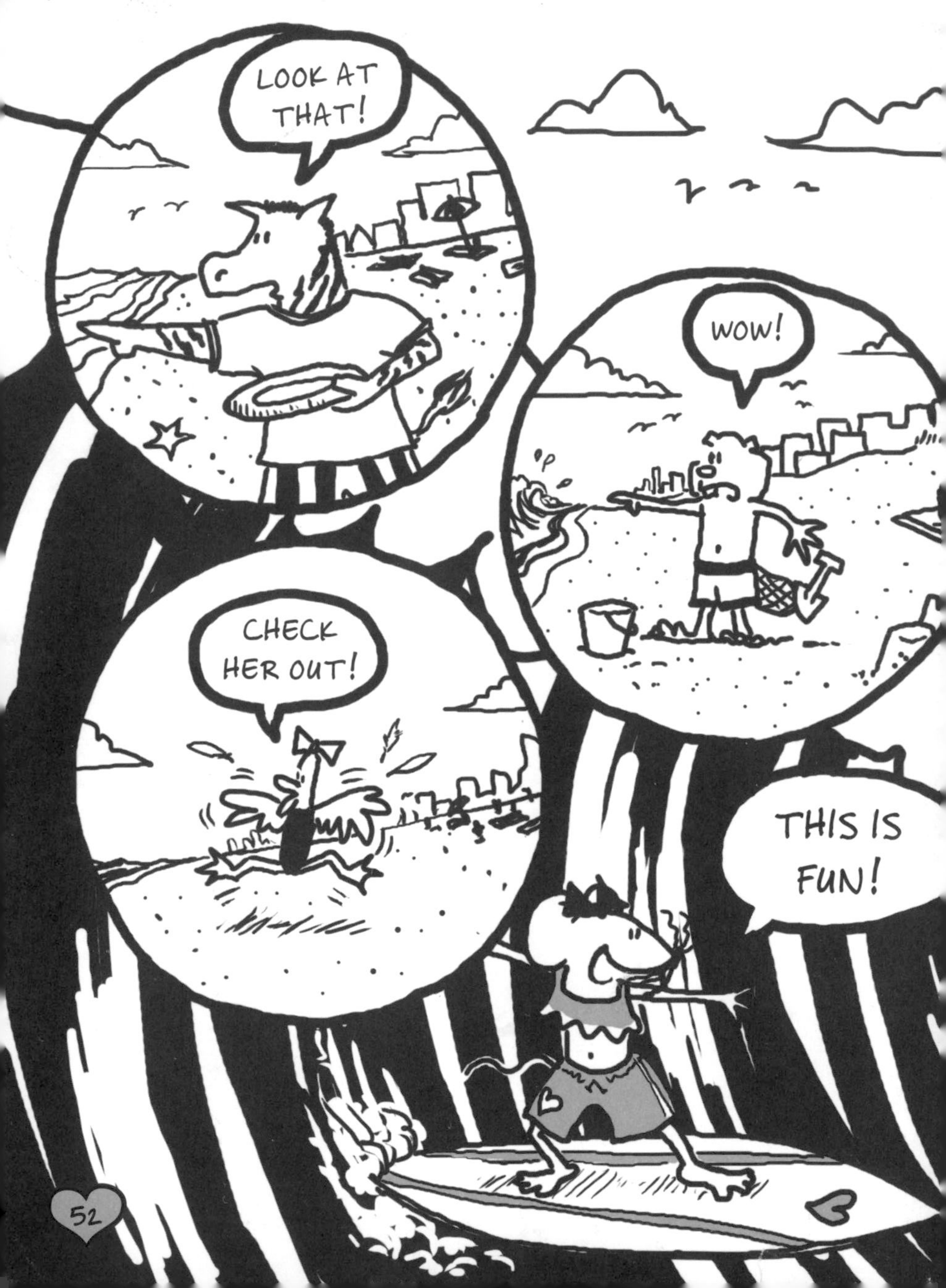
LOOK AT THAT!
WOW!
CHECK HER OUT!
THIS IS FUN!

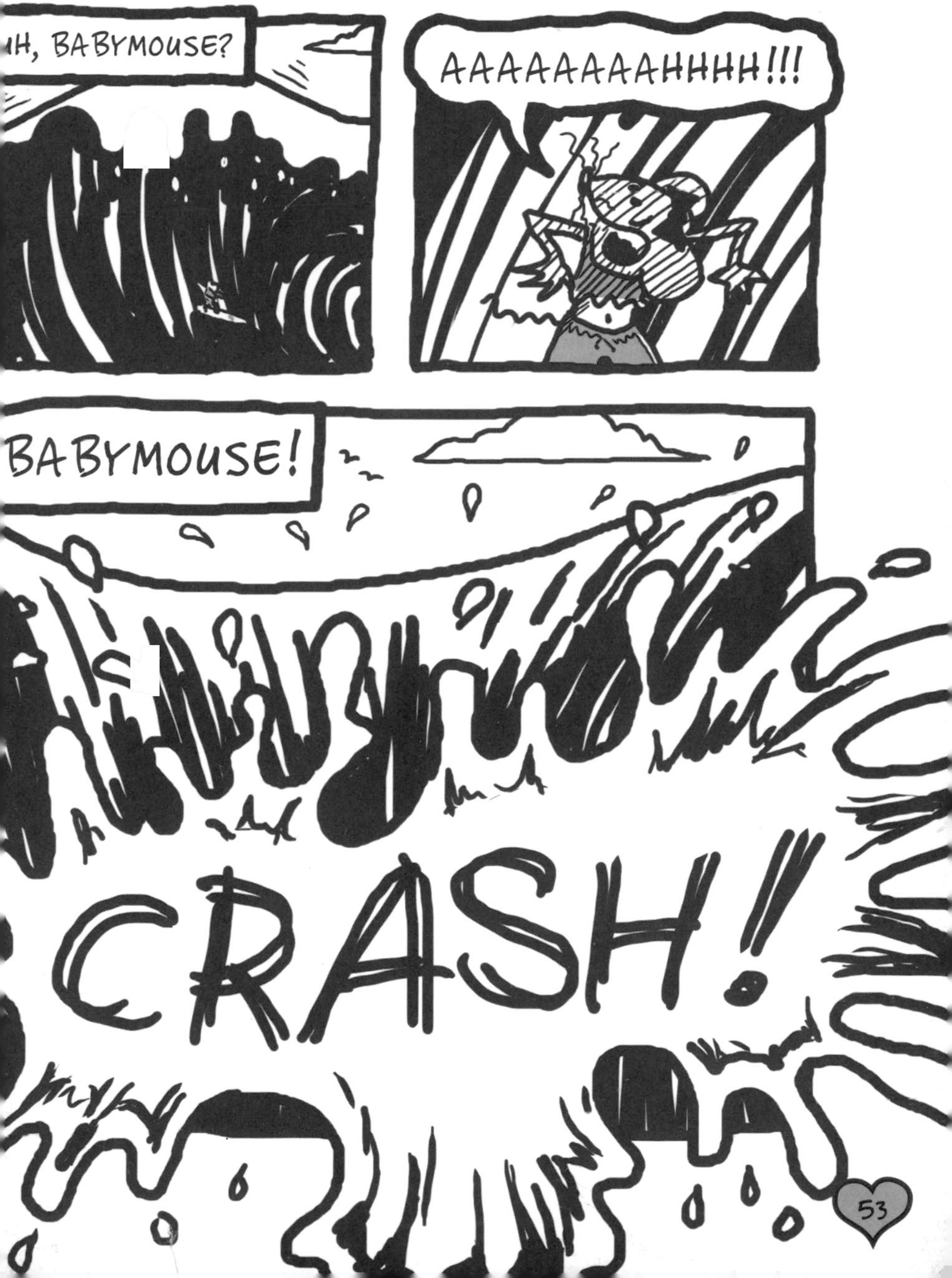
H, BABYMOUSE?
AAAAAAAAAHHHH!!!
BABYMOUSE!
CRASH!

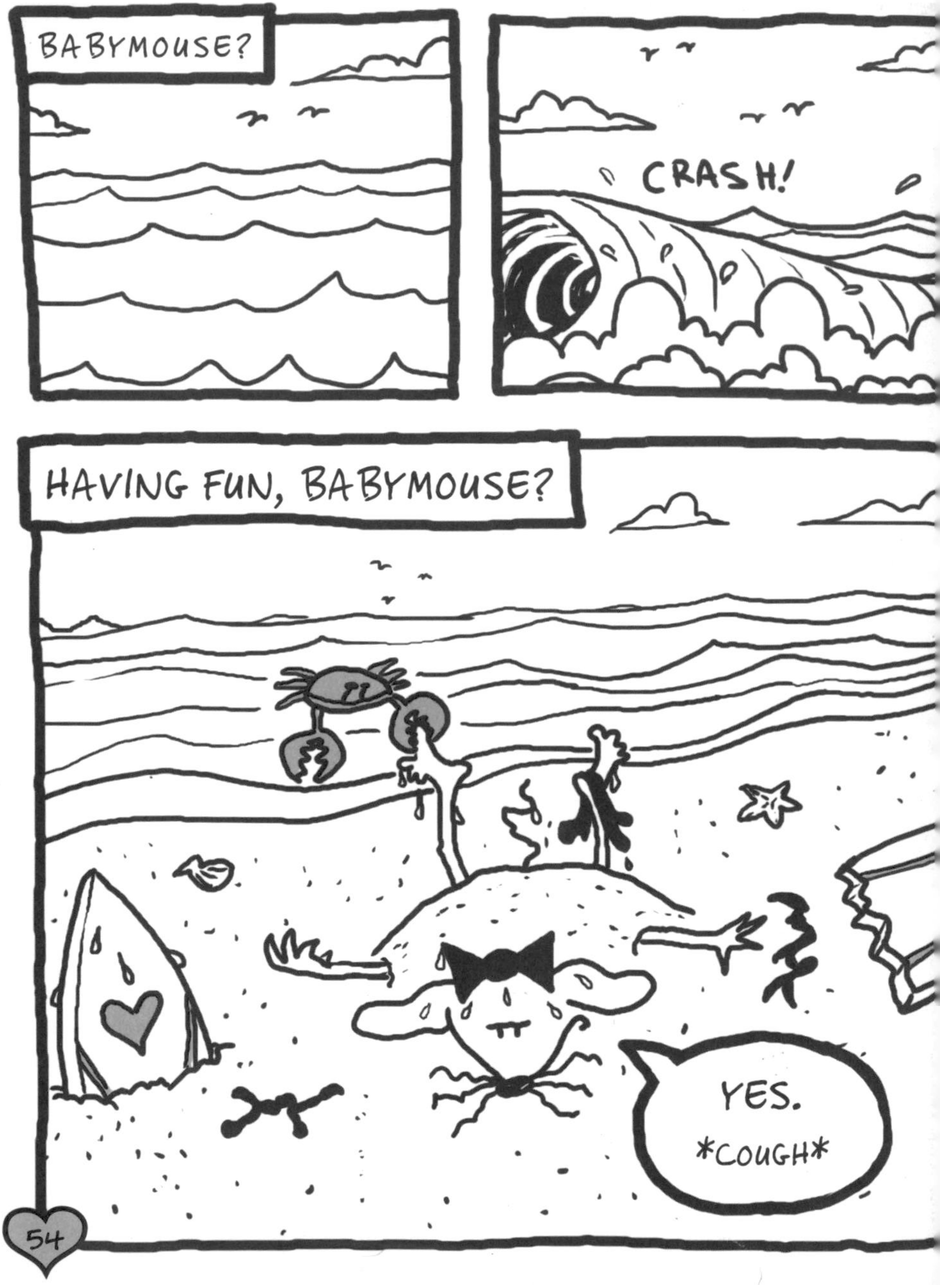
BABYMOUSE?
CRASH!
HAVING FUN, BABYMOUSE?
YES.
COUGH

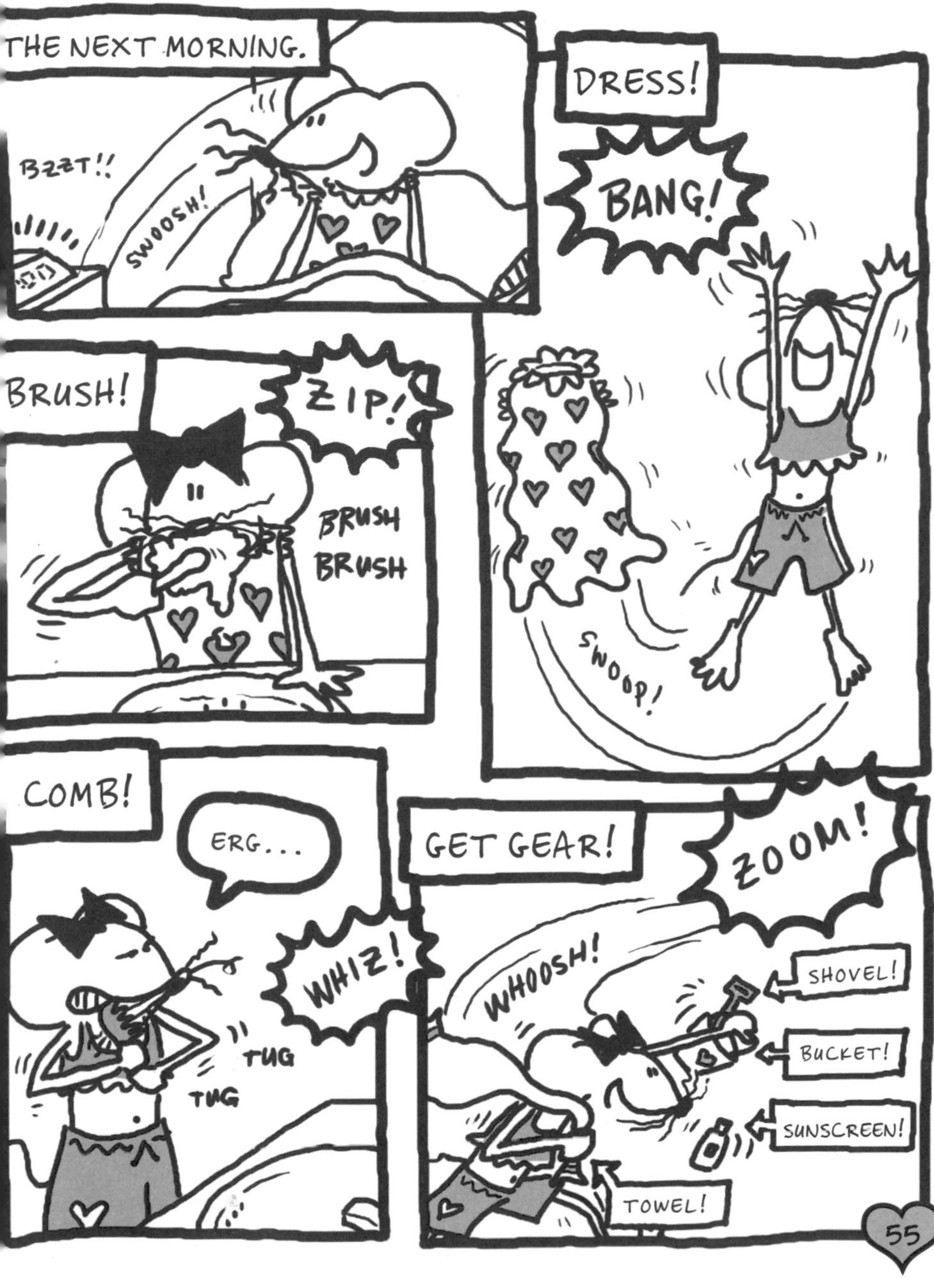
THE NEXT MORNING.
BZZT!!
SWOOSH!
DRESS!
BANG!
SWOOP!
BRUSH!
ZIP!
BRUSH
BRUSH
COMB!
ERG...
WHIZ!
TUG
TUG
GET GEAR!
ZOOM!
WHOOSH!
SHOVEL!
BUCKET!
SUNSCREEN!
TOWEL!

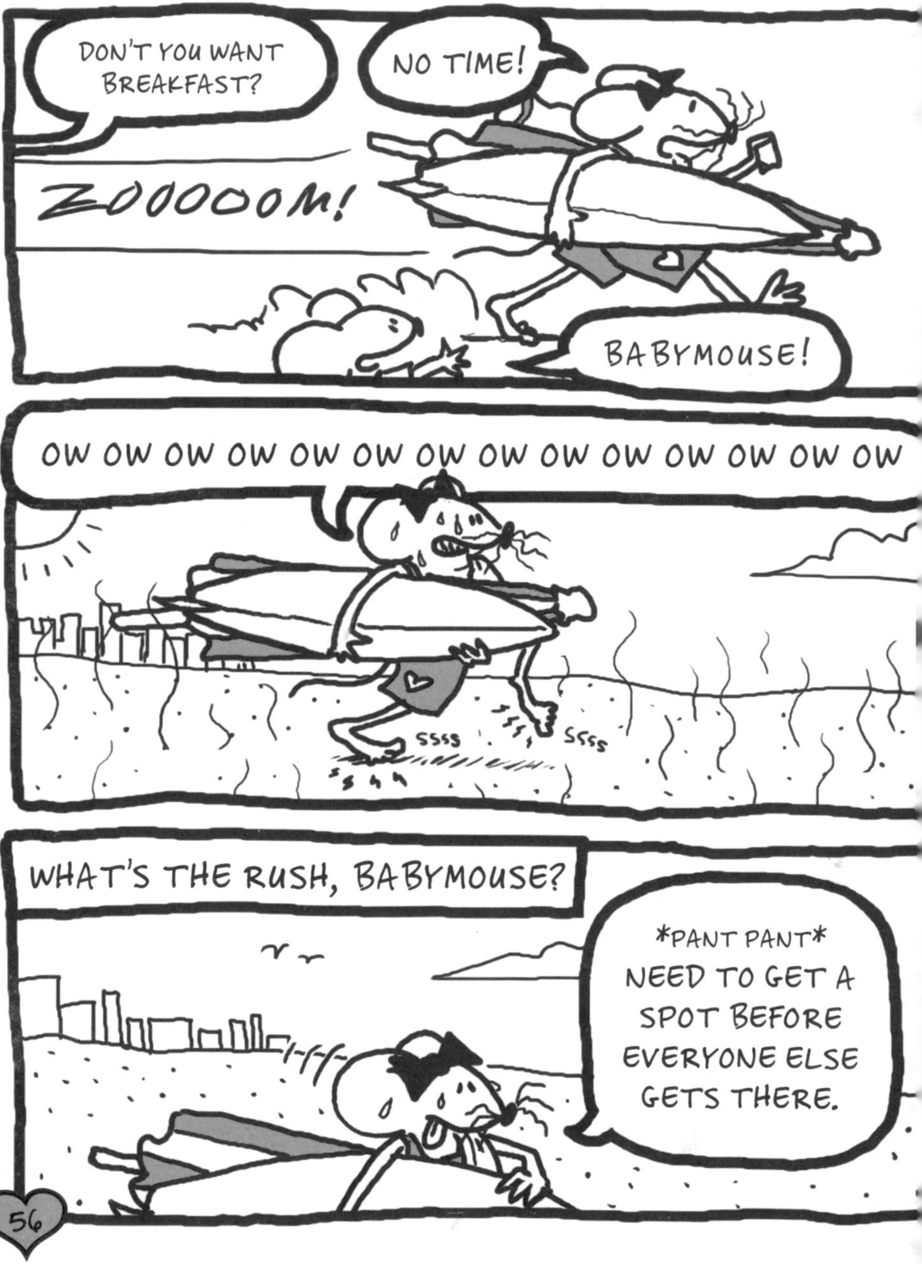
DON'T YOU WANT BREAKFAST?
NO TIME!
ZOOOOOM!
BABYMOUSE!
OW OW OW OW OW OW OW OW OW OW OW OW OW OW
SSSS
SSSS
WHAT'S THE RUSH, BABYMOUSE?
PANT PANT NEED TO GET A SPOT BEFORE EVERYONE ELSE GETS THERE.

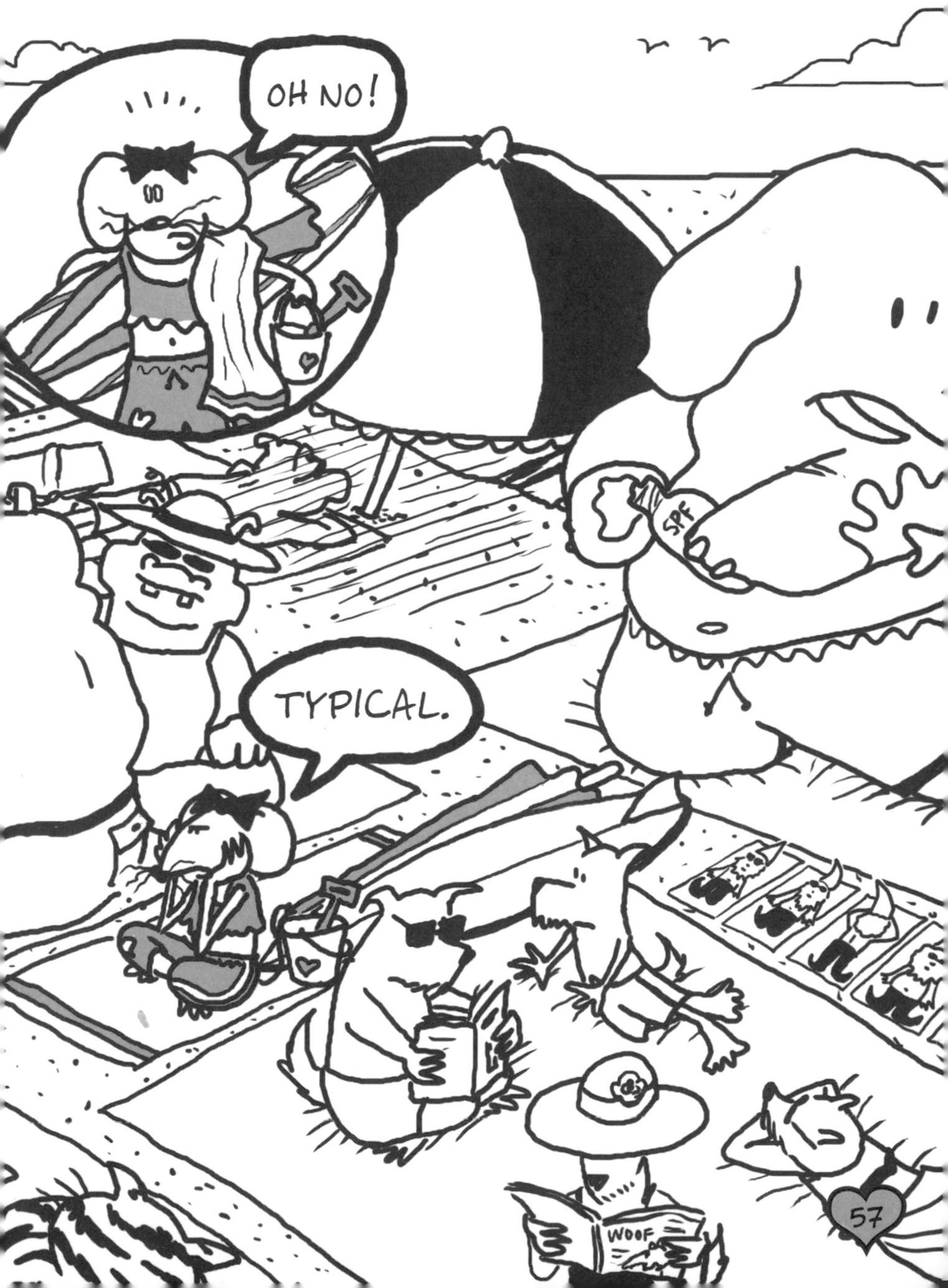
OH NO!
TYPICAL.
SPF
WOOF

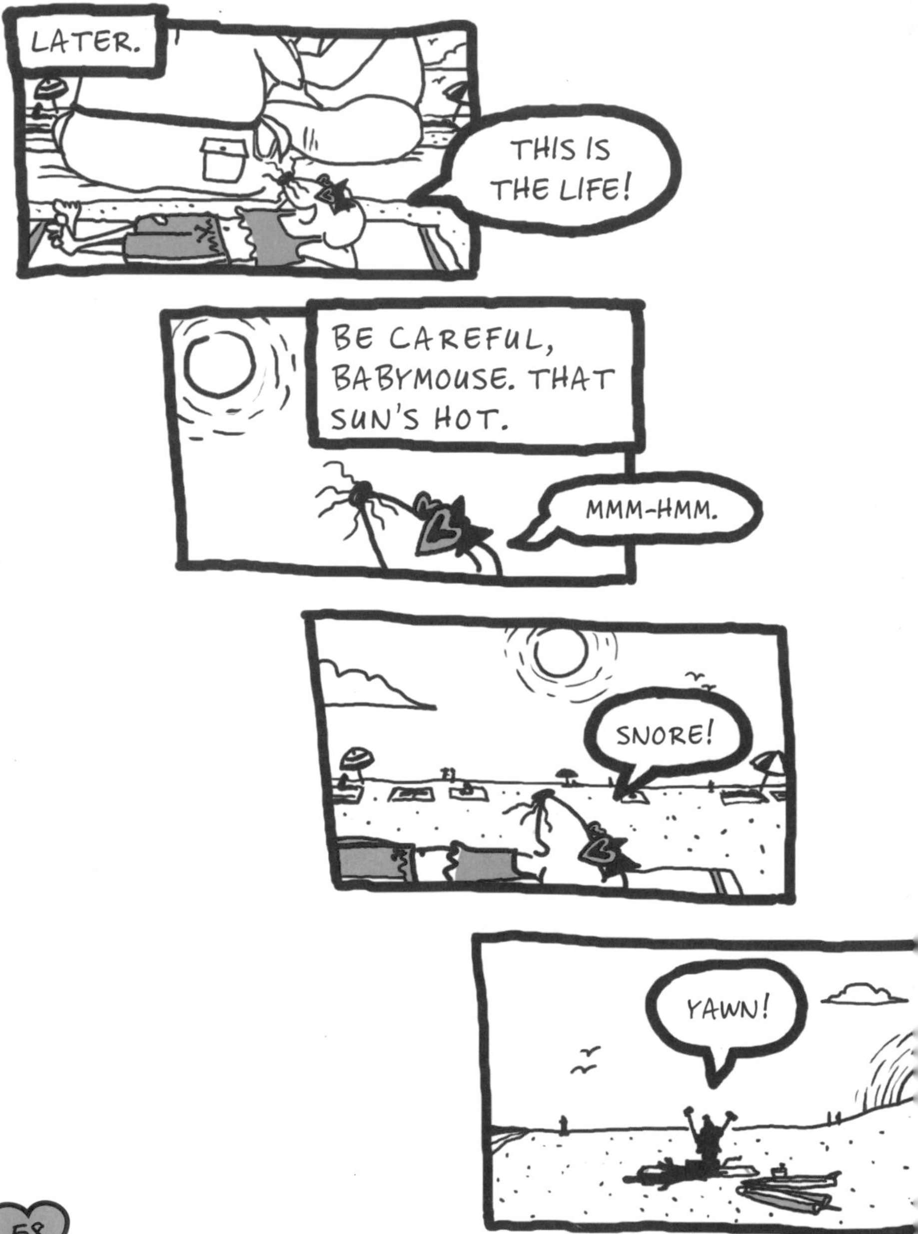

LATER.
THIS IS THE LIFE!
BE CAREFUL, BABYMOUSE. THAT SUN'S HOT.
MMM-HMM.
SNORE!
YAWN!

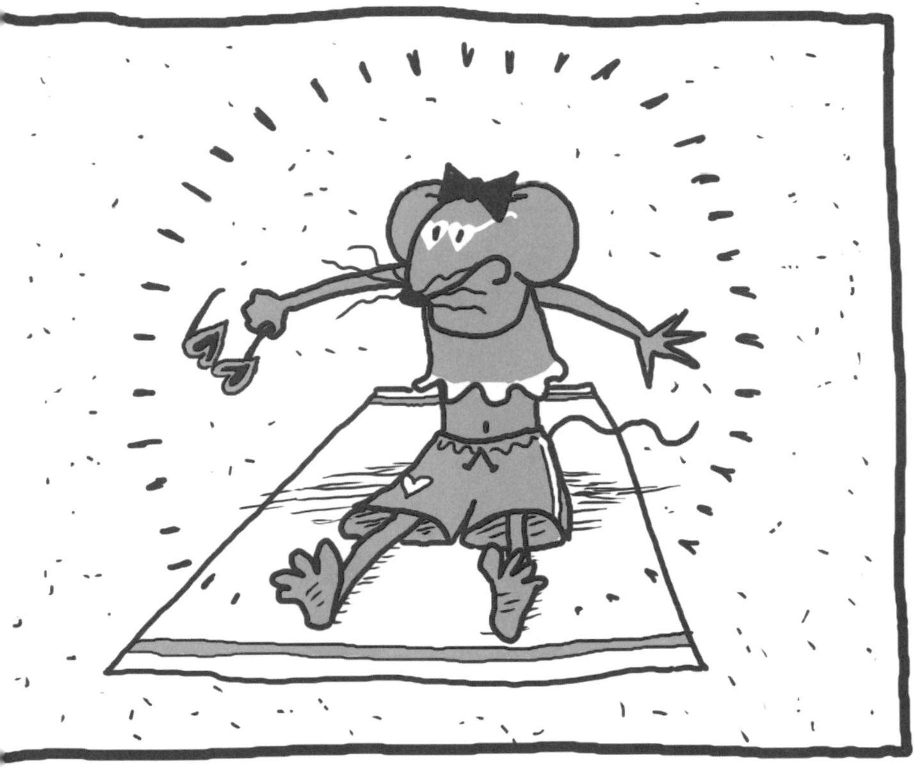

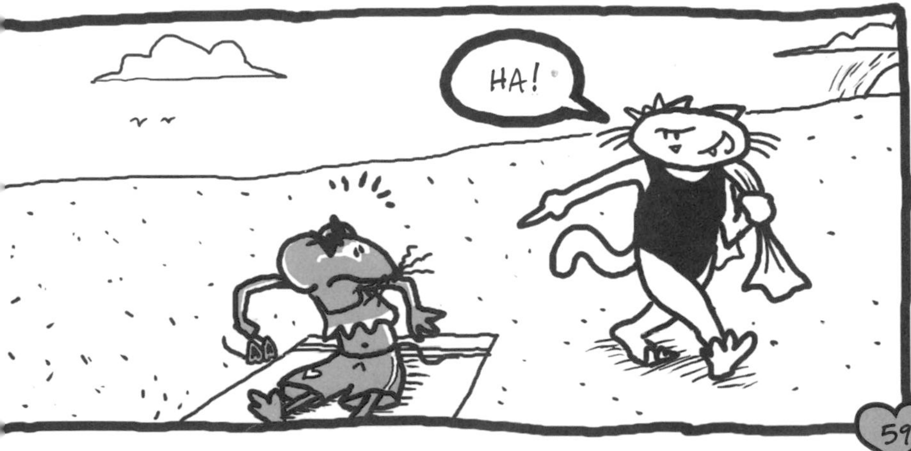
HA!

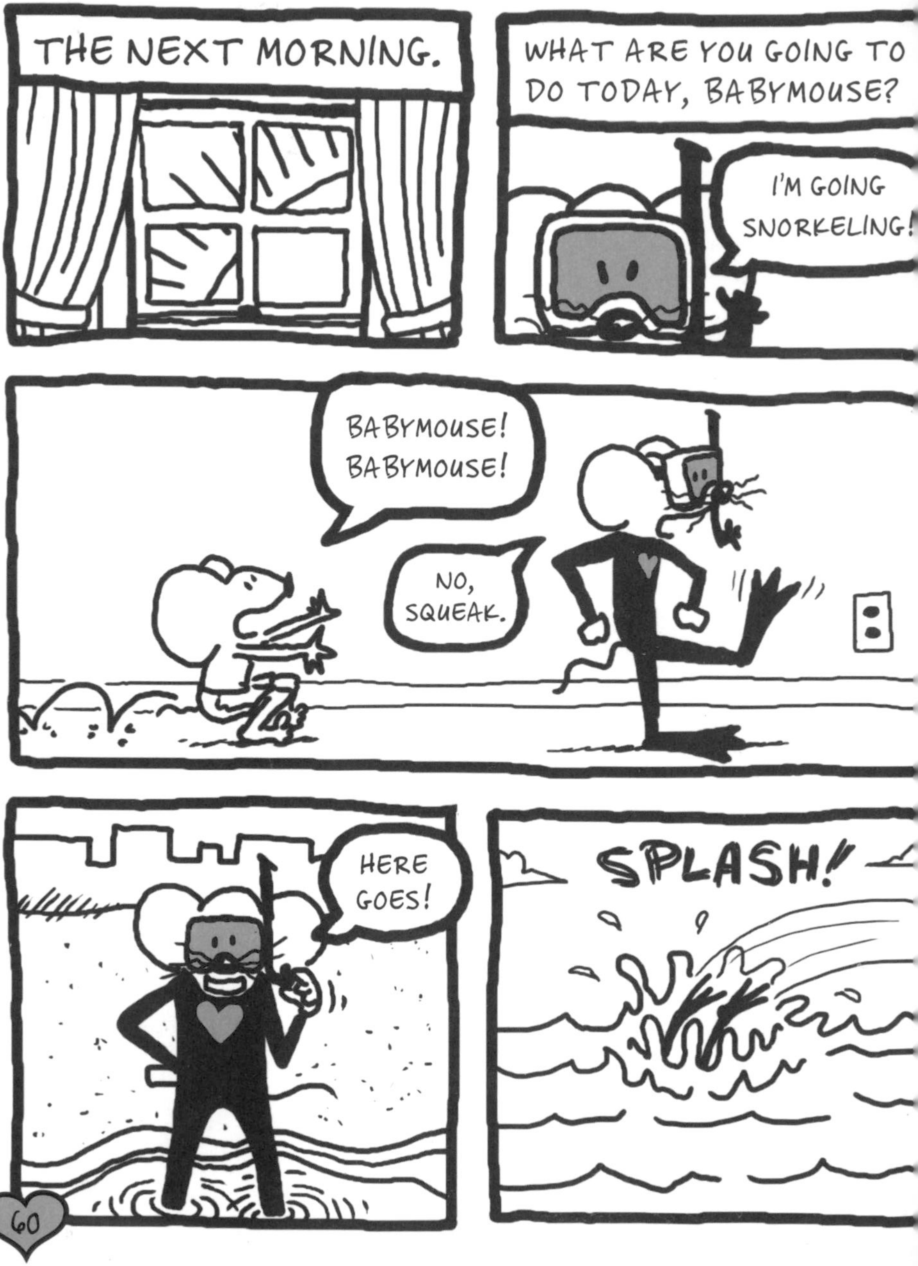
THE NEXT MORNING.
WHAT ARE YOU GOING TO DO TODAY, BABYMOUSE?
I'M GOING SNORKELING!
BABYMOUSE! BABYMOUSE!
NO, SQUEAK.
HERE GOES!
SPLASH!

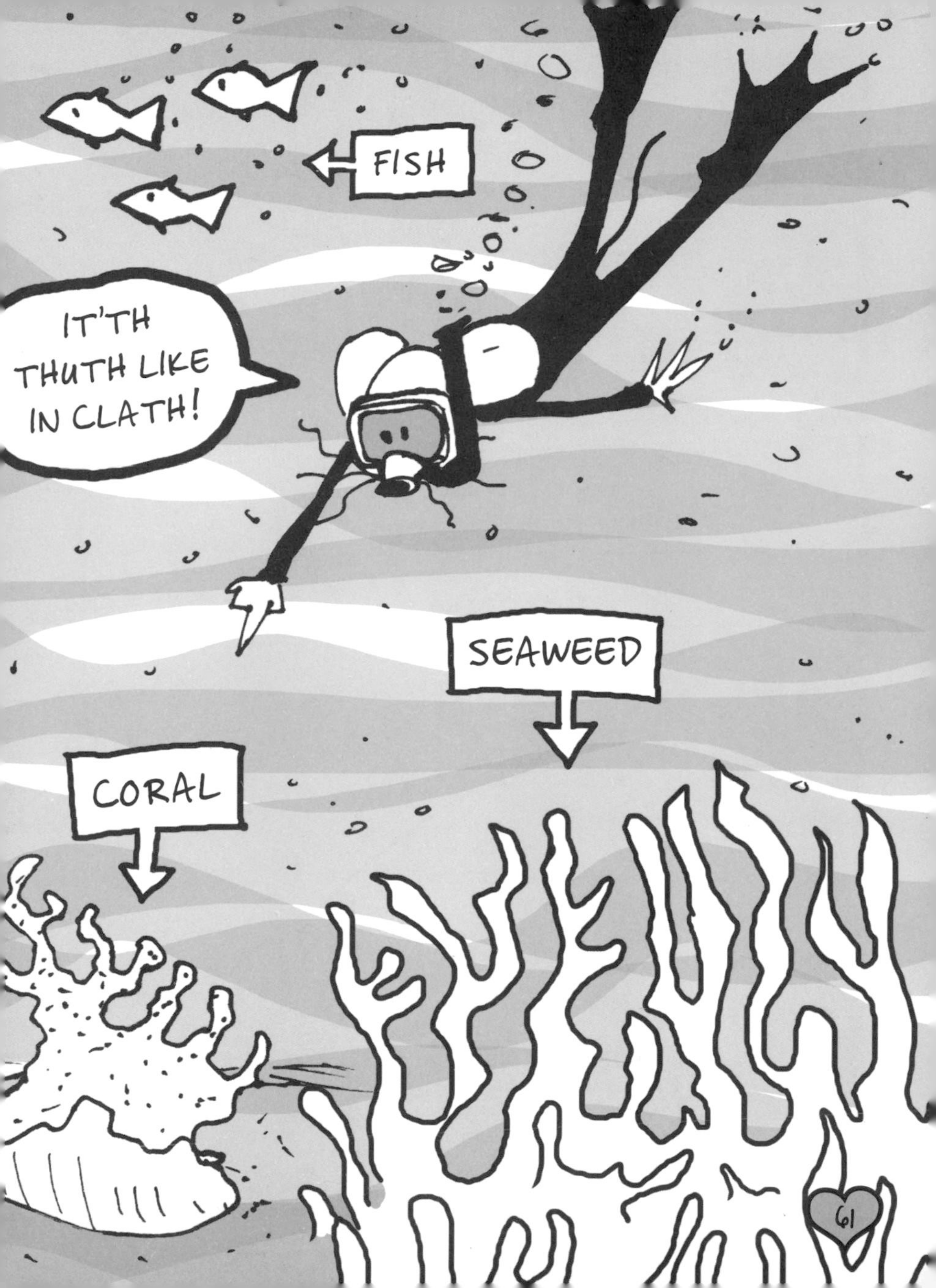
FISH
IT'TH THUTH LIKE IN CLATH!
SEAWEED
CORAL
61

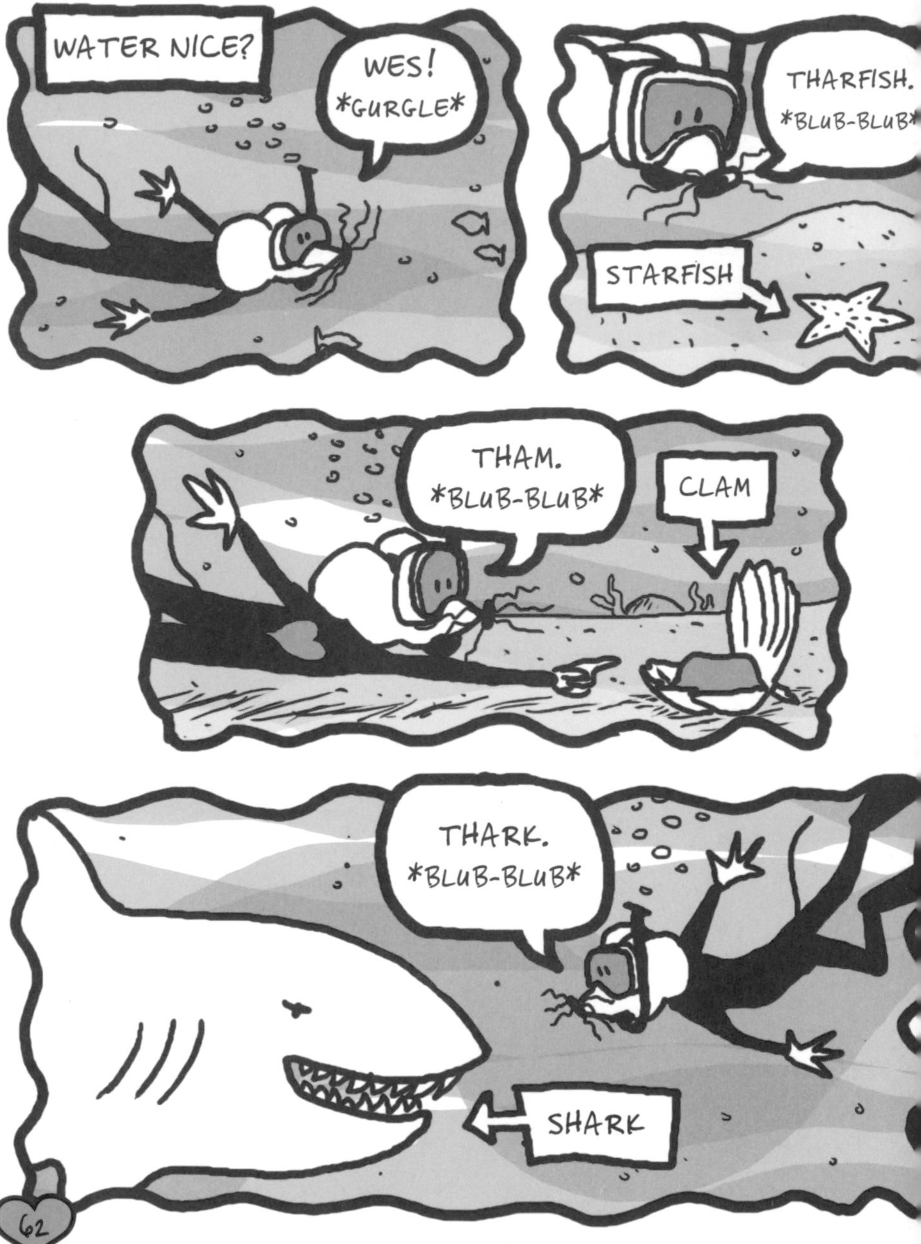
WATER NICE?
WES! *GURGLE*
THARFISH. *BLUB-BLUB*
STARFISH
THAM. *BLUB-BLUB*
CLAM
THARK. *BLUB-BLUB*
SHARK

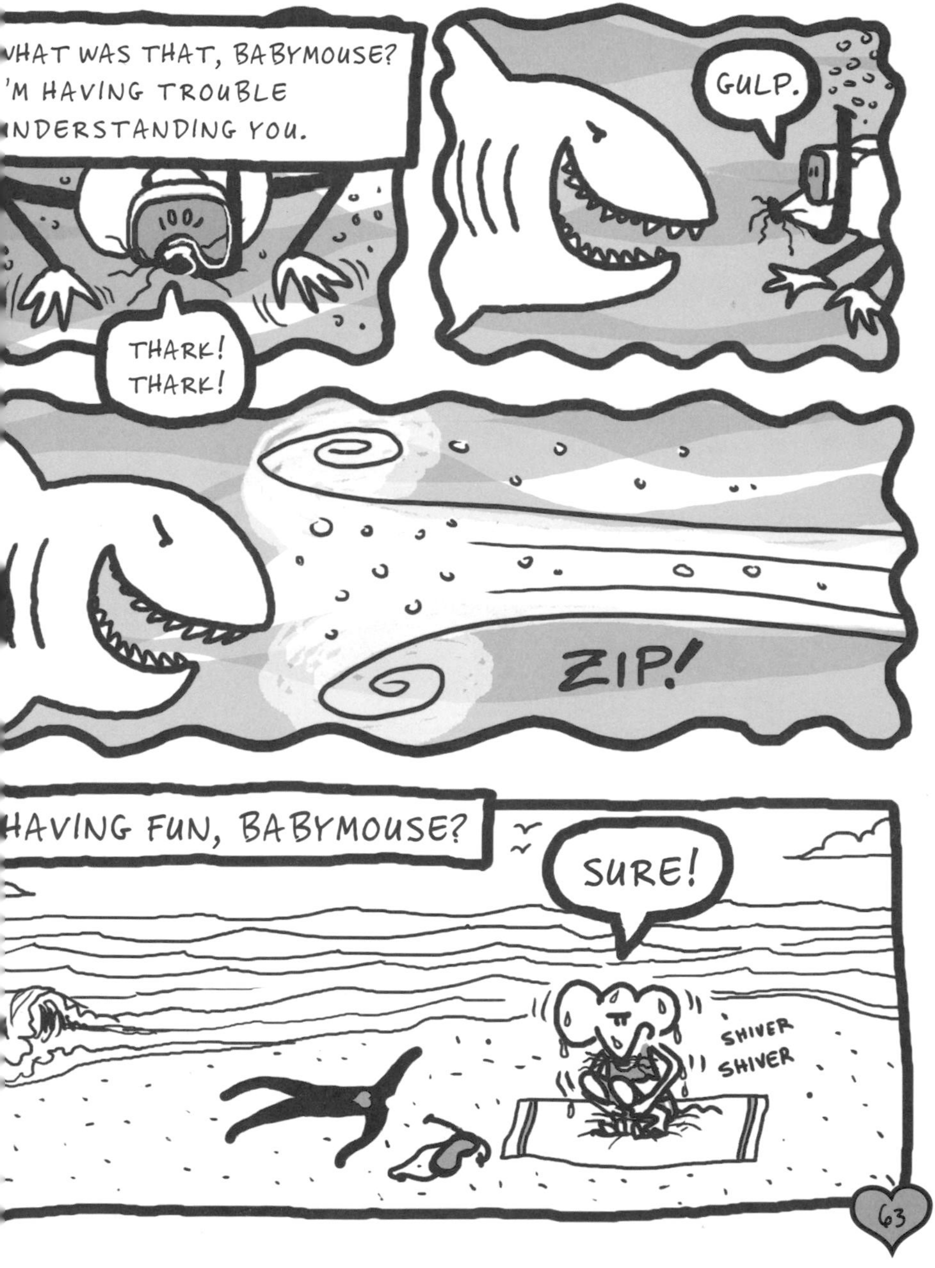

VHAT WAS THAT, BABYMOUSE? 'M HAVING TROUBLE INDERSTANDING YOU.
THARK! THARK!
GULP.
ZIP!
HAVING FUN, BABYMOUSE?
SURE!
SHIVER SHIVER

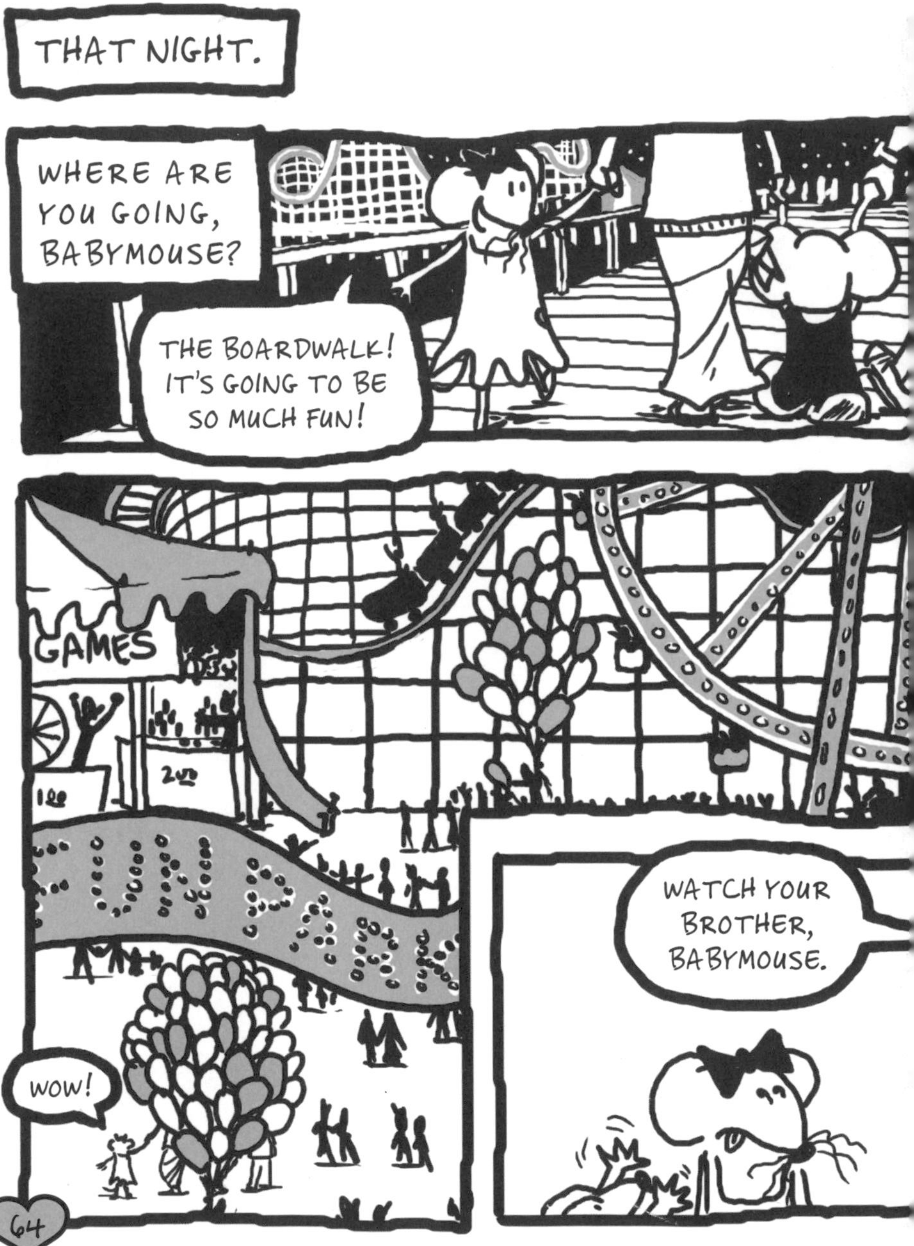
THAT NIGHT.
WHERE ARE YOU GOING, BABYMOUSE?
THE BOARDWALK! IT'S GOING TO BE SO MUCH FUN!
GAMES
FUN PARK
WOW!
WATCH YOUR BROTHER, BABYMOUSE.

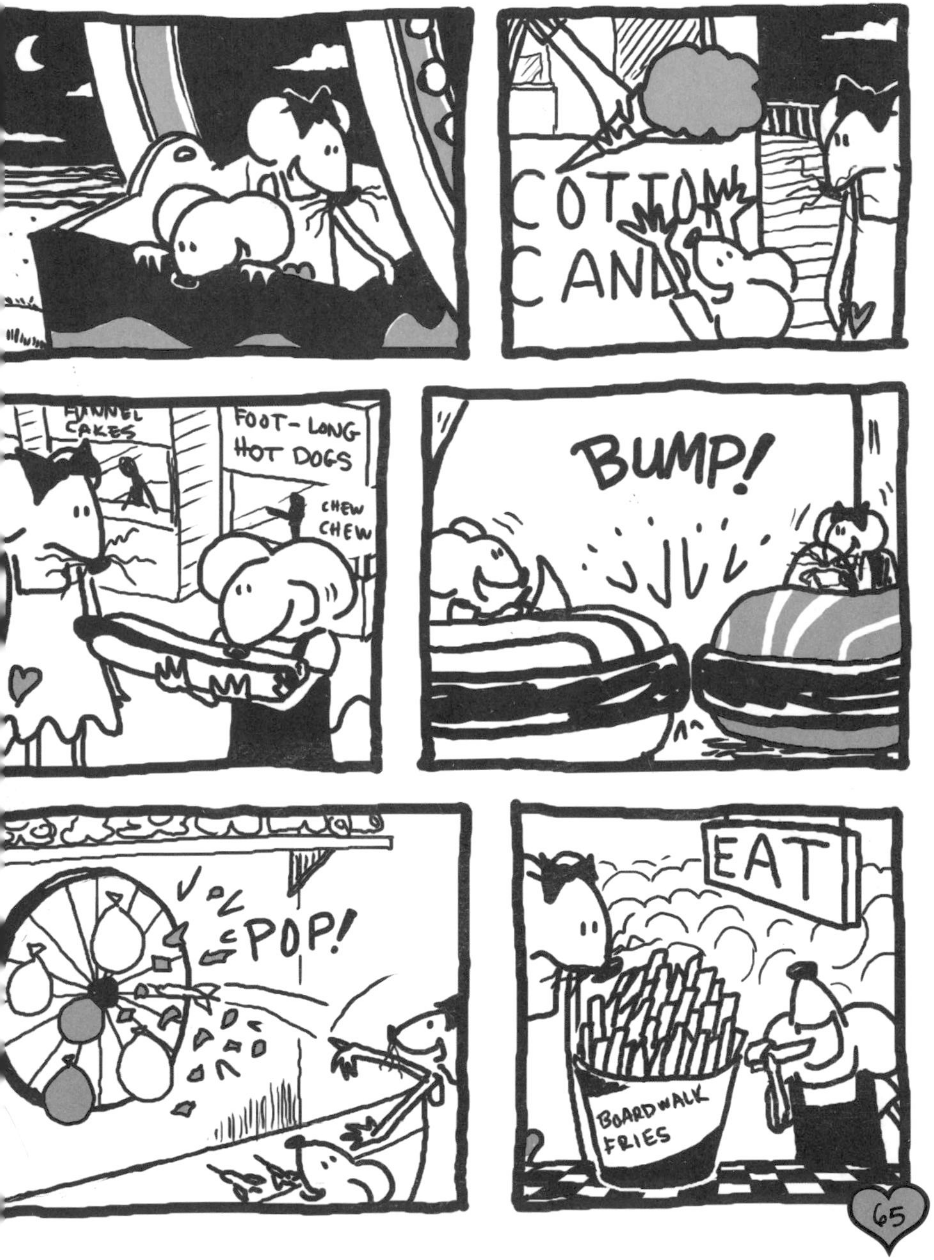
COTTON
CAND
CAKES
FOOT-LONG
HOT DOGS
CHEW
CHEW
BUMP!
POP!
EAT
BOARDWALK
FRIES

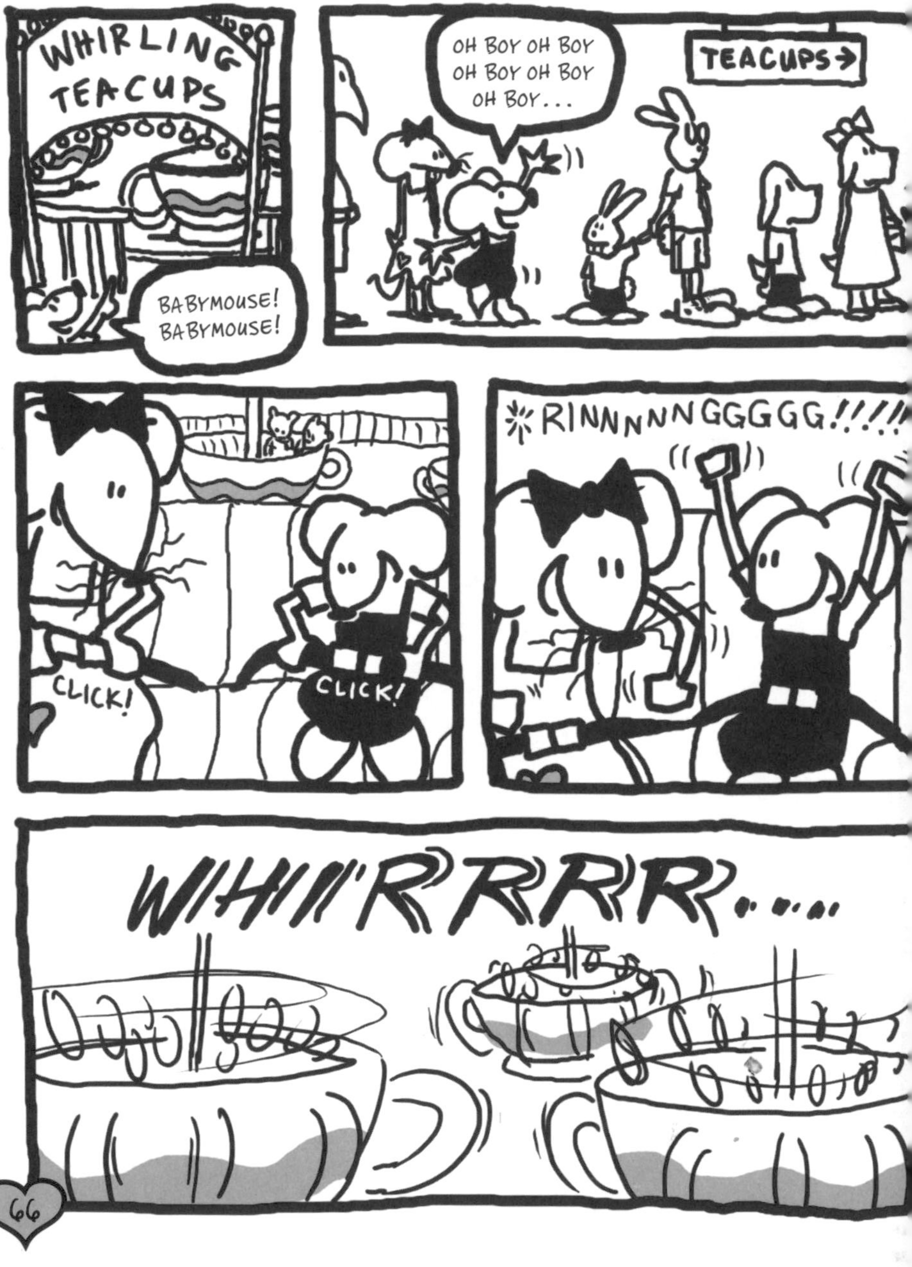
WHIRLING TEACUPS
BABYMOUSE! BABYMOUSE!
OH BOY OH BOY OH BOY OH BOY OH BOY...
TEACUPS →
CLICK!
CLICK!
RINNNNNNGGGGG!!!!!
WHIIRRRRR....

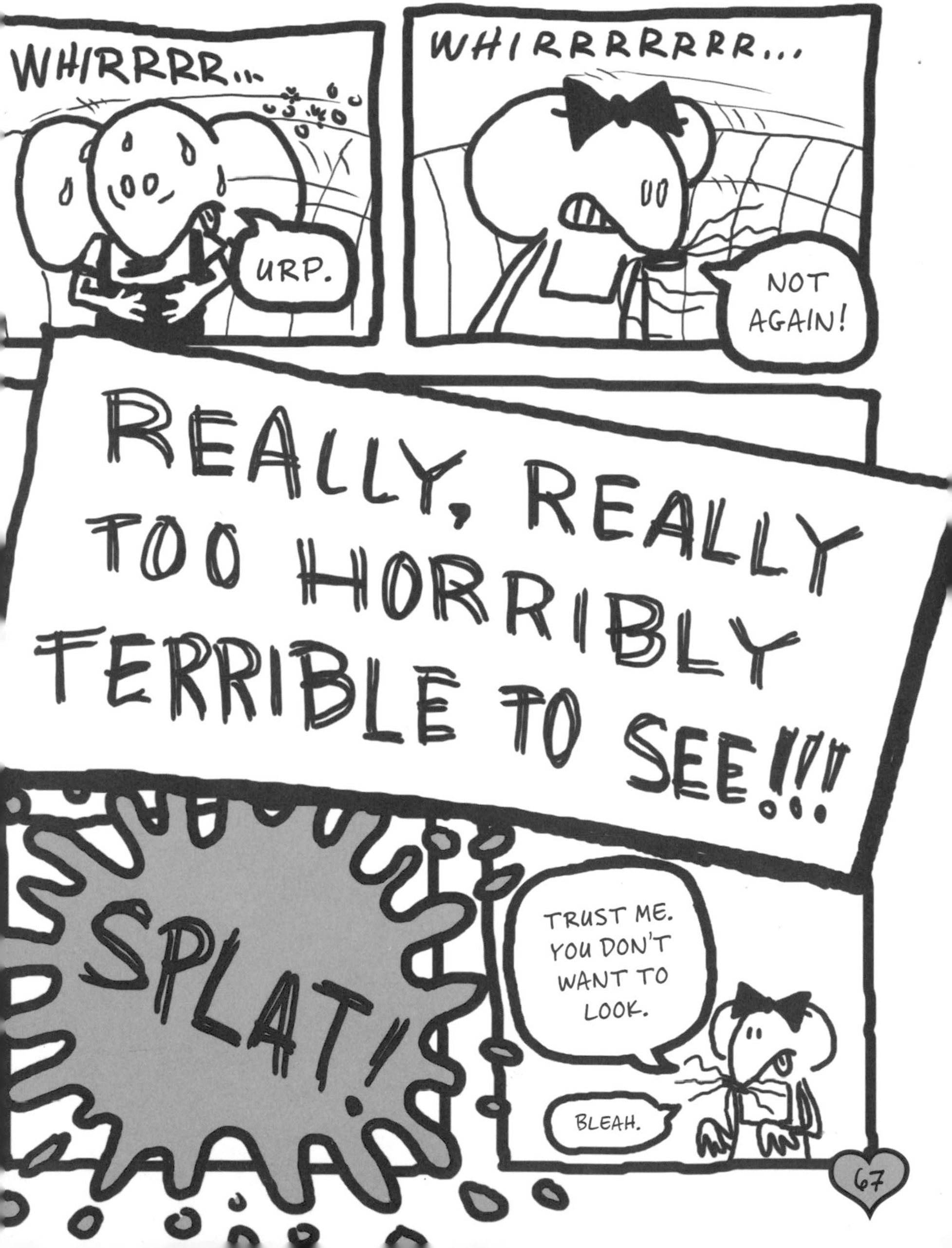

WHIRRRR...
URP.
WHIRRRRRRR...
NOT AGAIN!
REALLY, REALLY TOO HORRIBLY TERRIBLE TO SEE!!!
SPLAT!
TRUST ME. YOU DON'T WANT TO LOOK.
BLEAH.

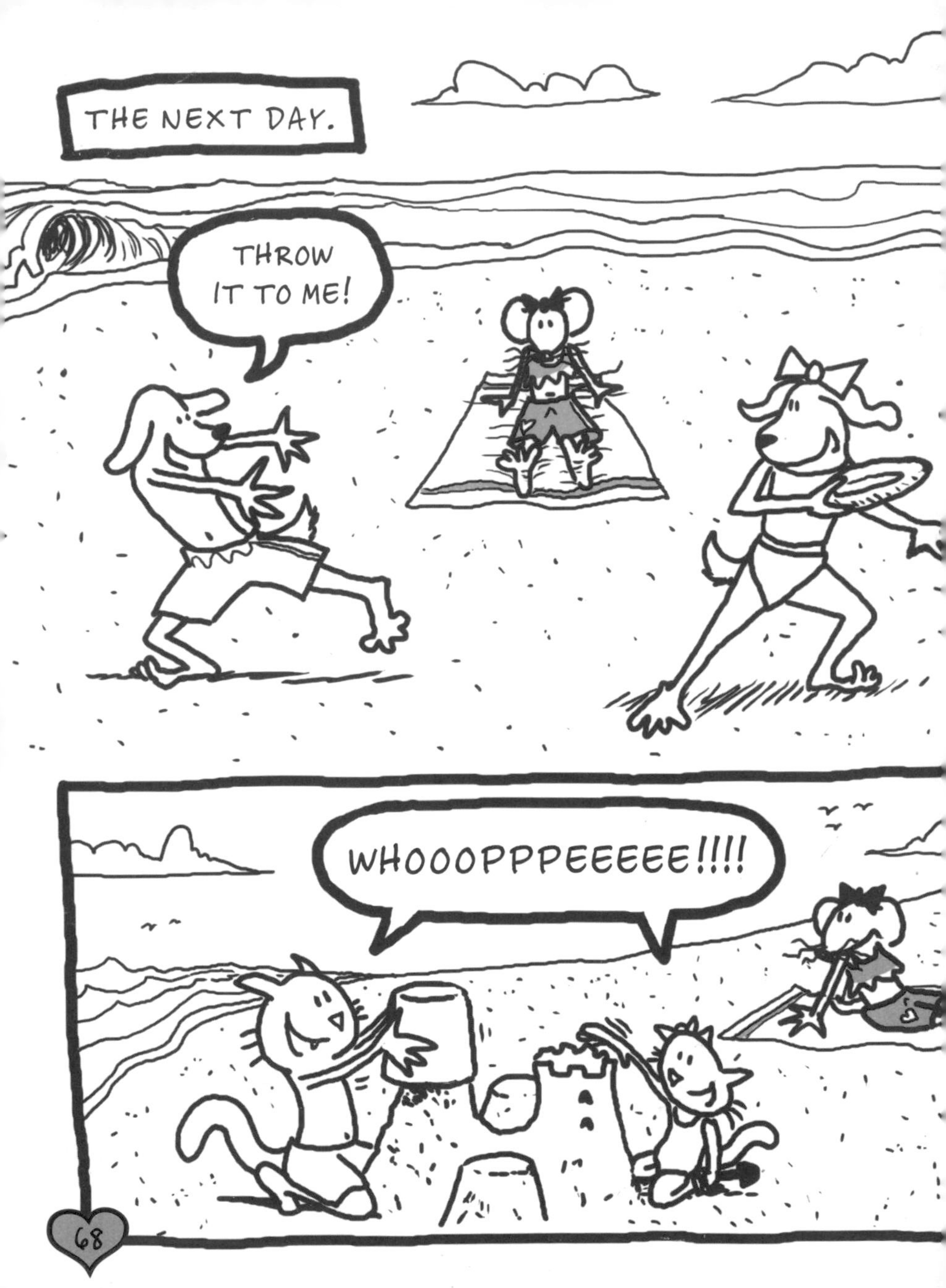
THE NEXT DAY.
THROW IT TO ME!
WHOOOPPPEEEEEE!!!!

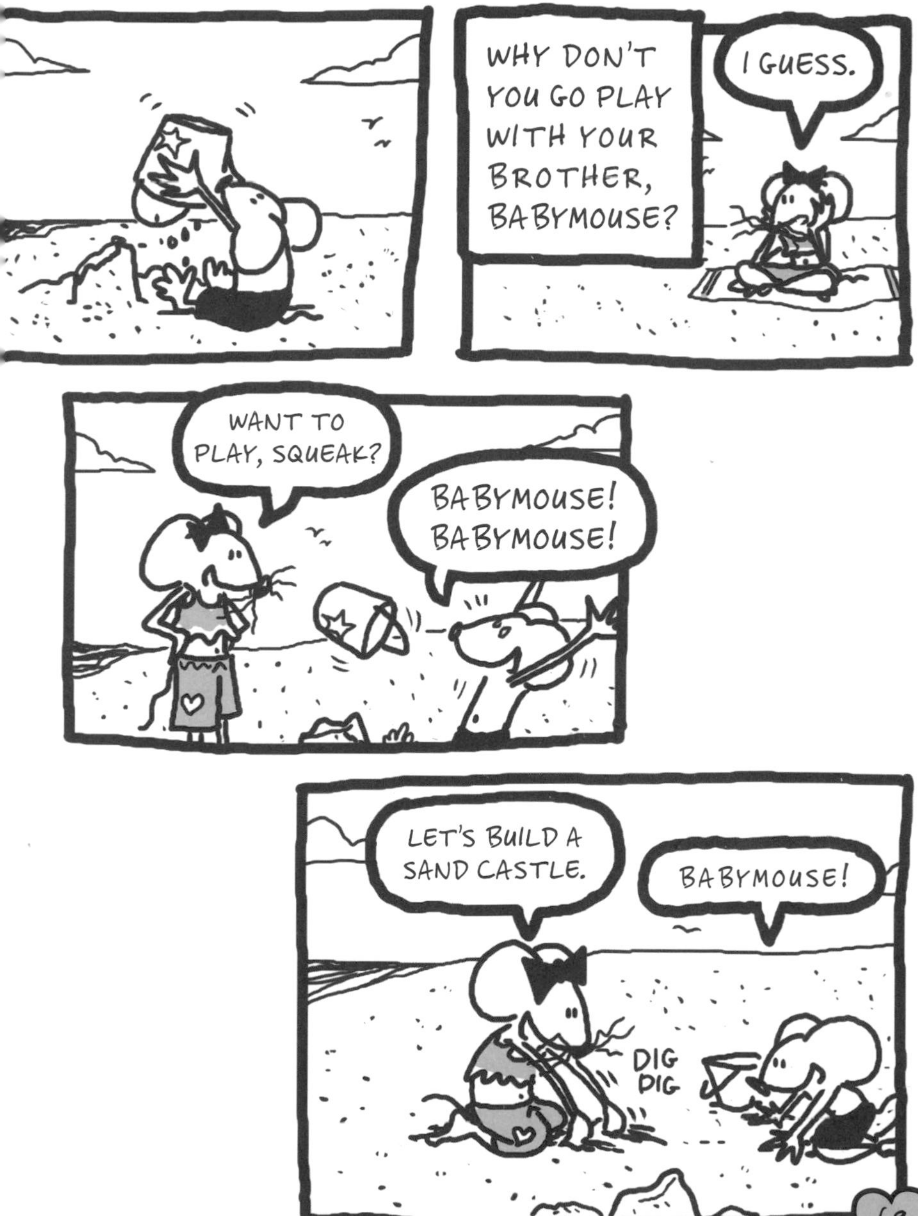
WHY DON'T YOU GO PLAY WITH YOUR BROTHER, BABYMOUSE?
I GUESS.
WANT TO PLAY, SQUEAK?
BABYMOUSE! BABYMOUSE!
LET'S BUILD A SAND CASTLE.
BABYMOUSE!
DIG DIG

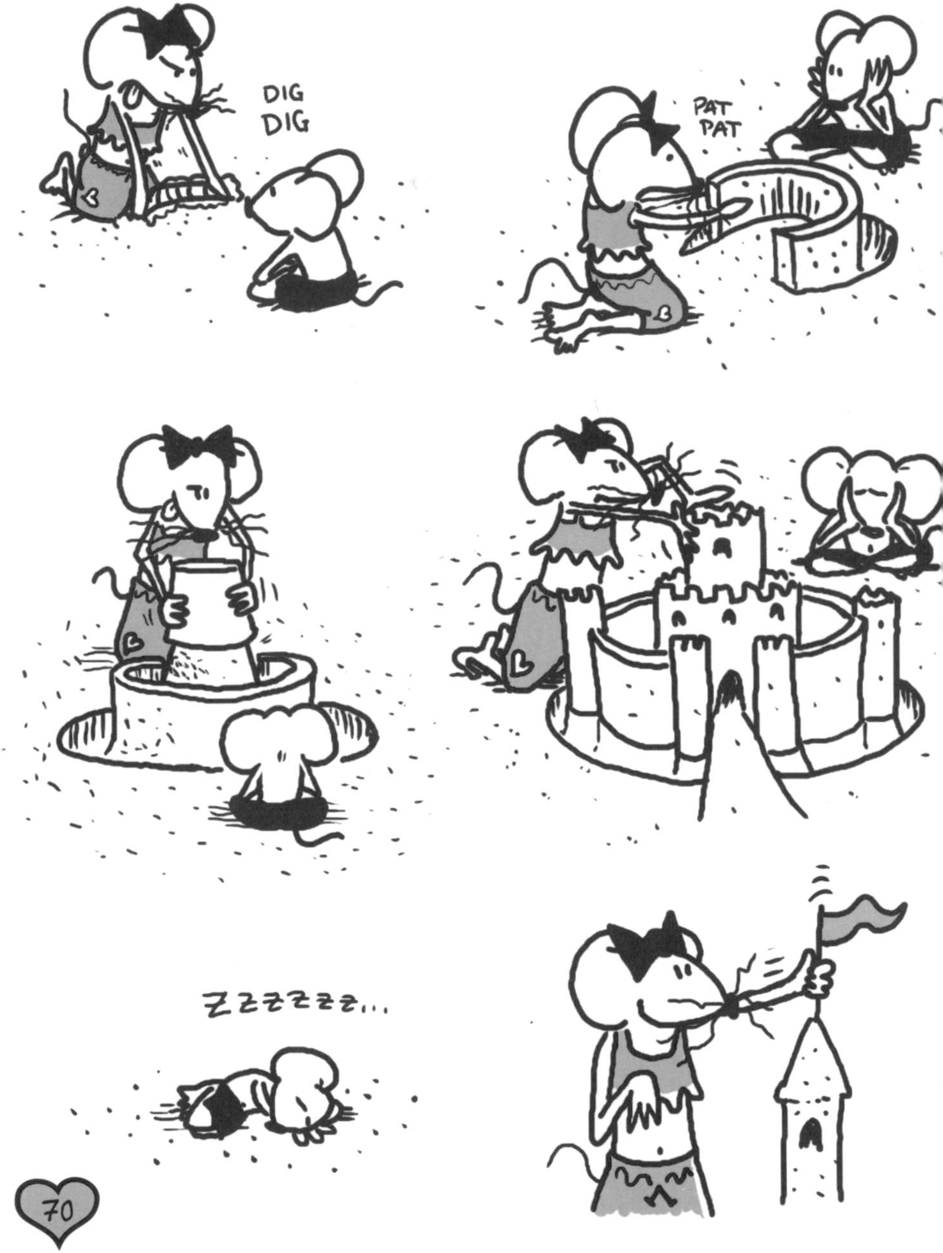
DIG
DIG
PAT
PAT
ZZZZZZZ...

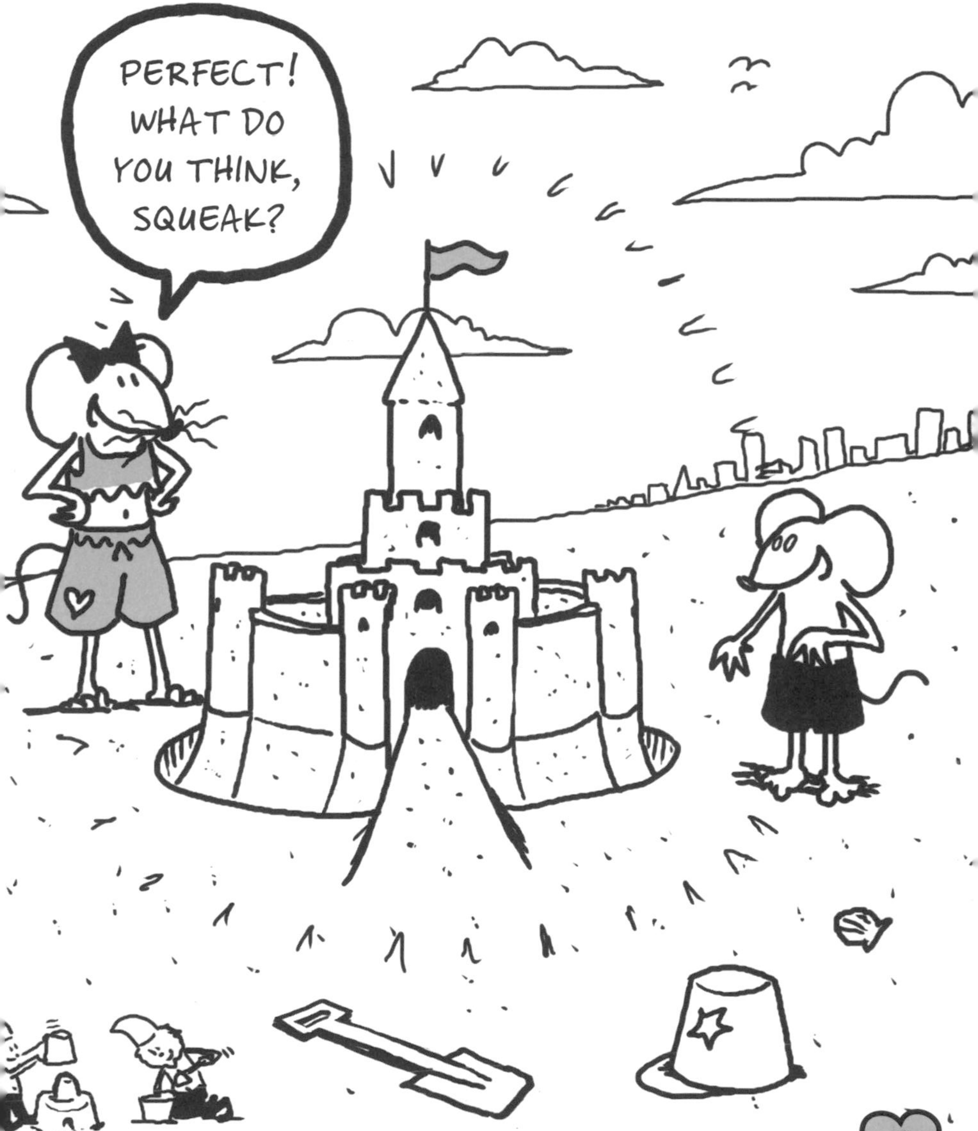
PERFECT! WHAT DO YOU THINK, SQUEAK?

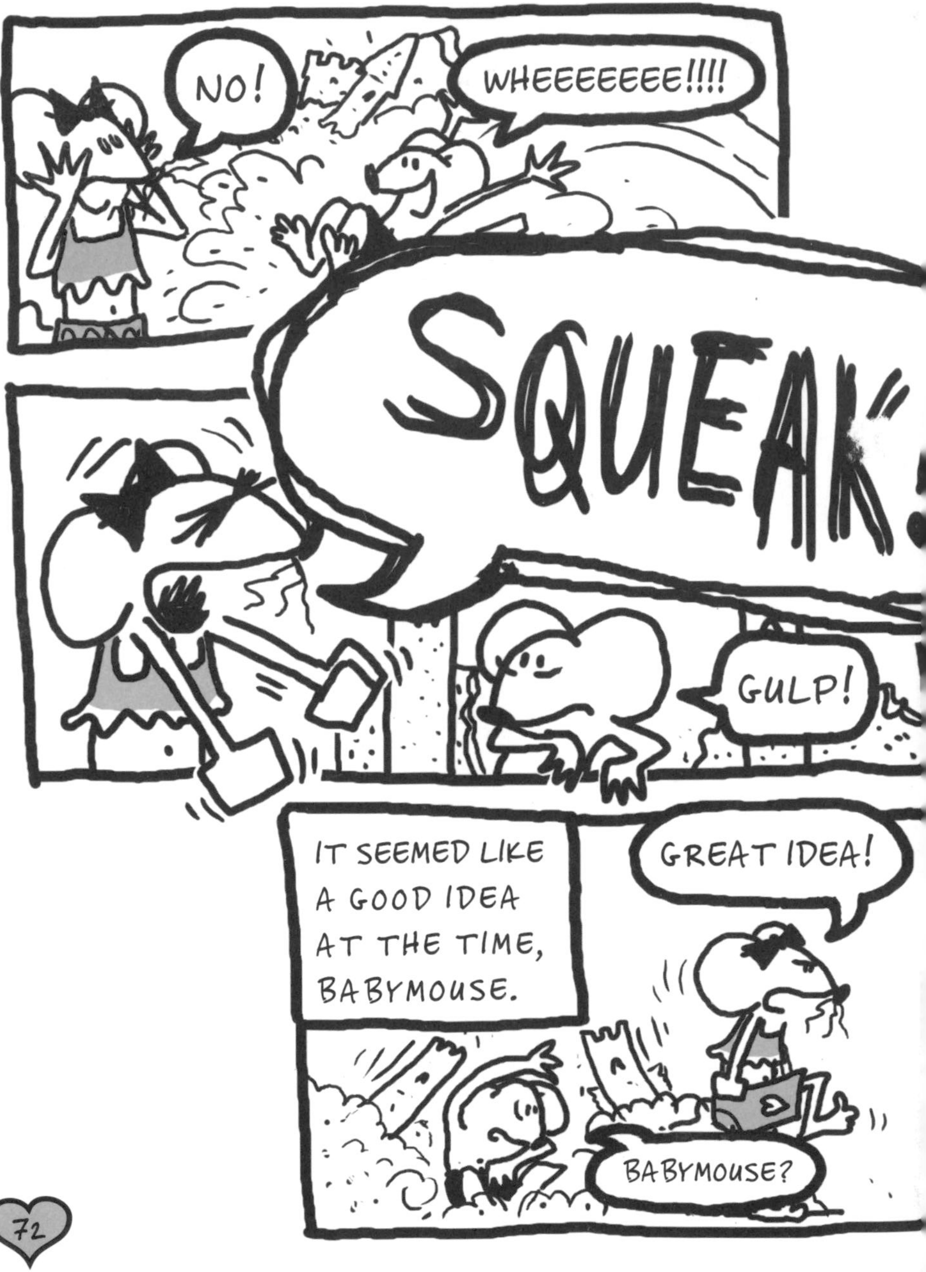

NO!
WHEEEEEEEE!!!!
SQUEAK!
GULP!
IT SEEMED LIKE A GOOD IDEA AT THE TIME, BABYMOUSE.
GREAT IDEA!
BABYMOUSE?

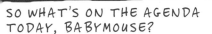
NEXT DAY.

SO WHAT'S ON THE AGENDA TODAY, BABYMOUSE?

I'M GOING TO COLLECT SHELLS!

AND **NO**, SQUEAK, YOU CAN'T COME.

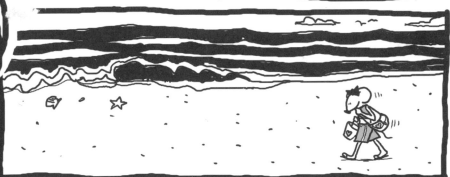

THAT'S A PRETTY ONE!

HEY!

SNAP!

73

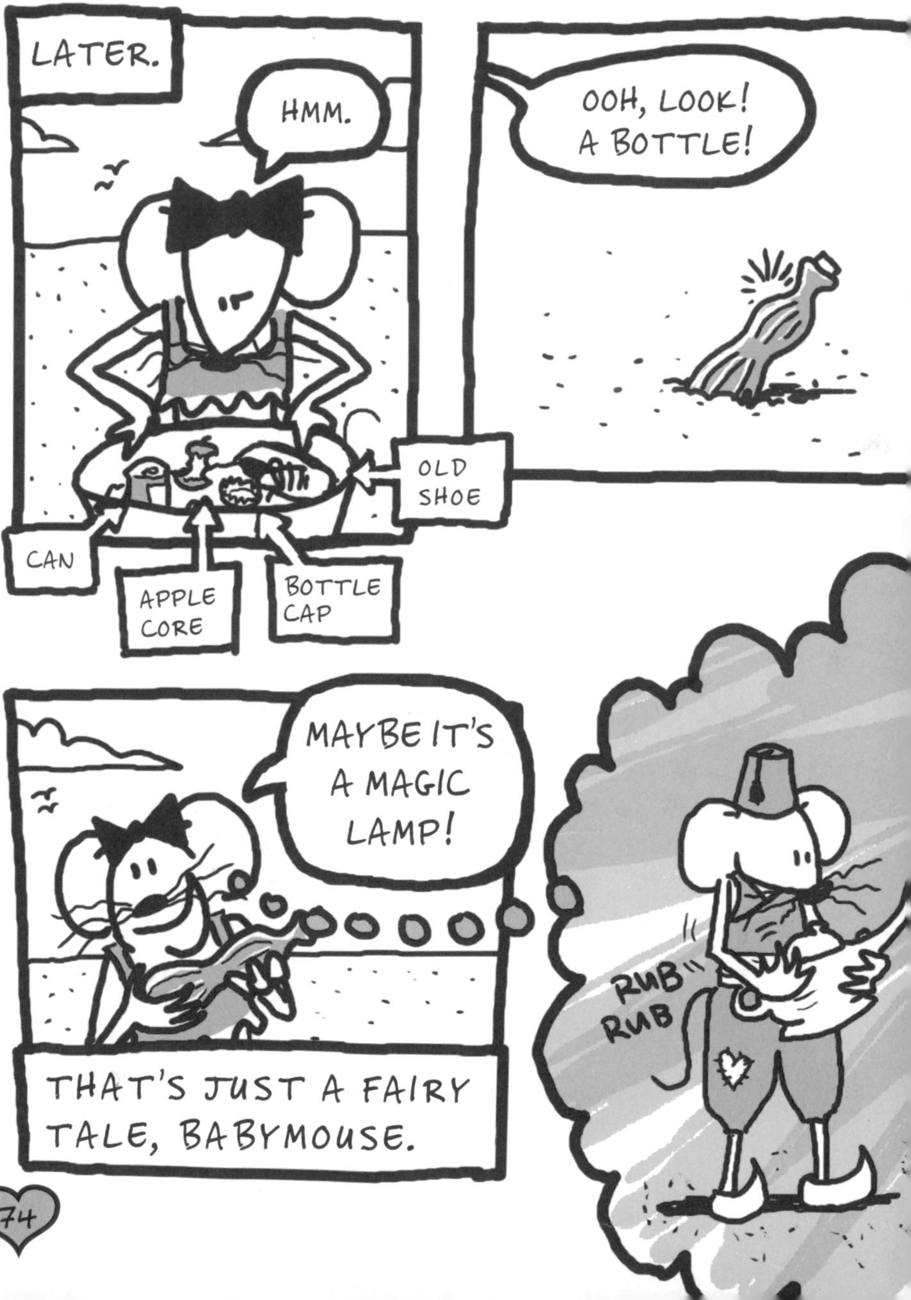
LATER.
HMM.
CAN
APPLE CORE
BOTTLE CAP
OLD SHOE
OOH, LOOK! A BOTTLE!
MAYBE IT'S A MAGIC LAMP!
THAT'S JUST A FAIRY TALE, BABYMOUSE.
RUB RUB

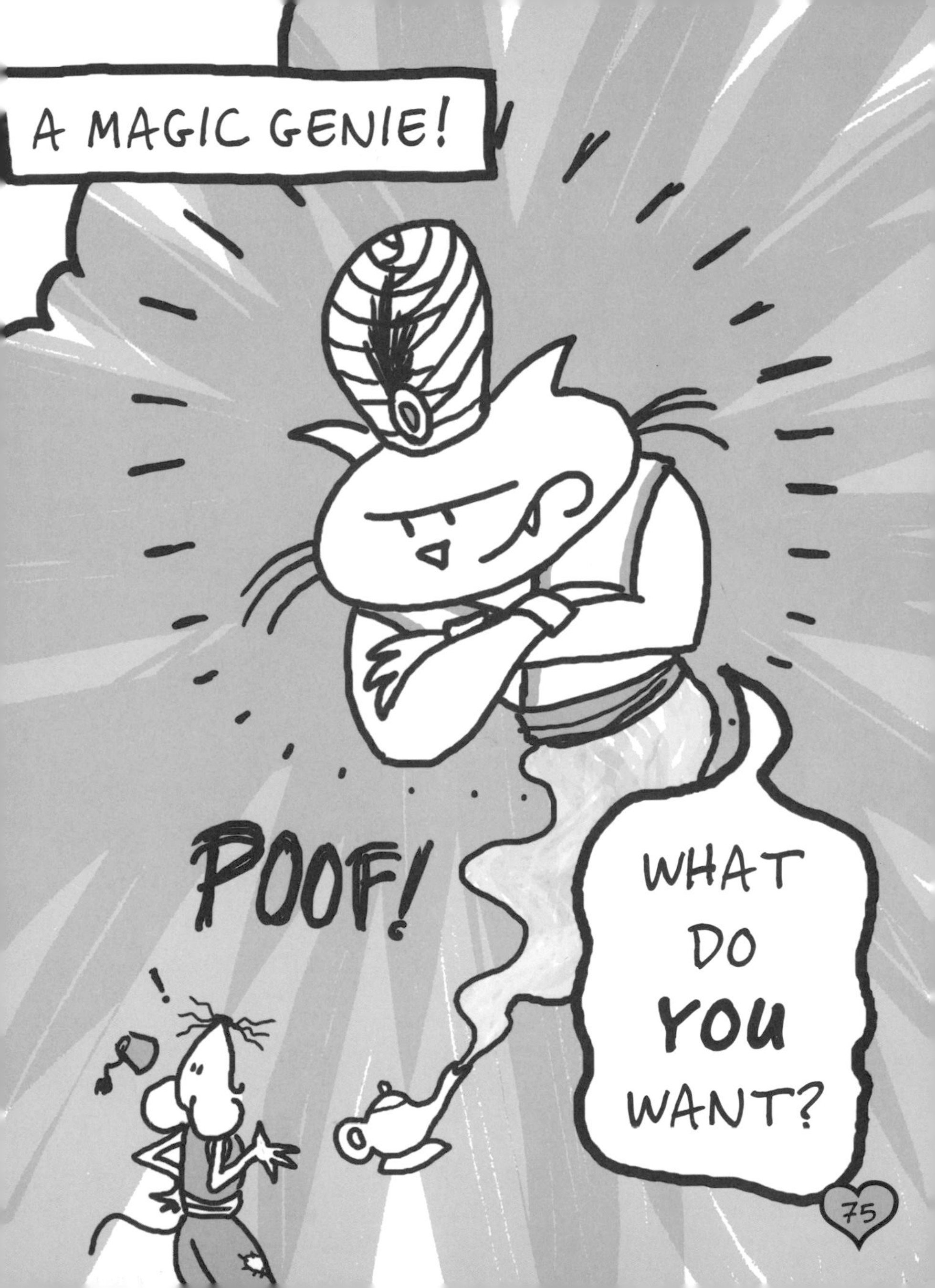
A MAGIC GENIE!
POOF!
!
WHAT DO **YOU** WANT?

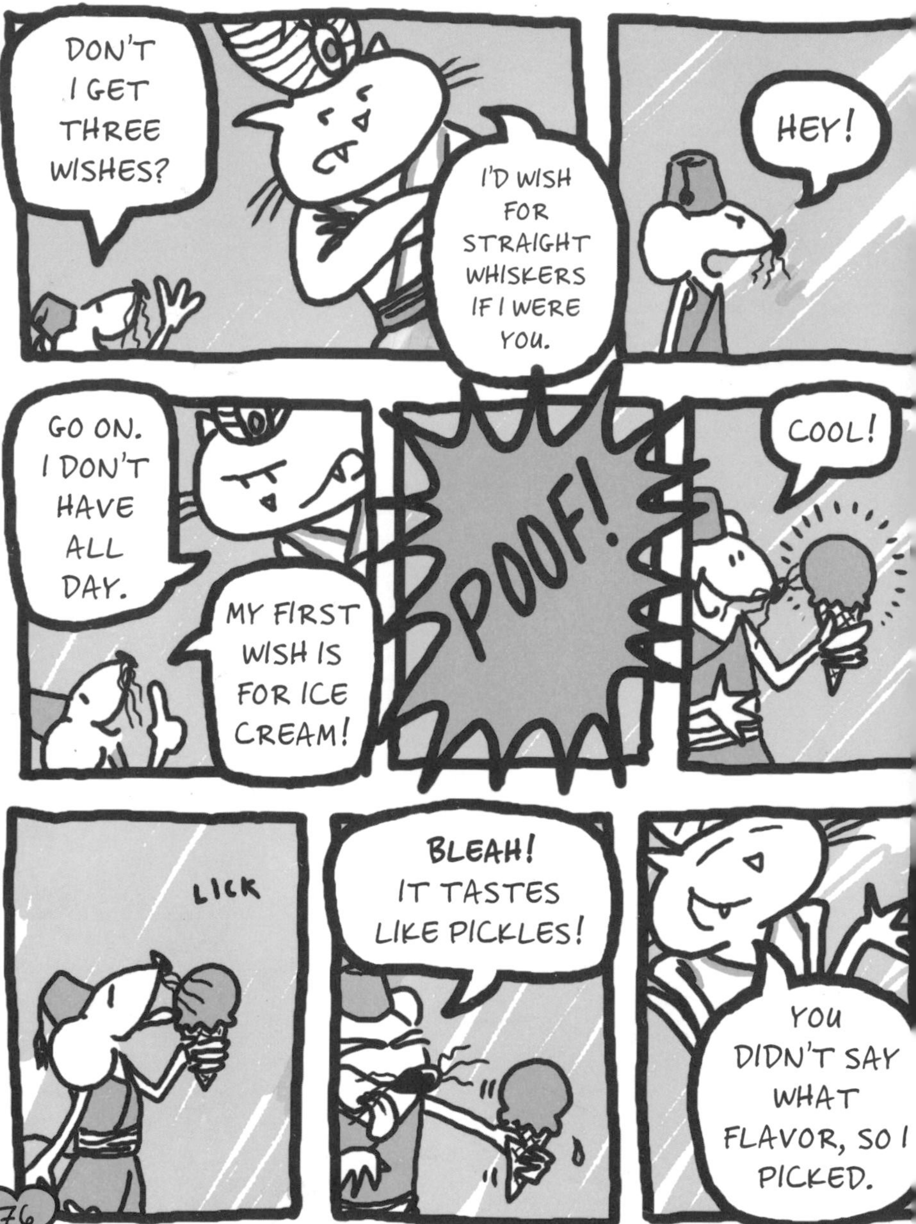
DON'T I GET THREE WISHES?
I'D WISH FOR STRAIGHT WHISKERS IF I WERE YOU.
HEY!
GO ON. I DON'T HAVE ALL DAY.
MY FIRST WISH IS FOR ICE CREAM!
POOF!
COOL!
LICK
BLEAH! IT TASTES LIKE PICKLES!
YOU DIDN'T SAY WHAT FLAVOR, SO I PICKED.

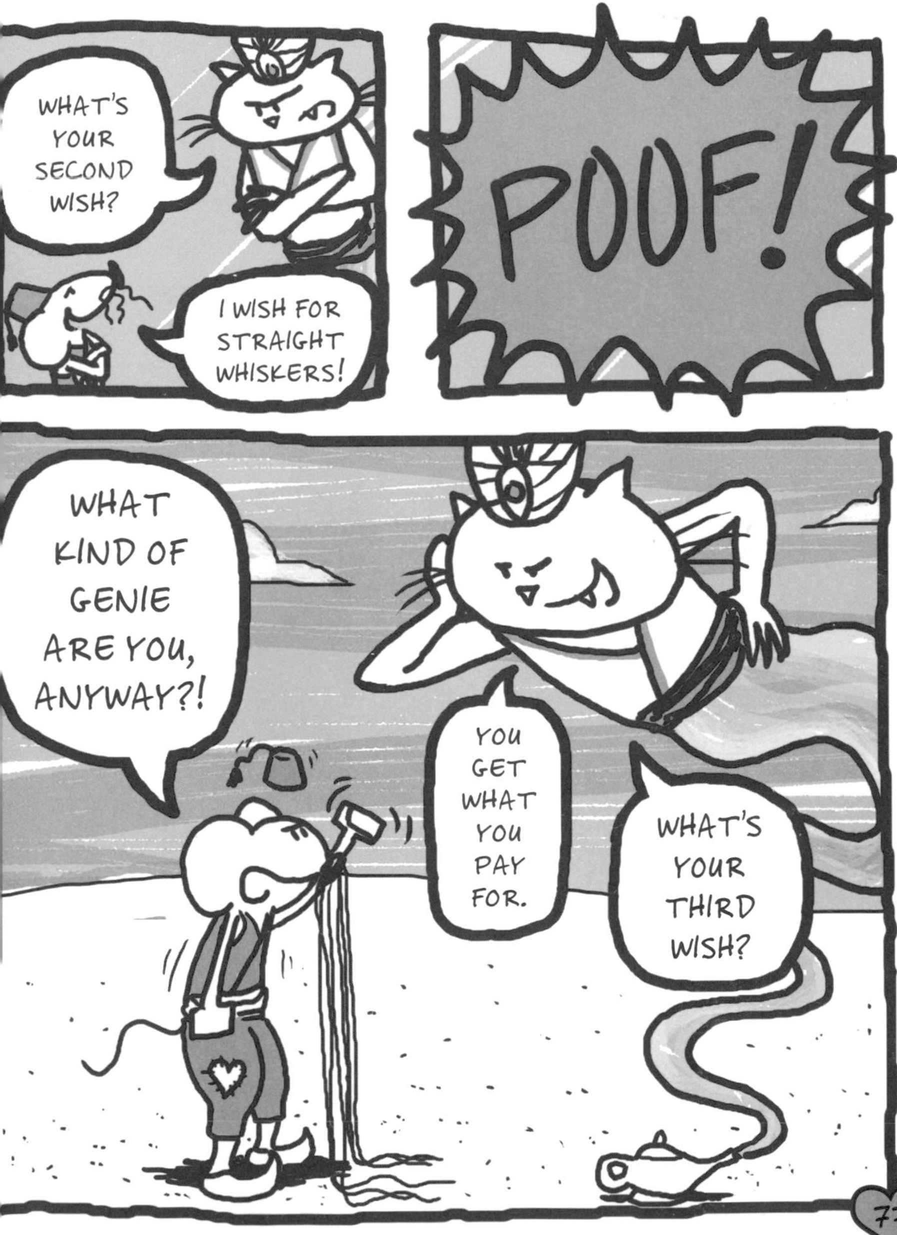
WHAT'S YOUR SECOND WISH?
I WISH FOR STRAIGHT WHISKERS!
POOF!
WHAT KIND OF GENIE ARE YOU, ANYWAY?!
YOU GET WHAT YOU PAY FOR.
WHAT'S YOUR THIRD WISH?

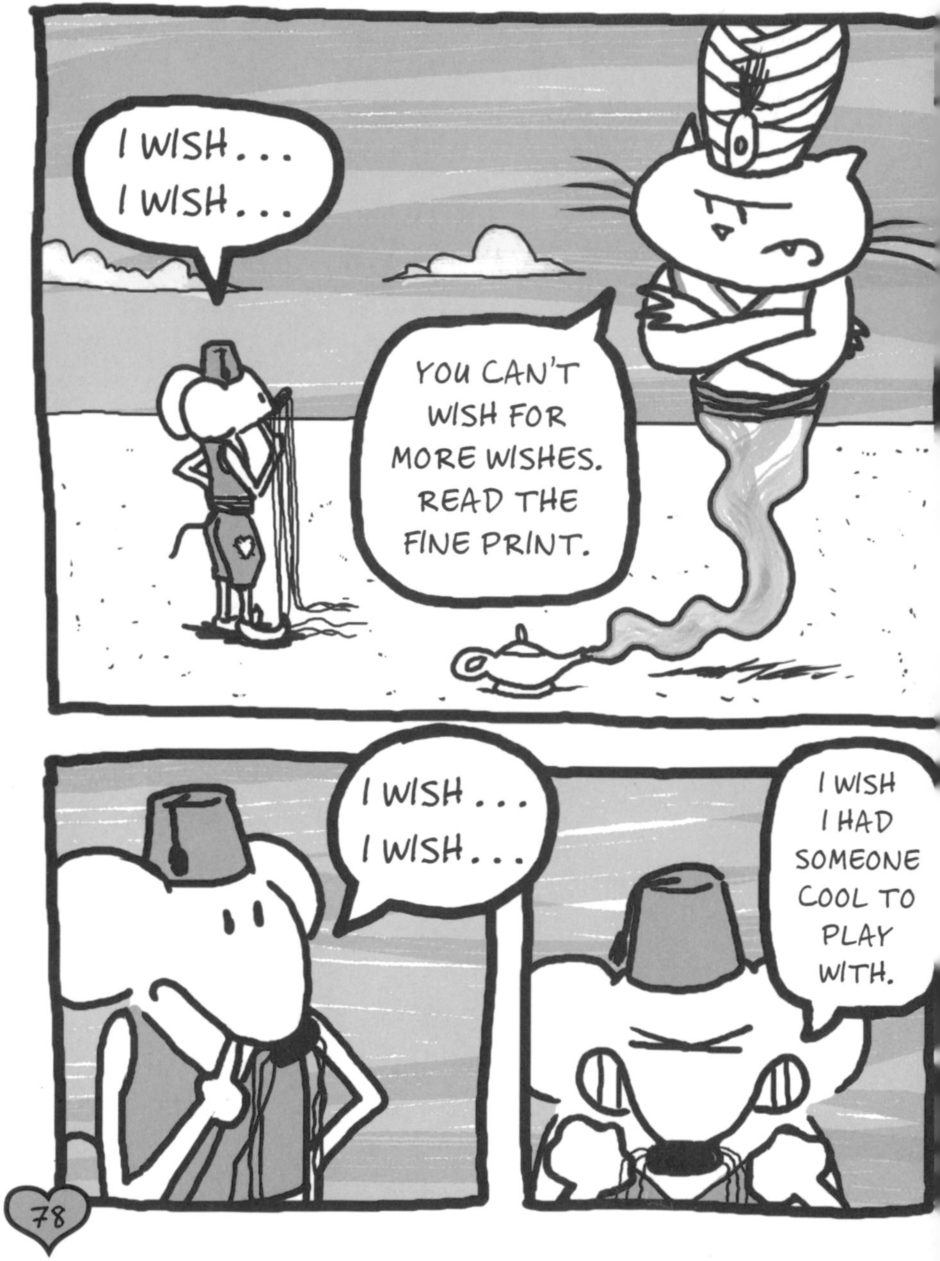
I WISH...
I WISH...
YOU CAN'T WISH FOR MORE WISHES. READ THE FINE PRINT.
I WISH...
I WISH...
I WISH I HAD SOMEONE COOL TO PLAY WITH.

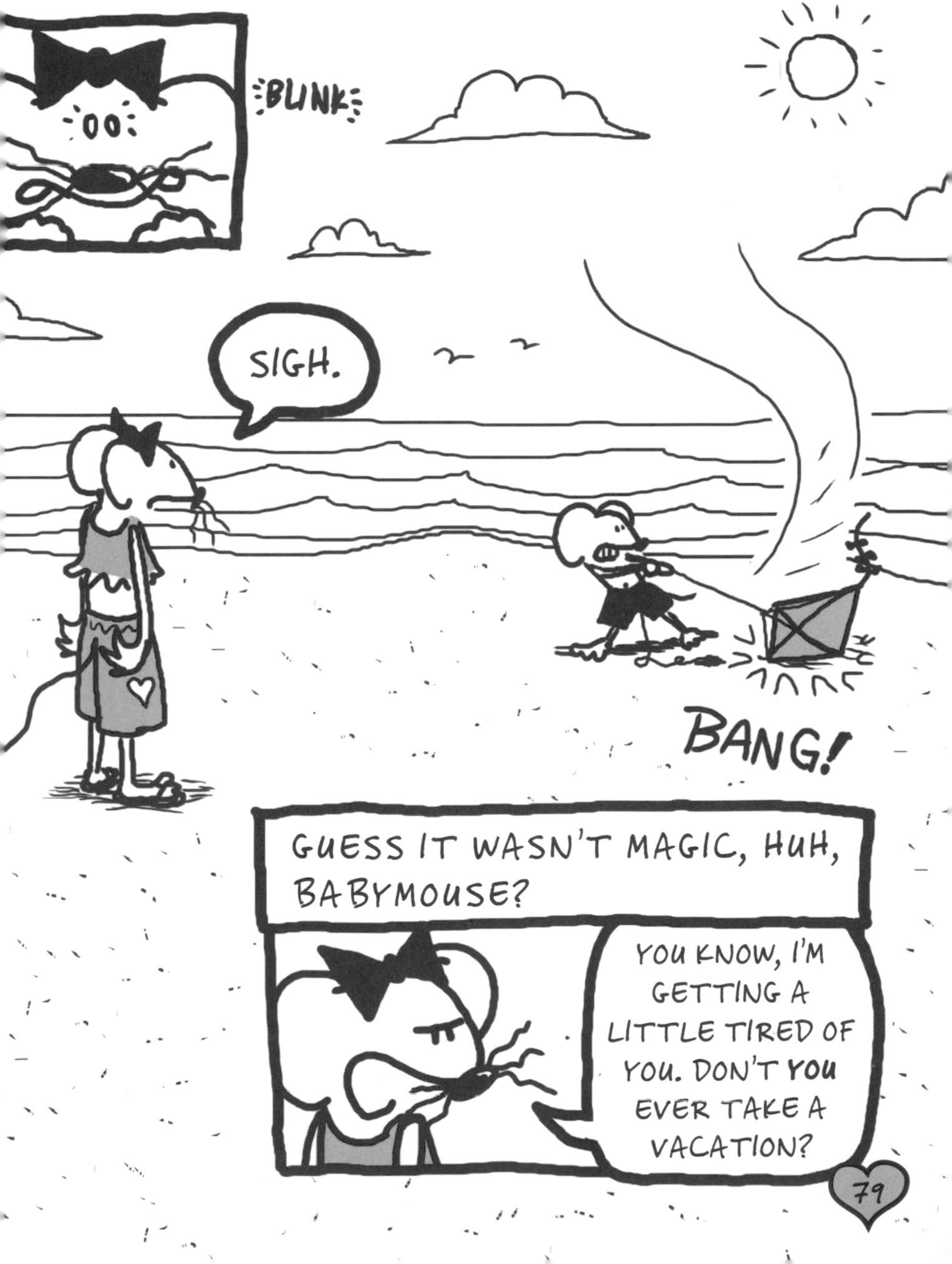
BLINK
SIGH.
BANG!
GUESS IT WASN'T MAGIC, HUH, BABYMOUSE?
YOU KNOW, I'M GETTING A LITTLE TIRED OF YOU. DON'T YOU EVER TAKE A VACATION?

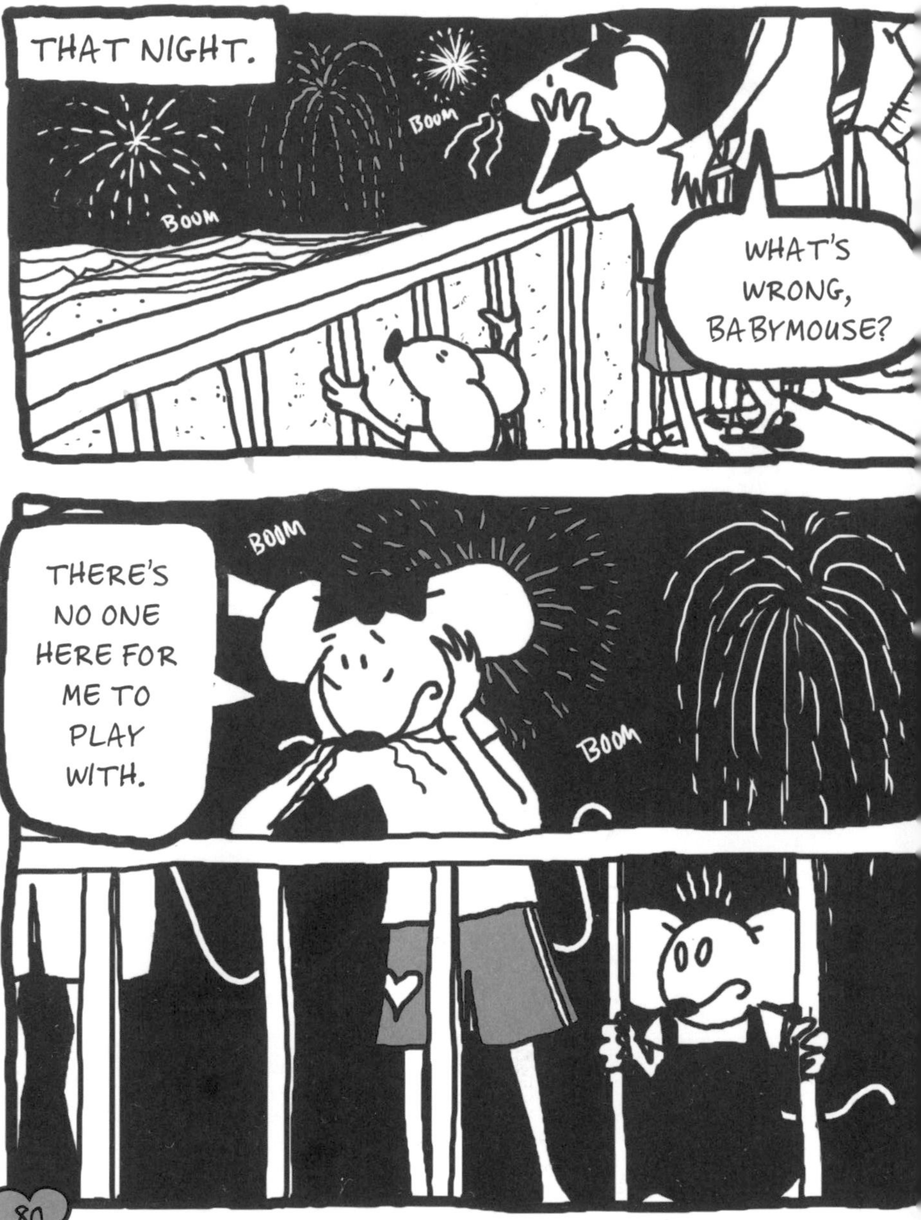
THAT NIGHT.
BOOM
BOOM
WHAT'S WRONG, BABYMOUSE?
BOOM
THERE'S NO ONE HERE FOR ME TO PLAY WITH.
BOOM

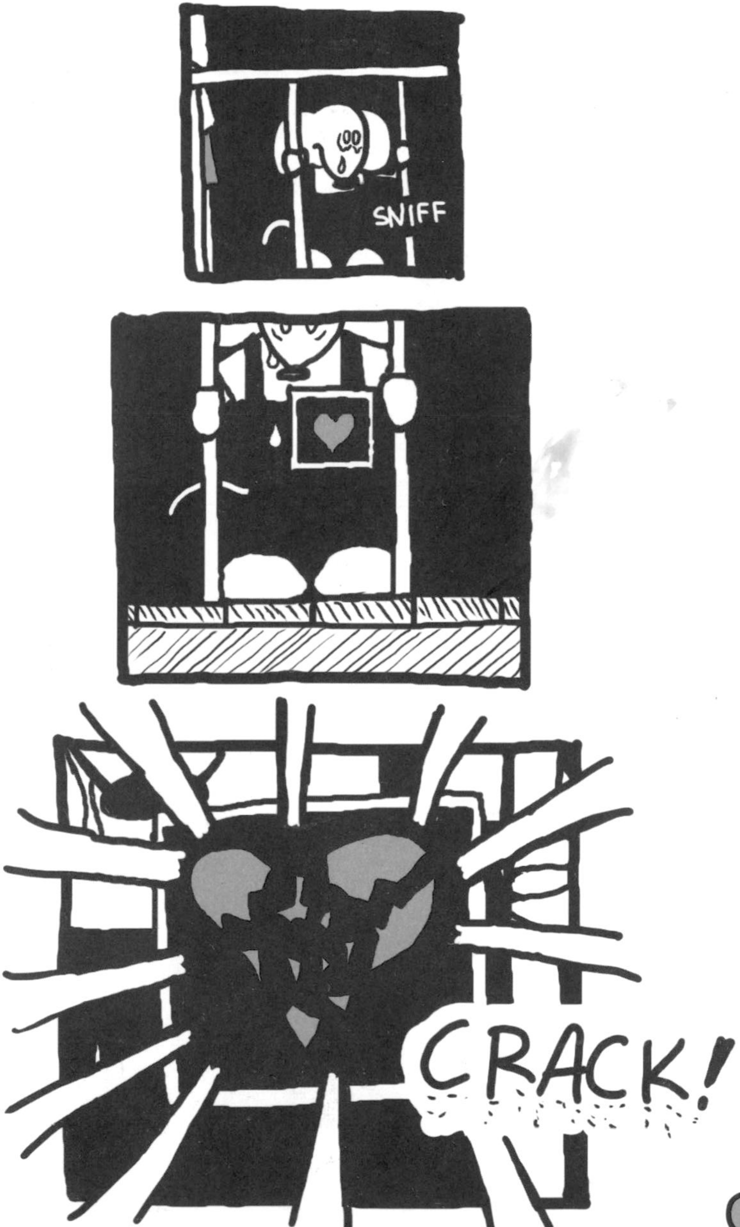
SNIFF
CRACK!

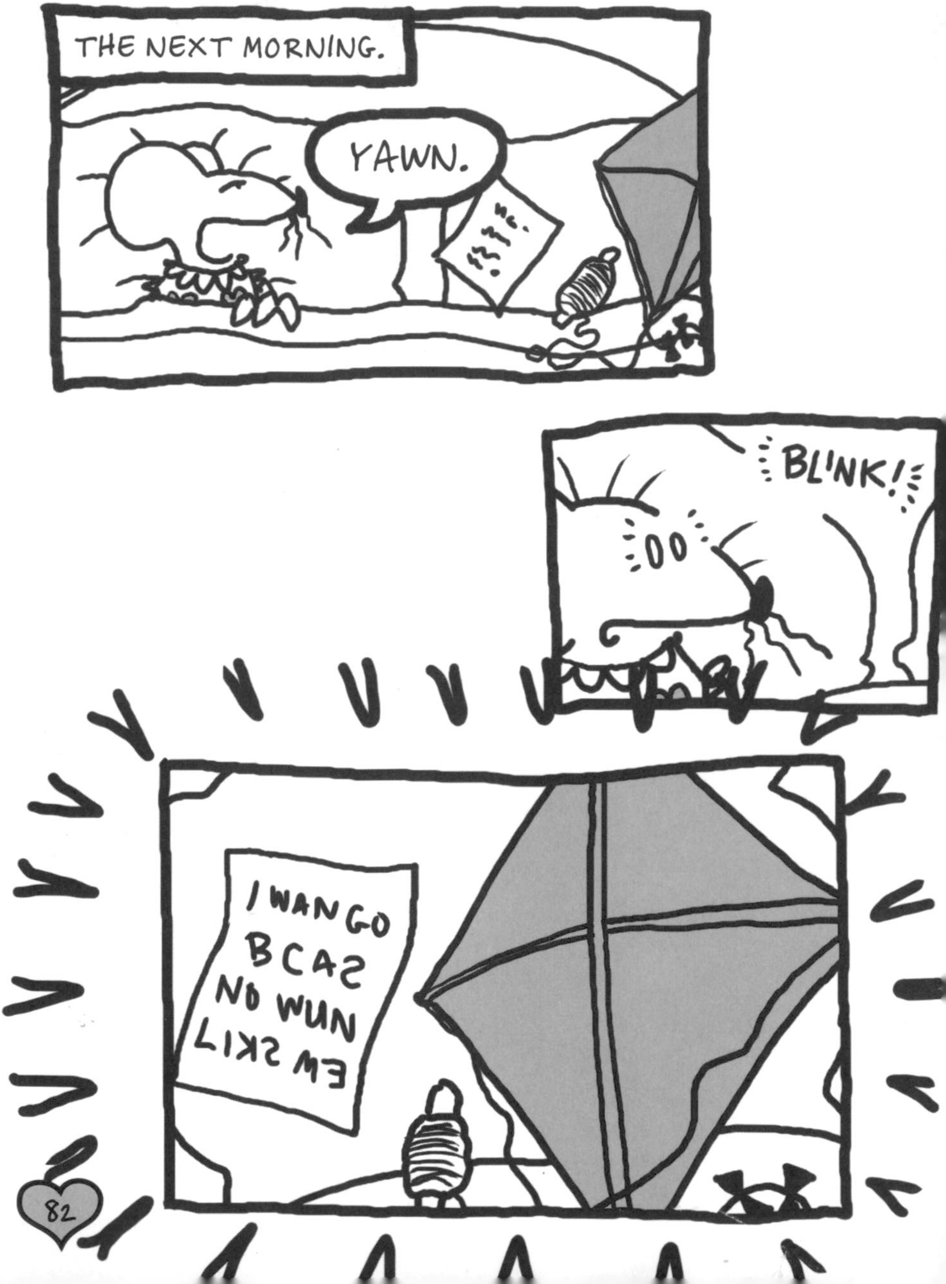
THE NEXT MORNING.
YAWN.
BLINK!
I WANGO
BCAS
NO WUN
LIKS EW

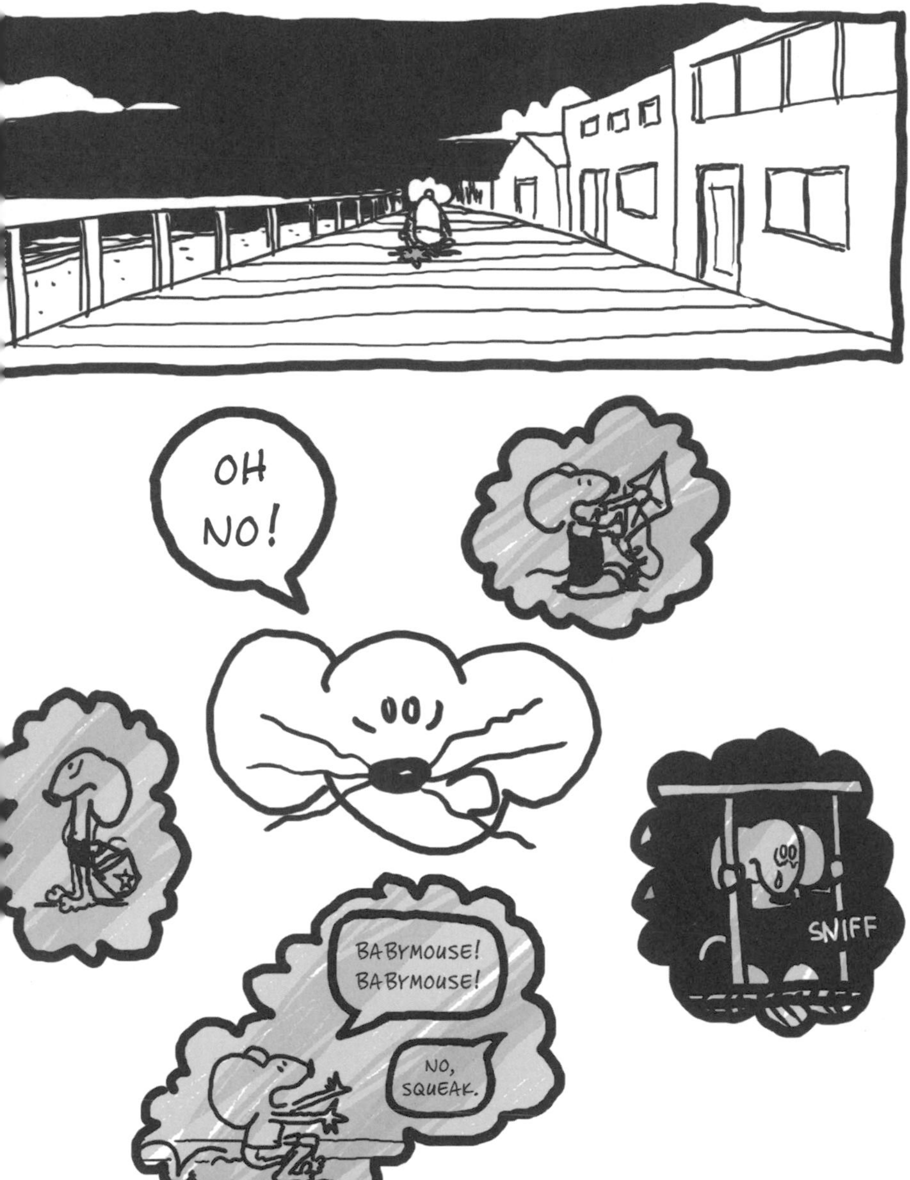
OH NO!
BABYMOUSE! BABYMOUSE!
NO, SQUEAK.
SNIFF

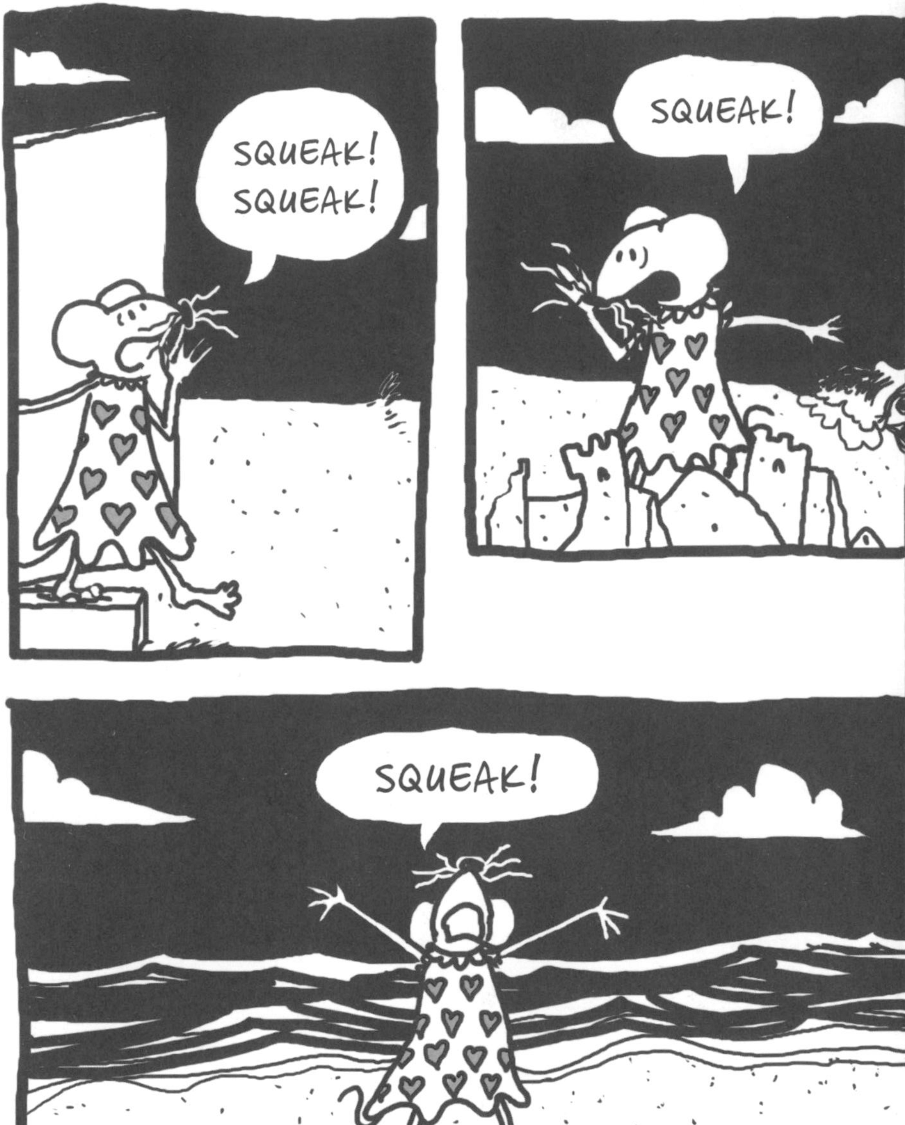
SQUEAK!
SQUEAK!
SQUEAK!
SQUEAK!

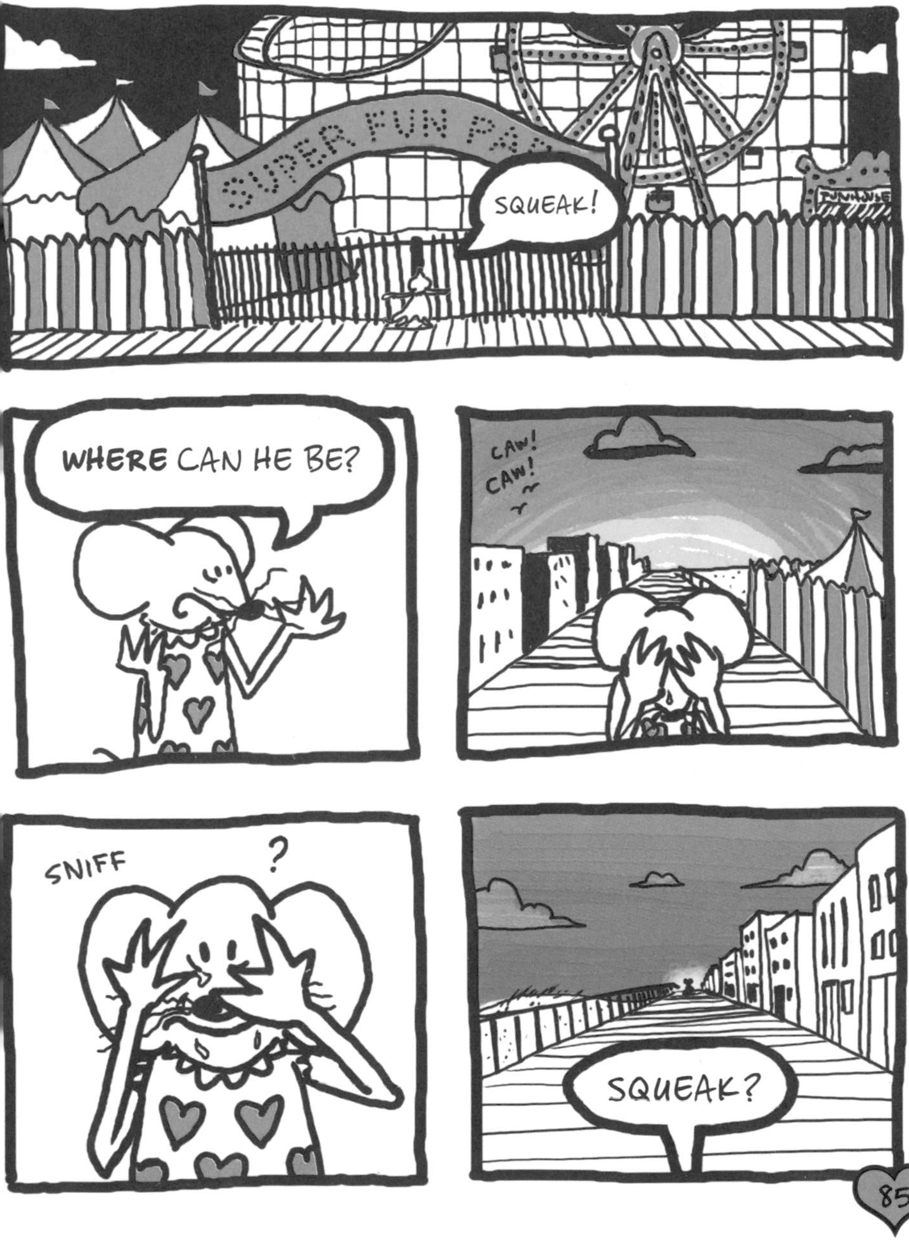
SUPER FUN PA
SQUEAK!
WHERE CAN HE BE?
CAW! CAW!
SNIFF
?
SQUEAK?

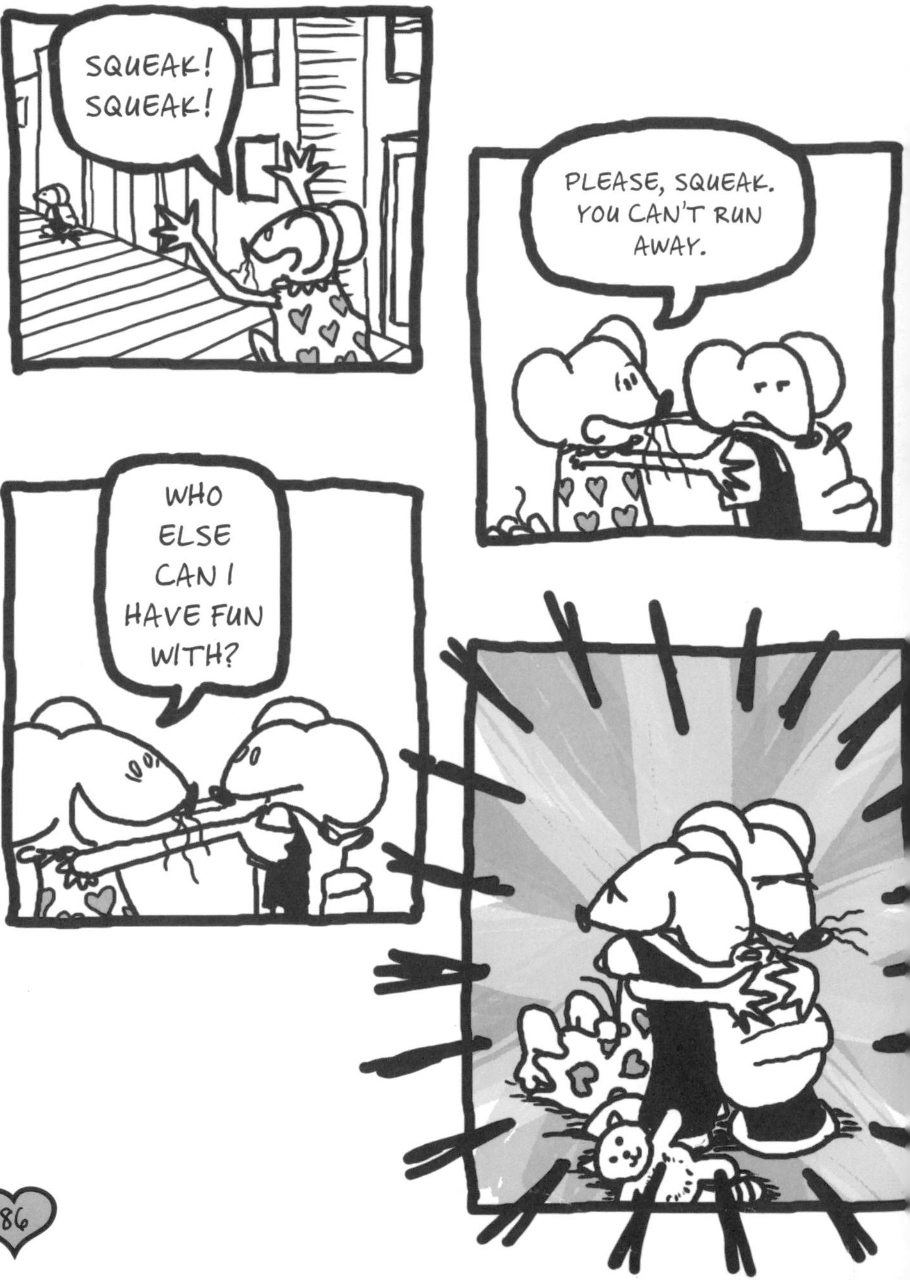
SQUEAK! SQUEAK!
PLEASE, SQUEAK. YOU CAN'T RUN AWAY.
WHO ELSE CAN I HAVE FUN WITH?

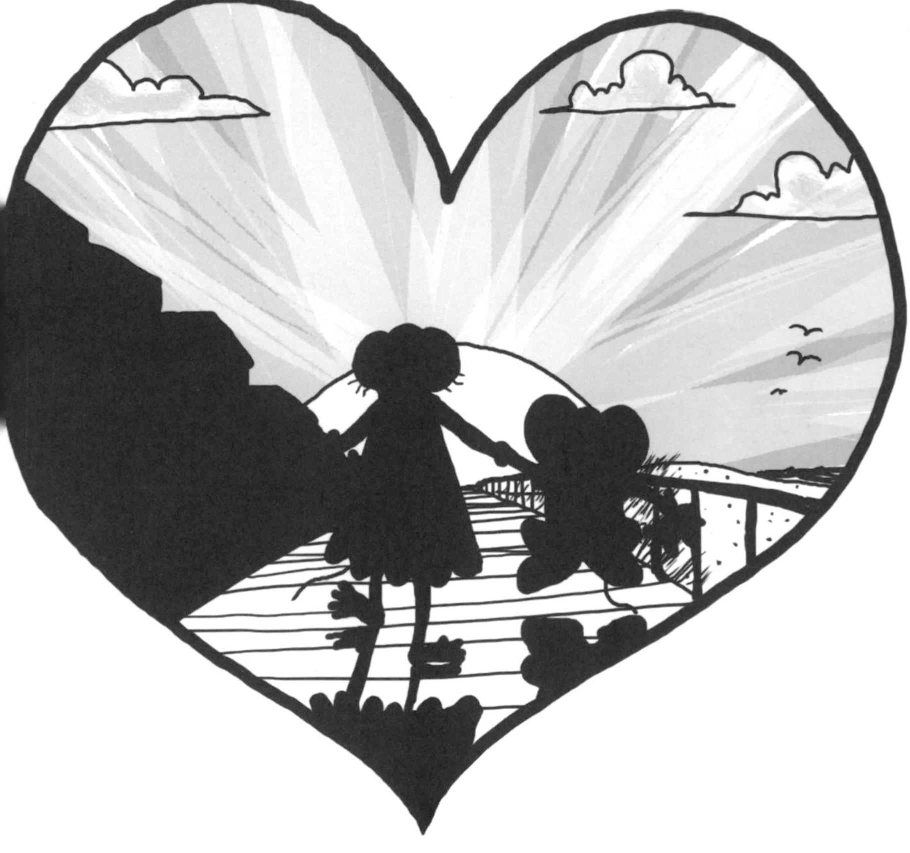

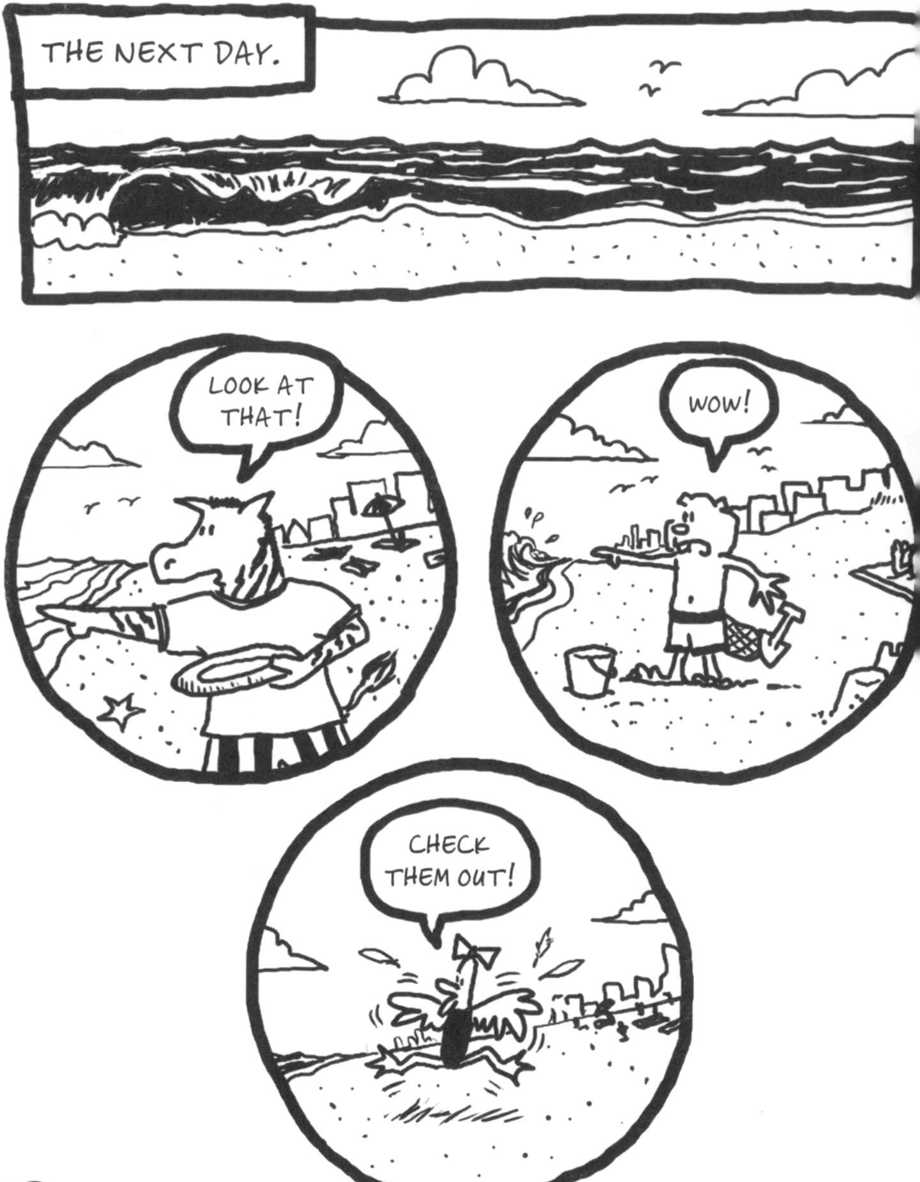
THE NEXT DAY.
LOOK AT THAT!
WOW!
CHECK THEM OUT!

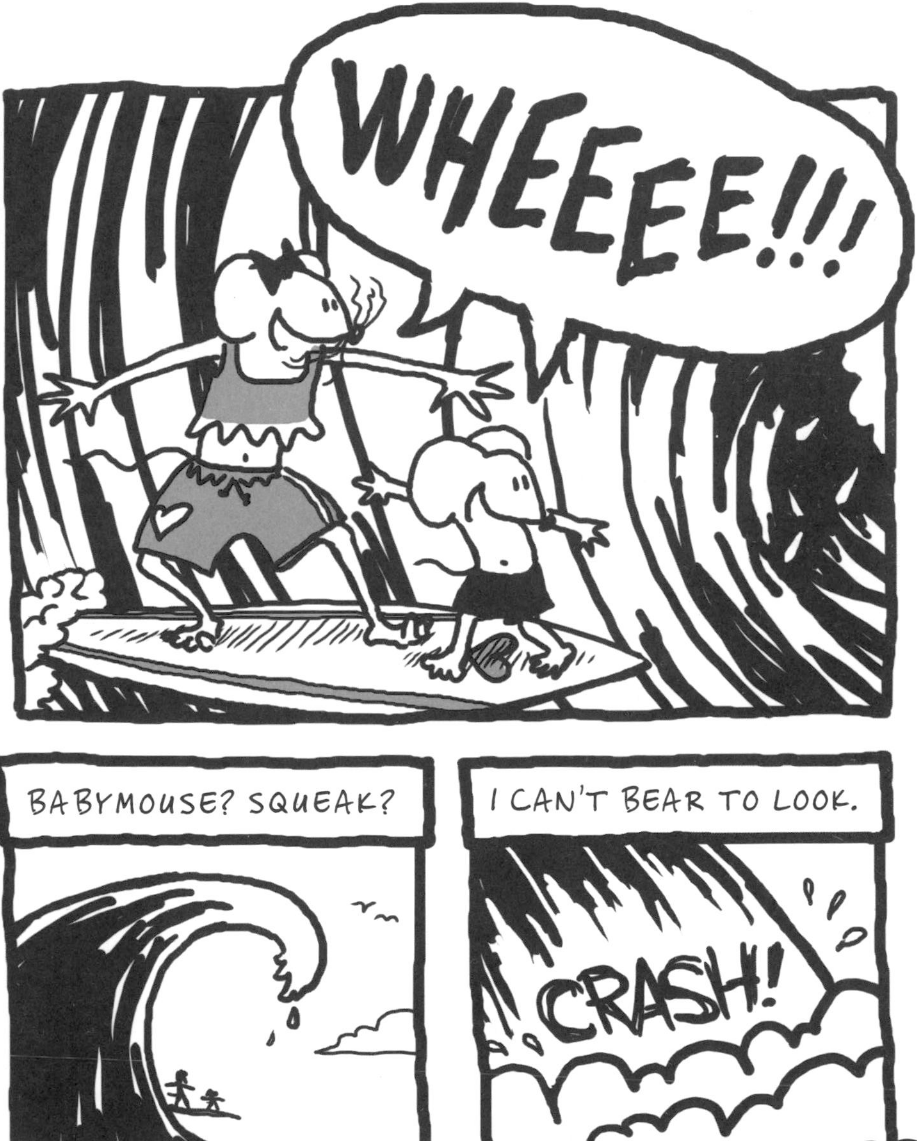
WHEEEEE!!!
BABYMOUSE? SQUEAK?
I CAN'T BEAR TO LOOK.
CRASH!

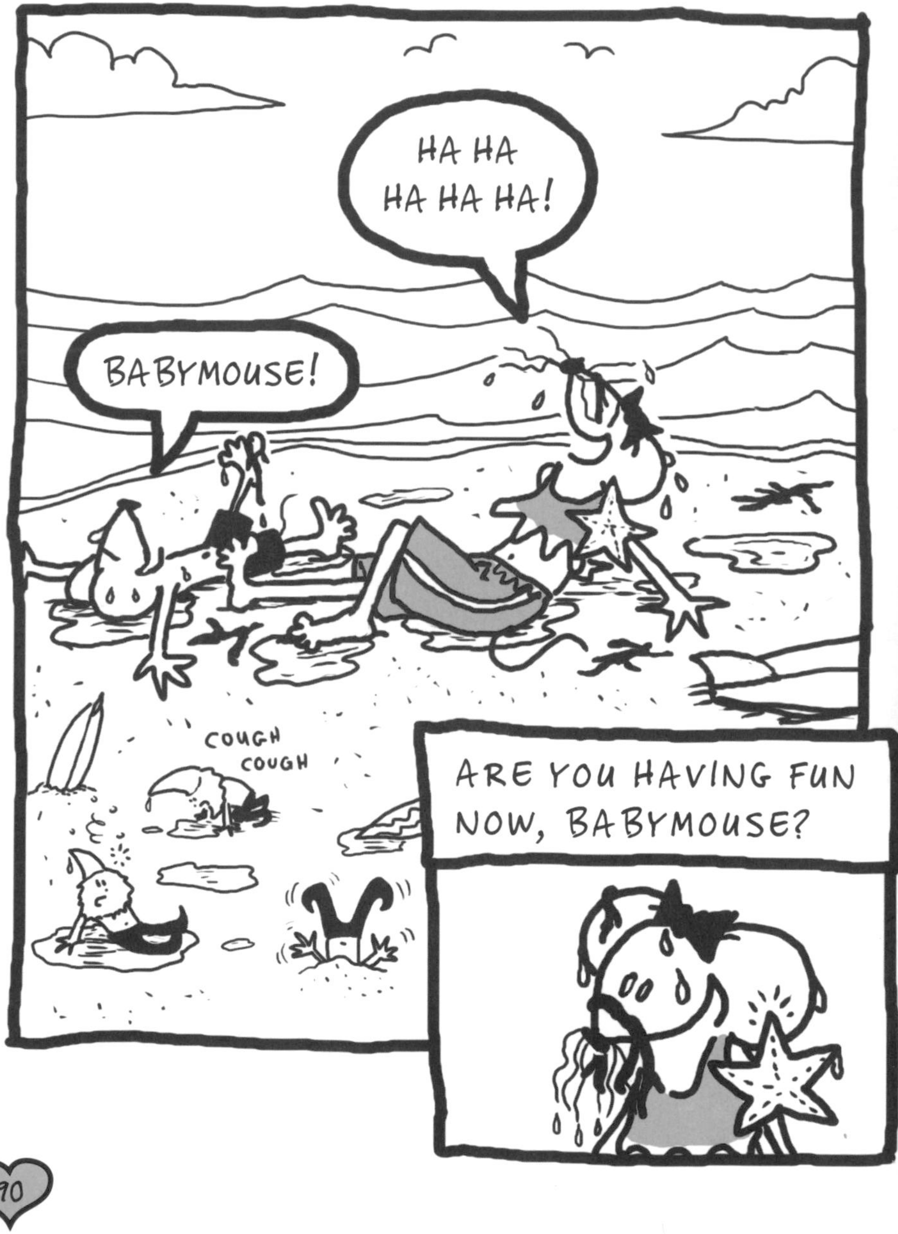
BABYMOUSE!
HA HA
HA HA HA!
COUGH
COUGH
ARE YOU HAVING FUN
NOW, BABYMOUSE?

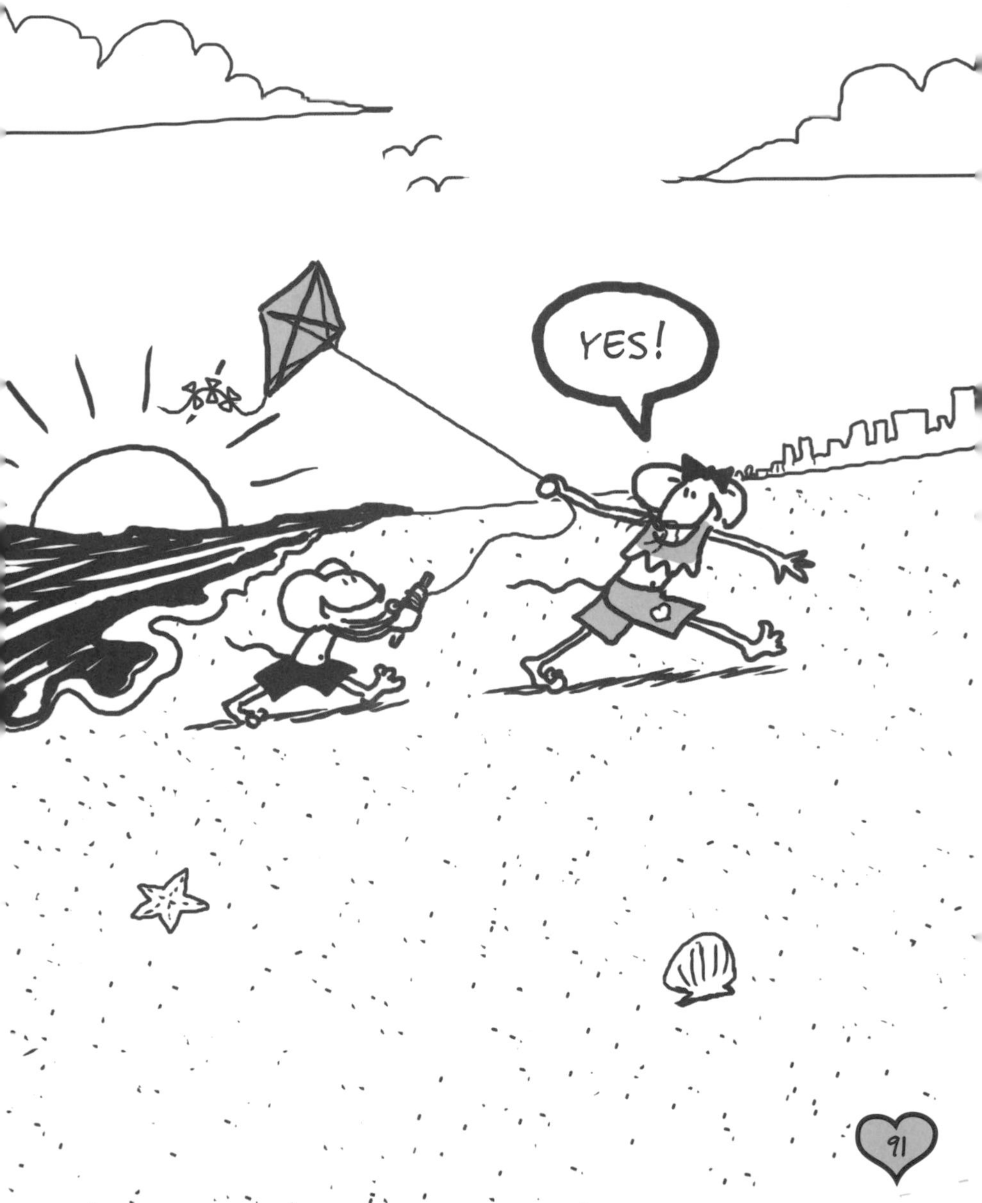
YES!

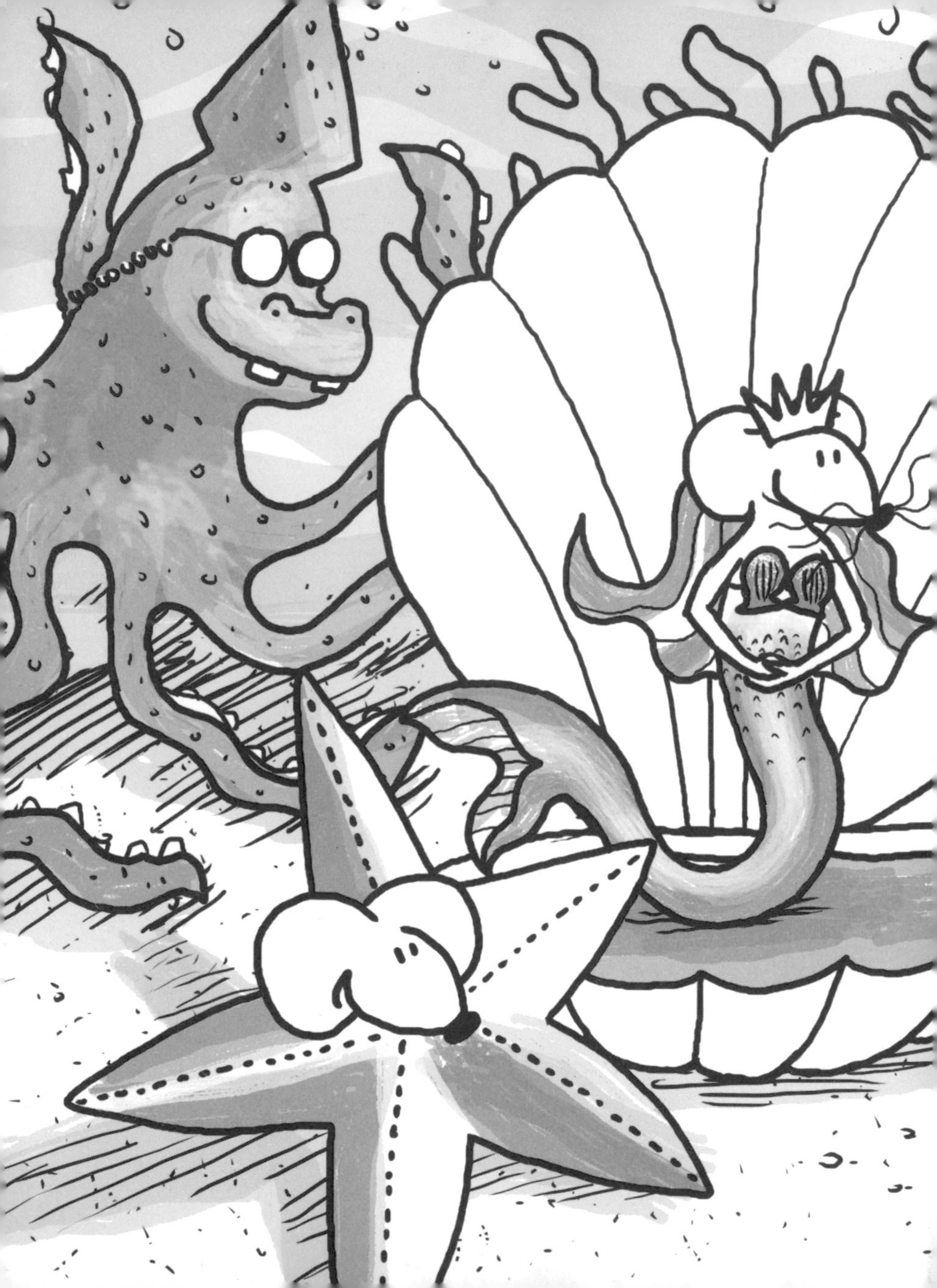

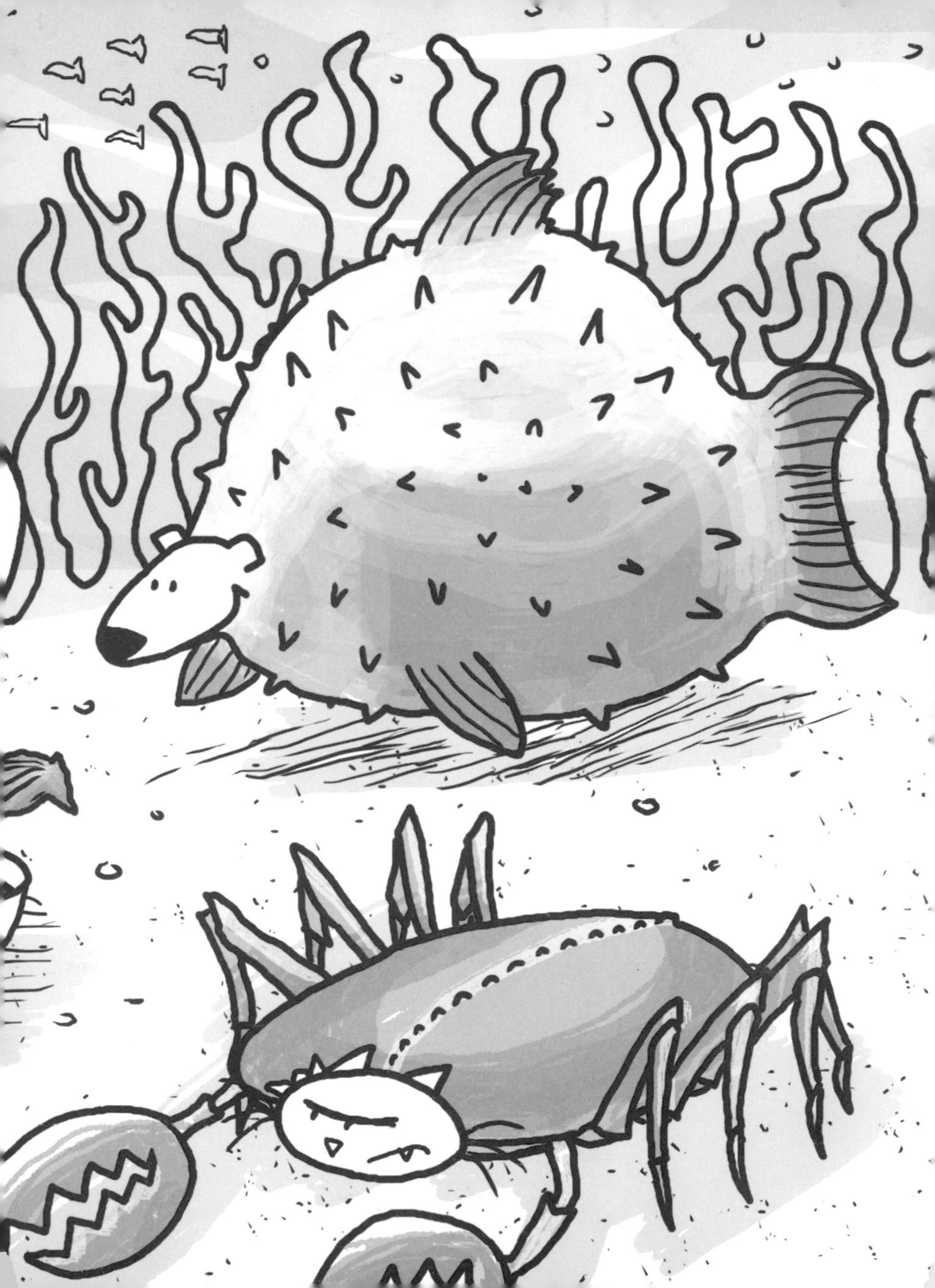

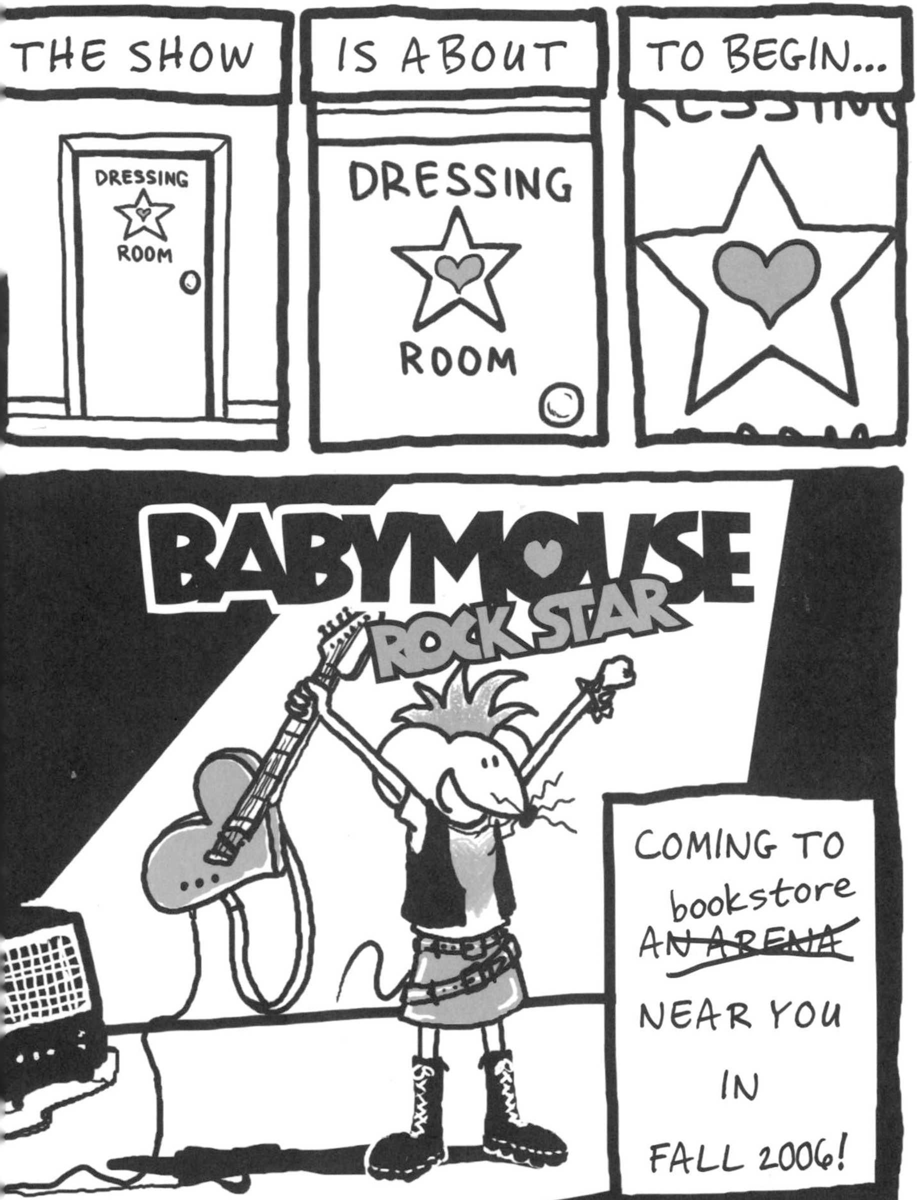
THE SHOW
IS ABOUT
TO BEGIN...
DRESSING ROOM
DRESSING ROOM
BABYMOUSE
ROCK STAR
COMING TO
bookstore
A~~N ARENA~~
NEAR YOU
IN
FALL 2006!

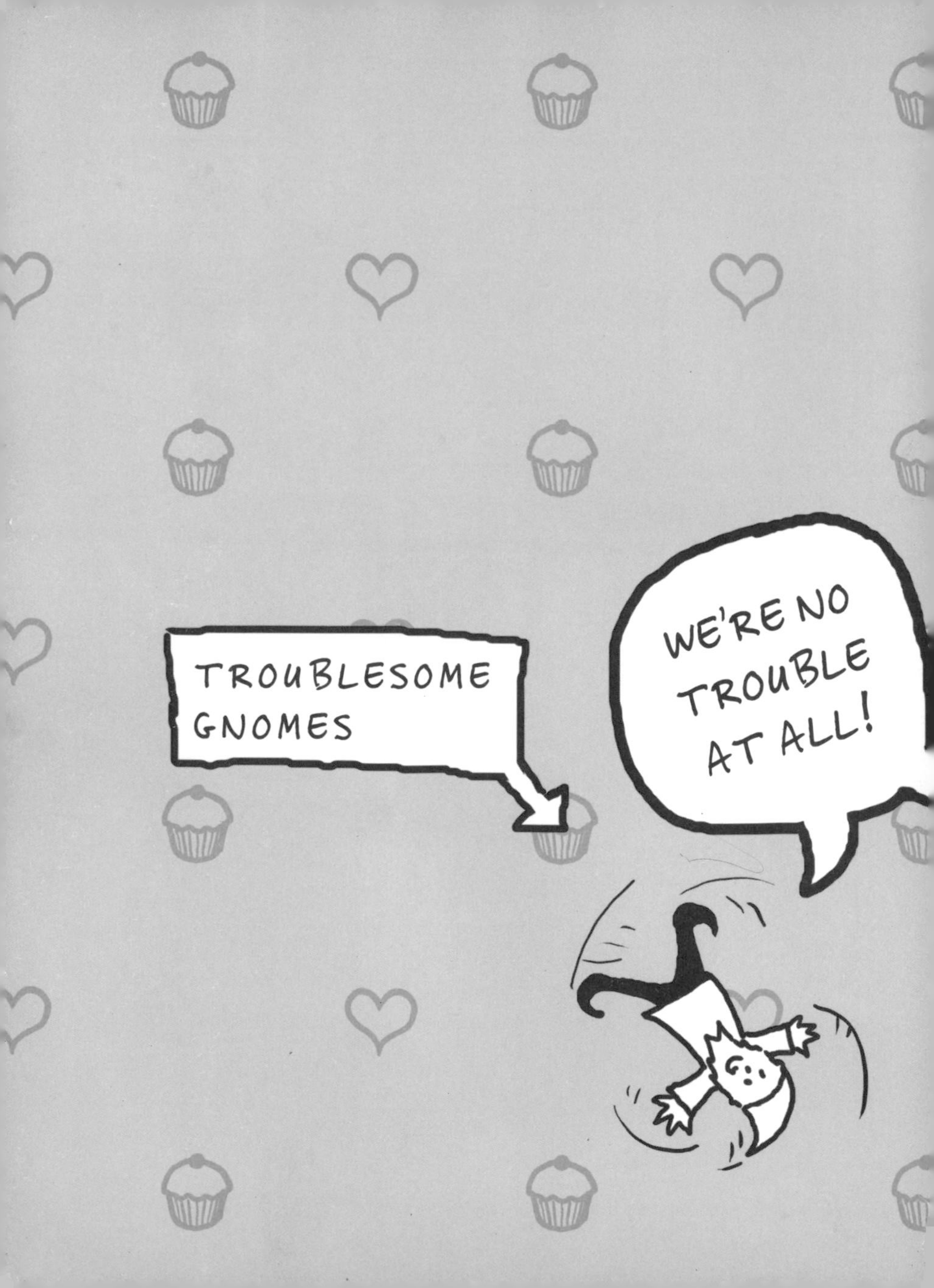
TROUBLESOME GNOMES
WE'RE NO TROUBLE AT ALL!